CW00847880

CONVERGENCE ZONE

SHIELDED HEARTS

ELLE KEATON

DIRTY DOG PRESS

ONE

"Are you *fucking* kidding me?" Carroll Weir bellowed, then slammed the connecting room door shut behind him. Tried to slam it. Fucking unsatisfying. The damn thing was on a pressure arm, which meant it continued hissing to a gentle close until the lock engaged with a quiet *snick*, mocking Weir's DEFCON red–level anger.

After working his ass off for months, he was rewarded by being stuck in this backwater fuck-town longer? "Fuck, fuck, fuck!" Just when he thought he was escaping the soggy, mossy shithole of Skagit, a Fish and Wildlife detective goes and gets himself killed. Murdered, even. "Goddammit!"

The Department of Fish and Wildlife was down to bare bones, only having had three detectives on staff for the whole state *before* Peter Krystad's murder. Weir was overreacting, but he had the nearly overwhelming urge to lie on the floor kicking and screaming like a toddler.

Couldn't the killer have waited until Weir had escaped back to a warmer, drier climate? Back to the beach? He was starting to feel itchy and closed in, what with the clouds pressing down from the sky and the mountains looming from the east.

Itchy was the wrong descriptor; *moldy* was more accurate.

He had been separated from the sun for far too long.

Late last fall Mohammad Azaya had assigned him to a child kidnapping case, partnering Adam Klay. Weir continued to have mixed feelings about Adam, who could be an ass but was also a dedicated and talented investigator. When Adam had gone on leave, Weir stepped in and took over, following the trail of evidence until it petered out. Only picking it up again when a neighbor made the connection between where the body was discovered and her creepy cousin, the one who drove a truck and had visited close the time of the disappearance.

There had been no time for a trip to LA and his stretch of beach before he had been sent to Skagit to partner with Adam again. They'd brought down a human-trafficking ring that resulted in an internal affairs investigation of the entire Skagit Police Department. Led by Weir. A team of investigators was still trying to untangle all the details, but Weir's part was finally done. He had been released from that special assignment two days earlier, and he was ready to go. His bags were already packed, for crying out loud. He'd been on the road so long the plastic plant in his living room was going to die from neglect.

He wrenched open the bathroom door, really wanting something to slam, but was interrupted by his cell phone. He bristled at the cheerful ring tone. Answering it five minutes ago had put him in this crappy mood. Stalking over to the desk where it rattled along like it was possessed, he glanced at the screen. Mohammad. Great.

"Weir." He closed his eyes and practiced some deep-breathing tactics. He liked and respected his boss, but right now he was afraid he might say something stupid. His mouth got him in trouble more often than not.

"I was hoping to talk to you before Adam did. My apologies." Weir pulled the phone away from his ear so he could stare at it and confirm that Mohammad was on the other end. Yep.

Well, damn, that took the wind out of his sails. It was hard to remain mad when his boss was apologizing to him. He sat on the edge of his unmade, uncomfortable hotel bed.

"This case is a bit tricky."

"Aren't they all?"

"Yes, but this one is especially problematic. Normally, Fish and Wildlife would investigate this themselves, but they are down manpower. Then it would most likely fall to ICE investigators. However, because we have been in Skagit for months now on the Matveev case, we are in a unique position for it to appear that you are still part of that investigation, while in reality you are on loan to Fish and Wildlife."

"So." Weir stopped to consider his words. Maybe the deep breathing was helping? "So, am I undercover? Why all the secrecy?"

"In a manner, yes, you will be undercover. Whoever had Detective Krystad murdered believes they have gotten away with it."

"All right, what are you not telling me?"

"You will continue to act as if you are dotting i's and crossing t's on the Russian case, but in fact we need you to start researching gooey-duck smuggling and anything associated with Peter Krystad."

"Gooey *what*?"

"G-e-o-d-u-c-k. A large bivalve, often smuggled from the Pacific Northwest to Asia. China specifically. A Canadian company was caught poaching them and was banned from fishing in US waters several years ago. Start there. Start with the locals who were suspected of working with them. The Fish and Wildlife files will be coming your way soon."

After clicking off the call, Weir did a quick Google search on the geoduck. Jesus Christ, the thing looked like a giant cock. It was kind of disgusting, and Weir *liked* cock.

Maybe that was why he was out of sorts. He liked cock, and it had been forever since he'd gotten any. Skagit wasn't exactly bursting at the gills with gay bars, though there was one. He sighed. The Loft was... well, it was okay, but there wasn't a lot of inventory to go around. Plus Sterling, the regular bartender, got on his nerves.

He couldn't put his finger on what it was about Sterling that bothered him. They'd run into each other a few times since Weir had come to town, at the Booking Room and even at Buck Swanfeldt's New Year's party—where Sterling had been caught semi-cheating at some card game that seemed to involve sex and bluffing. Weir had forgotten about that.

Weir left their encounters generally irritated. He decided that, like most people who didn't know him, Sterling didn't take him seriously. They saw a young guy with an even-younger-looking face and dismissed him. Most people did, to their detriment. It was one of the many reasons why he was so successful at what he did.

AFTER SPENDING the remainder of the day researching the giant clam and those who sought it, he found himself heading for the Loft anyway. What could he say? He'd had a long dry spell. He ditched his suit, because nothing screamed "trying too hard" more than a man in a suit after five o'clock in Skagit. Actually, a man in a suit in Skagit any time of day stuck out like a sore thumb.

Weir normally didn't mind wearing suits for work. For one thing, he knew he looked damn hot in one. Tonight, though, he'd prefer if people would forget he was a federal agent. Hopefully his favorite olive cargos, a gray hoodie paired with a red flannel shirt, and a pair of Vans wouldn't be too much for the locals. Grabbing his card key and wallet, he debated for a minute before deciding to walk.

He knew not being able to get out and exercise on a regular basis was central to his frustration. When he didn't get outside, away from everything, his brain tended to ambush him. Running was more enjoyable and cheaper than therapy, although he'd done that, too.

The Loft was packed.

It was a Tuesday night, for fuck's sake. All he wanted was a couple drinks, see if anyone caught his eye. He had supplies tucked in his back pocket. If something happened, nice; if not, eye candy would do.

Standing in the entryway debating wasn't helping his mood. People bumped into him from all directions. After making it in the door, he thought he might as well grab a drink before leaving to sulk in the silence of his hotel room.

When it wasn't packed to the gills, the Loft was a pretty cool place. It had a kind of speakeasy vibe. An exquisite mahogany back bar stocked with glittering bottles of liquor dominated the space. A long mirror behind it reflected the multitude of bottles, making patrons' choices appear endless. Three light fixtures hung over the bartender's workspace, beautifully wrought stained glass with art deco touches. The dance floor, currently hidden under a sea of bodies, was parquet. Weir thought someone had mentioned it had been recycled from an old dance studio in town. Along the other side, booths catered to casual diners and there were tulip-shaped wall sconces, the lights kept low, adding to the atmosphere.

Semi-politely elbowing his way through the throng, he still couldn't see why the place was so full. Was it possible that every gay man in Skagit was in the same building tonight? Seriously, what was going on? As he drew closer to the bar he spotted a clue, a banner reading: HAPPY BIRTHDAY TO THE LOFT! TEN YEARS OLD!

Crowds had never been his thing. Too many people, too much

noise and he got twitchy—his skin started to feel tight. He had a vague memory of being at Disneyland and having some kind of epic meltdown; he didn't recall the details now. These days, usually, as long as he knew in advance, he could handle it.

Squeezing into the last open spot at the bar, he ordered a drink from his least-favorite bartender in Skagit and proceeded to brood. If he had turned around and left, the detachment he generally wore like a shield wouldn't have failed so spectacularly. It would have stayed where it belonged: simmering, lurking, protecting him. Mostly unacknowledged, but still providing a modicum of safety from the world at large. Instead, a heavy melancholy snuck up on him while he sat nursing his drink, stripping his defenses.

It was a peculiar kind of self-torture to sit and listen to a bunch of strangers interact. Day-to-day emptiness was one thing, but he was generally busy, and work was a good distraction. It was different when he was suddenly faced with every gay couple in Skagit. Jesus, even non-couples were paired up; he recognized Seth Culver sharing a beer with a guy Weir didn't recognize.

He found himself engrossed in watching Sterling work. As busy as it was, he never lost his stride, preparing one specialty drink after another. His sleeves were rolled up, showing off his sinewy forearms as they flexed while he shook the cocktail mixer or used a hand press for fresh orange or lime juice. The show was hot and well choreographed. Weir upgraded Sterling on his inner ranking system from a four to about a seven. The jury was still out on his personality, but there was nothing wrong with the sense of authority he exuded. Surely he had all the boys at his beck and call.

Weir decided to call it a night, tossing back the remains of his vodka-cran before pushing his empty glass forward to try to get Sterling's attention and the check. The guy was slammed with orders but was managing to chat with a sweet-looking man at the other end of the bar while he mixed drinks. Irrationally, Weir felt his temper rise.

When the strip-o-gram guy walked in "wearing" a tunic measuring no more than one inch by one inch, carrying a bow and arrow, his body covered with rainbow glitter, Weir deduced something else. It was fucking Valentine's Day. He wanted to put his head down on the bar top in surrender. How had Valentine's Day slipped by him, even if it was his least-favorite holiday? What an amazing investigator he was proving to be.

A second drink landed in front of him. Weir didn't question it, even though he had been planning on leaving. He nodded semi-gratefully in Sterling's direction. He needed another drink before he fought his way out through the throng.

A tingling he hadn't felt in years sizzled between his shoulder blades, slowly making its way up the back of his neck. Damn. His muscles tightened, and he twitched his shoulders and cracked his neck to try and stop the sensation.

The crowd had grown exponentially since he'd sat down. He regretted turning around to see how many people were between him and the front door. Crap, he really should leave. He'd known more revelers had arrived, because he was getting jostled and bumped as patrons moved from the bar to the seating area and dance floor, but he hadn't actually seen the writhing mass. Fuck.

Weir had to be the only single person in the bar. Even the strip-o-gram was getting some love. Cupid was being passed above the crowd on the dance floor, like an old-school grunge crowd jumper.

As he took another gulp of his drink, he realized his hands were shaking. Enough that cool liquid sloshed over the rim of the glass onto his fingers. Deep breathing, he reminded himself. His shoulders clenched again, and he hunched closer to the bar, fighting the familiar yet unwelcome sensation of *everything* being too much. The back of his neck was hot and pinched, the top of his scalp tight. The sensation of being trapped increased. He needed to get outside or risk a full-blown panic/anxiety attack. Shutting his eyes against the crowd, he concentrated on his breathing and the glass of alcohol cool and damp against his palms.

A noisemaker screamed into his right ear, the high-pitched sound taking him completely apart.

TWO

Sterling's feet were killing him. He'd been running like crazy all night long. The combination of Valentine's Day and the bar's anniversary was a killer. Tonight was wilder than last year. He was going to kill whoever had hired the stripper, candy-gram, what-the-fuck-ever, with his bare hands. He had a few suspects. Or maybe he and the aloof, sexy federal agent sitting alone at the other end of the bar could get together and investigate the case. The fed looked good in his civvies tonight.

Yeah, no. Sterling didn't date customers. An excellent rule, one that kept him from sleeping with the entire gay population of Skagit. Kept him from dating, because he didn't do that, either. Dating meant giving up too much of himself. He didn't see it happening. After fifteen-plus years of having his life under his own control, he saw no reason to change.

The bar was so busy he didn't have time to make small talk. Kevin Smith, one of his part-time bartenders who was smart enough not to have signed up for this shift, stood at the drink station for a while trying to shoot the breeze, but soon enough even he had been driven away by the constant jostling of thirsty revelers and having to yell over the thump and grind of the sound system. At the Loft, Valentine's Day looked more like Mardi Gras than a traditional candlelit, romantic dinner.

Kevin vanished into the writhing mass of dancing bodies— mostly men, although there were a few women tonight. The stripper was being passed around like a piece of candy. Sterling hoped no one dropped him. He could feel insurance rates rising the longer the guy was in the air.

Hands busy muddling fresh mint, making the twenty-jillionth mojito of the night, he kept his focus on the room. Kent, his door guy, was good, but a crowd like this needed attention at all times.

Something funky about Weir's body language had Sterling keeping one eye on him while he worked. Weir seemed to be relaxing a little after the second stiff drink Sterling had poured him, until some asshole he didn't recognize leaned in and blew a fucking noisemaker right in the guy's ear. Without conscious thought Sterling was in front of Weir, leaning across the bar and grasping the man's wrists with both hands.

Unseeing brown eyes stared through him. Weir was shivering, but not pulling away. Okay, he could work with that. He'd been a bartender since he turned twenty-one. He had seen and dealt with almost every situation.

Kent forced his way through the crowd, finally making it to the bar.

"Help me get him into my office, then get back out here and confiscate every fucking noisemaker you can find. It's Valentine's Day, not New Year's Eve. And send Kevin up here; he can show off his chops for a bit."

Ignoring patrons waving for drinks, he came around the bar, moving to one side of Weir while Kent took the other. Slipping an arm around Weir's narrow waist, Sterling whispered into his ear, "Come back to the office for a few minutes, okay?"

He received a slight nod, and when they stood, Weir turned into him, using Sterling's body as a shield. Between them, he and

Kent edged Weir around the end of the bar toward the small office hidden behind it.

The office was Sterling's not-so-secret hideaway. He figured he spent enough time in it, he might as well make it comfortable. After he'd fashioned a desk out of a wooden plank and a couple of sawhorses and added a fancy, ergonomically correct roller chair he'd spent way too much money on, as well as a small couch with red faux-velvet upholstery and a plush area rug, the little room had become his refuge. Sterling waved Kent back out to the front.

Weir mumbled something unintelligible. Sterling gently nudged him onto the couch before crouching down in front of him. Taking a deep breath, Weir sagged into the seat, his head lolling against the back cushion. "Well, that was awkward," he whispered. "I haven't had one of those in a long time. Sorry about that."

"What happened? Aside from the jackass blowing a noise-maker in your ear."

"Slow down a fucking minute. Lemme catch up," Weir groused.

Sterling figured if the guy was bitchy, he'd survive whatever the little episode had been. Pushing himself to his feet, he stood over Weir, assessing his general bearing.

The guy looked worn out, frayed at the edges. Dark circles had taken up residence under his eyes, and his skin didn't have the same healthy tone it had the first time they met.

They'd hung out on New Year's Eve at Buck Swanfeldt's house, but Sterling had seen him around before that. Probably at Sara Schultz's place. Weir was good-looking, had the SoCal thing going for him, especially with his outfit tonight. Not the type Sterling usually hooked up with, but good-looking enough. Probably not more than mid-twenties, though tonight he looked older.

"You want some water?" He'd never seen such dark brown eyes with blond hair before. It was... disarming. Weir stared up at him, unguarded for a moment, unaware and exposed. A vein in his neck throbbed. A flicker of some unnamed emotion crossed his face, gone so quickly Sterling couldn't catalog it.

"Yeah, I'll have some water."

Sterling handed over a bottle from the stash under his desk. He was going to assume the "thanks" was silent. Weir took a drink, and the weird silence grew longer, more taut between them. Weir's knees bumped against Sterling's shins, and yeah, he was still standing between the guy's splayed legs. For whatever reason, Sterling still didn't move. They had gone from panic attack to playing an erotic game of chicken. He was taken by surprise by a surge of heat, low in his groin.

"I don't think I'm in any state to return the favor, but I've heard an orgasm goes a long way toward bringing someone down from a panic attack. Endorphins and shit like that." Weir waved a languid hand toward his groin.

"That so?"

"Yeah." He grinned, revealing something else Sterling had never seen before. At Buck's Weir had been reserved and quiet. The grin changed him; Sterling had a glimpse of a goofy, boyish demeanor Weir hid behind a professional mask. Weir was handsome any day of the week, but the grin elevated him to fucking gorgeous.

It was madness. Pure madness. Faint sounds from the bar penetrated the office. Good-natured yelling, and then somebody bumped up the volume on the sound system and the pounding lyrics of the Arctic Monkeys' "Do I Wanna Know" drifted into the small room. He did, kinda, want to know. Fuck. He hadn't been drinking, couldn't blame this crazy on alcohol.

Weir watched him while he stood there weighing the pros and cons of a blow job. *Really*, he asked himself, *cons?* Weir's expression, still unguarded, sparked with a smoldering heat. They both wanted this.

Sinking to his knees and thanking his own forethought when he hit the area rug, he reached out a surprisingly steady hand to tug open the button of Weir's cargos. The music thumped louder, egging him on together with the soft, drowsy expression on Weir's face.

Oh, and he was commando. Jesus fuck. Sterling fished Weir's semi-erect cock out of hiding, pushing his pants down around his hips as he did so. Weir was cut, long, slender, gorgeous. Sterling leaned closer, pressing his nose into Weir's groin. There was almost nothing he liked better than the smell of man, a musky tang unique to each guy he had ever blown. He had to reach down and adjust himself, his own hardening dick at an awkward angle in his tight jeans.

"Fuck." Weir drew out the word, as if it was too much work to enunciate. "It's been so long, I'm… Yeah." His hips twitched upward, his cock growing harder in Sterling's fist. Oh. Yeah.

Sterling hadn't put his mouth on him yet. He had an excitable boy in his hands. Nice. Inhaling his scent again, enjoying the caress of Weir's shaft against his cheek, he let his tongue trace a path to the plump mushroom tip where he teased the slit, holding onto the base with one hand, opening his own jeans with the other. It was hard to jack two dicks at once, but Sterling needed a hand on himself, even if it was his own.

He took as much of Weir into his mouth as he could. He loved giving blow jobs, but he had a terrible gag reflex. Tragic story of his life. Weir didn't do any controlling shit like grab his head or pull his hair, which Sterling appreciated. Opening wide and pushing down as far as he could, he sucked that thing like a Kirby —or was it Hoover? His cheeks hollowed as he sucked and licked, losing himself in the soft sounds Weir was making, the scent of him, the soft skin under his tongue.

Fingers touched his cheek, caressing it. Sterling looked up through his lashes at Weir, his head still against the back of the couch, only the one hand touching Sterling's face. Weir's hips jerked. In a moment he was coming into Sterling's mouth. Tangy, bitter come exploded across his tongue, and he swallowed what he could. Tugging his pulsing shaft, he came with a rush into his own hand.

The room was silent except for their quiet breathing while they pulled themselves back together. Sterling slid down onto his ass, his dick still semi-erect.

"Sorry," Weir said.

"Sorry? For what?"

"I didn't ask, you know, before I came. But I'm negative." He waved vaguely toward his cock, which was still not tucked back into his cargos. The man looked like he would have lost a fight with a limp noodle.

Oh. Sterling waggled his eyebrows suggestively. "Ah, and now you know you don't have to ask."

After snagging a tissue from his desk to wipe off his hand, Sterling stood up and rearranged himself, tucking his shirt and other important parts back into his jeans.

A sharp rap on the office door intruded on their... whatever this was. "Sterling, Kevin's drowning out here," Kent yelled through the door. Fuck.

"Be right there." He looked at Weir, who was still sitting there, gathering himself. "I gotta go. The back exit is farther down the hall. Be careful in the alley." Sterling checked himself in the small mirror—no come on his face, hair mostly behaving, smile in place—and left his sanctuary for the madness awaiting him.

THREE

Hundreds of hours of research and surveillance later, Weir drifted along in a bleary haze. It had been weeks since Peter Krystad was murdered. There were no solid leads. No smoking gun. No emails to, or from, bitter rivals. No jilted lover or spouse (that Weir could find), no connection to geoducks. And yet, someone had carefully planned his murder and gone to great lengths not to be discovered. The perp had made no mistakes. Yet.

Hunger plagued him, but nothing appealed. Especially not clams, or maybe any kind of seafood. Ever again. His exhaustion was weighty enough for it to be difficult for him to focus on the computer screen on his desk. Tracking these smugglers/killers down was proving to be a lesson in persistence and patience. The Fish and Wildlife contact he was working with, Tom Poole, pestered him relentlessly. Krystad had been his partner and long-time friend. Poole wanted justice.

It was hunger that finally drove Weir to the Booking Room later that morning. Also, he wanted to talk to Sara about Krystad. From the number of empty to-go cups in his office, Krystad had a serious Booking Room habit.

The café was busy, as usual. Weir could see the draw. Even a few local cops were enjoying a coffee break before heading back to fight Skagit's crime. Those who were left, anyway, after the internal investigation that followed the exposure of Matveev and the shits who had been in his orbit.

The chance of Weir being able to head to the café and *not* know anyone there was vanishingly slim. He'd been in line for just a few moments when Sara's dad, Ed, hailed him over to "his" table. Ever since a few months ago when the café had been targeted by teens paid to vandalize the shop, Ed had been there every day. He wasn't fooling anyone, but Sara was sweet enough to pretend she didn't know he was trying to protect her and her employees.

The table closest to the espresso machine was unofficially Ed's. If a new, or unaware, customer made the mistake of sitting there before Ed arrived, he would sit down with them. Sara had given up trying to get him to behave. Unsuspecting customers received a coffee on the house. And Ed? Ed made new friends.

Normally Weir tried to avoid the "codger table," as Sara called it. He could only handle so much random gossip. Today, however, Ed fit perfectly into his hastily laid plan to see if the Skagit gossip underground knew anything about Krystad. The key would be making it casual. Although he questioned Ed's capacity for subtlety of any kind.

"Carroll." Ed smiled at him. Weir was going to murder whoever had told Ed his first name. The old man insisted on using it whenever they met. "Haven't seen you around. Thought maybe you'd left without sayin' goodbye."

Ed was laying it on thick. "Nope, still here." He'd considered leaving without saying goodbye, but didn't get out quick enough. Now his bags were unpacked again.

"You look tired."

"This new case is keeping me busy."

Ed nodded. "You working on the Krystad case?" This was like taking candy from a baby.

"Yep." Weir sat down at the table. "Did you know him?"

"Nah, that's not really the kind of trouble I got into." Ed chuckled. "I knew him a little, of course. Hard not to; he was here almost every day when he was in town."

Weir scooted his chair closer, out of the aisle. "Did you ever talk to him? What kind of person was he?" Weir had read the notes, talked to Krystad's partner and coworkers, but still didn't have a good feel for who the man had been.

Ed looked thoughtful. "He was nice enough. Sara says he always tipped. He'd order a coffee, sit and work for a while, then order another one to go." That would explain all the empty cups at his office. "Probably was the cop part of his job, but he wasn't overly friendly, kept things on the surface."

"Did he come in here before he was killed? That day, or close to it? Maybe meet someone?" The very definition of grasping for straws, Weir thought.

The noise level had grown. A mom was having some kind of argument with her teenaged son at the front of the line. Whatever they were talking about, it was holding up the line, which now snaked past Ed's table and out the front door.

"Not that I ever noticed." Weir refocused on their conversation. "He came, had coffee, and left."

"What about Tom Poole, his partner?" He raised his voice a bit so Ed could hear him over the background chatter.

"Thomas Poole. There's a name I haven't heard in a while. He used to be quite a troublemaker. Everybody was surprised when he went away to school and came back part of Fish and Wildlife. His family, they were some of the original survivalists around here. Living off the land and all that. Poached all the time, they did. I think he's the only one left. His mama died of cancer a few years ago, I know for sure."

And that, it appeared, was all the information he would get out of Ed. He stayed for a little while longer, chatting about nothing. Learning that a new casino and resort was in the planning stages. That the VFW was hosting a local beer tasting and art auction in honor of poetry month. Ed rambled on while Weir watched customers as they came and went, happily clutching Skagit's best handmade coffee drinks.

He tossed a mental coin as to whether to wait until things calmed down and Sara might have time to talk, before deciding to head back to the hotel for more computer time. The walk might help him come up with a different angle. It wasn't until he opened the door to his room that he realized he'd never ordered anything to eat. Later. For now he would relook at the facts. Again.

Krystad had been working a late night in his local office. Sometime between midnight and two a.m., a person had taken careful aim through the scope of a rifle and pulled the trigger. He was dead before he hit the floor, a single bullet straight through his left temple. The angle of the entry wound was such that the CSIs believed the shot came from one of the buildings across the street. The whole thing had a surreal, action movie aspect to it. Weir had seen plenty of crime scenes in his short career; this one left him scratching his head.

The deceased detective had primarily been working the geoduck smuggling case, but there were plenty of other open cases with equally viable suspects. Not that they had pinpointed a suspect yet. Mohammad and Tom suspected geoduck smugglers. Weir respected Mohammad's intelligence and experience, so he continued to focus primarily on that angle, but he couldn't help thinking that it didn't *have* to be those disgusting giant clams.

Krystad's notes were littered with doodles along the margins, half-finished thoughts, and coffee stains. Seriously, who wrote stuff on paper anymore? Peter Krystad. Dozens of spiral-bound notebooks were stacked on the shelves of his office, and they were all full of notes. Weir couldn't tell if the doodles were part of the investigation or if Krystad had had a busy mind that needed to be kept on task.

There were phone numbers, all of which checked out as legitimate businesses and individuals. There were weird curlicues, smiley faces, and several notes that appeared random: "Call DOT," "Check with Randy," "Lunch/sushi!" He'd been planning a backcountry hiking trip for the summer; there was a reminder to apply for a hiking permit for Mt. Rainier along with gear he wanted to remember. Other doodles were less enlightening, circles and letters comingled. Who knew, Krystad could have had his own code, and unless they found the key it probably wouldn't be cracked. But nothing that pointed toward a smoking gun. The easiest clue to decipher was the significant amount of coffee rings and empty Booking Room paper cups stacked up around his office, indicating a big part of his budget went to coffee.

Some of his notebooks were dated. Weir put the older ones aside and focused on the newer and undated ones. Not only did Krystad investigate crimes against the state's resources, he and Poole volunteered for a variety of community education projects, visited the state forest camping areas during high season to deliver educational lectures, and helped local residents identify strange animals that wandered into their yards. The two were multipurpose state employees.

The exposure both Poole and Krystad had to the public was extensive. They attended a multitude of conferences to speak out against poaching and illegal harvesting, and had arrested hundreds of perpetrators over the course of their careers. In a small community like Skagit it was more of a question of who *hadn't* they pissed off at some point? Yet Poole was still alive.

Privately, Krystad was pretty boring. Hadn't been married, no kids, no strange debts. No red flags. He'd been respected, if not well liked, by other Fish and Wildlife employees. Typically, some thought he was too intense and focused on rules and regulations, while others felt he hadn't pushed hard enough to change archaic thinking about public lands and how they should be managed.

Poole was… *interesting*. Weir wasn't certain he liked him.

Prematurely bald, as in all the way, billiard-ball bald, yet strikingly handsome. Weir could only hope if he went that way he would look that good; the man had a nice head. When they were introduced, Poole had been wearing his dark-green Fish and Wildlife uniform, heavy boots, and glittering aviators. At 6'4" and two hundred twenty pounds, he was imposing.

A local guy, also not married, no kids, Poole lived well within his means. Normally, Weir would wonder if the two of them had been in some kind of relationship. They had worked closely together for over ten years. Even though Weir had a poor record when it came to picking out less-obvious gay men, Poole's vibe wasn't one that translated to *gay* in his head. The men had been very good friends, and that, he believed, was the end of it.

Part of what bothered him about Poole was that they had been indoors when they met. People who wore their sunglasses inside, in Weir's opinion, had something to hide or were trying to be intimidating. At any rate, Weir took an instant dislike to the big man.

A week ago, an anonymous tip had been called in about a potential illegal geoduck harvest sometime in the next few days. Since then, he and Poole had spent hours every night steering a Fish and Wildlife patrol vessel through dark, choppy waters with no running lights, Weir armed only with a set of night-vision binoculars, trying to spot floating debris and buoys in the pitch-dark, while Poole navigated the bitterly cold waters of Skagit Bay and the Strait of Juan de Fuca, searching for other vessels out and about with no lights. Weir now knew more about geoducks and the people who smuggled them than he cared to.

Poachers dove at o'dark-thirty, often using pressure hoses, spraying down the underwater geoduck beds to expose the mammoth clams. Sometimes they would harvest them right away; other times the geoducks would be bagged up and left for later retrieval. Current market value in China was over $150 a pound. A single geoduck averaged around two-and-a-half pounds.

One of the FW guys Weir had interviewed said harvesting geoducks was "like picking twenty-dollar bills off the ground."

Weir was in the wrong fucking business.

After spending all those nights together, Weir eventually conceded that Poole, rather than being a possible suspect, was absolutely driven to catch whoever had killed his longtime partner.

Poole did remove his sunglasses at night. Weir still didn't really like him but could see where his unusual eyes would be a distraction or perhaps even disturb some people. Poole had one distinctly hazel-green eye while the other was ice-blue. Weir had seen people with little chunks of different color before, but nothing like Poole's eyes.

"Ask your question," Poole had said.

Weir was puzzled. "What question?"

"Don't you want to know how I got this way? Do I know that I have eyes like a dog's? Or, my favorite, am I a witch?"

"Uh. I was wondering what the statistical probability of complete heterochromia is. My assumption is, very low?"

Poole looked at him for a minute before answering. "Less than one percent."

Okay then. "A witch?"

"A witch." A wolfish grin crossed his face, "In case you were curious, I'd rather be a warlock."

And also possibly had a sense of humor hidden somewhere on his person.

It was a good thing Weir didn't get seasick. Poole was a maniac, pushing his craft's small engine to the limit as they criss-crossed Skagit Bay. The water was always extremely choppy, and the impact of the hull slamming against the waves jarred Weir's knees and back. How Poole managed to stand at the wheel, a solid and unshakeable avenger, was beyond him.

Each trip out they stopped several boats with no running lights, but all proved to have legitimate business on the water in the middle of the fucking night. All Poole could do was remind them they needed to be using some kind of special white night-fishing lamp.

Sighing, he changed his search parameters *again*, hoping to get something, anything. There were so many variables. Krystad had been deeply invested in the hunt for a specific group of poachers; the office had gotten an anonymous tip that someone was harvesting a lot of the giant clams. There were a few blurry snapshots, but they could have been of anyone, anywhere on Skagit Bay.

The computer screen began to blur, and rubbing his eyes didn't help. Fuck. The computer clock said it was past seven. Where had the day gone? People who thought investigative work was fun and exciting had never fought the unending boredom of a stakeout or hours of following leads that went nowhere. Leaning back in the uncomfortable chair provided by the quasi-residence hotel that had become his home away from home, Weir stretched his arms out and leaned back. The satisfying pop of his spine was spoiled when the lever holding the chair in position released, bringing the seat crashing down with a hard snap. He needed to get out of this room; it was plotting to kill him.

Making sure he had his phone and his keycard in his pocket, Weir stepped out into the evening drizzle. He grudgingly admitted a couple months made a difference in Skagit. At least it was light almost twelve hours a day now. The constant cloud cover was depressing, and the rain still kept him inside more often than not, but it was brighter than it had been. Although at this rate the hotel gym was going to need to replace its treadmills by the time he left town.

FOUR

Walking aimlessly, running numbers, angles, and thoughts through his head, Weir wasn't conscious of wandering down Steele Street until a happy patron stumbling out of the Loft almost ran into him. Weir hadn't been back since Valentine's Day. Thrusting the memory of that incident aside, he decided to go in. He was hungry and thirsty. If Sterling was there, well, they were both adults. They'd made no promises.

Weir had nearly fallen asleep in Sterling's office that night. It had been close. After finally summoning the energy to pull himself together, or at least to put his dick away and zip his pants, he'd made a quiet exit out the back and hadn't seen Sterling around town since. The whole experience had an unreal tinge to it, like a dream. Except there was no doubt he'd had Sterling's lips on his cock. Thinking about it was giving his dick ideas.

He pushed open the door and did an internal fist-pump; it wasn't a holiday he had been unaware of. No banners flying, no crowd. In fact, he saw only four or five groups sitting at tables and three people at the bar. Sterling was behind the bar, of course. As Weir scanned the room, deciding where to sit, he caught Sterling's glance and a slight facial movement that might have been a smile.

Sterling was older than Weir by a bit. Weir thought he was in his early thirties. He hadn't paid much attention to him before the notorious Valentine's Day Blow Job. Sterling seemed a little goth. Frankly, Weir was tired of that look. Although maybe he should reconsider, because Sterling looked good. His pale skin glowed next to his usual somber clothing. Short black hair, deep-blue eyes. Weir had already experienced the lips, and they were as soft as they looked. He shivered, catching Sterling's glance again. He knew the guy was on to him. Whatever, he was a guy, sex was on his mind a lot.

"You look like shit." Sterling eyed him head to toe. "Worse than the last time you were in here."

"Thanks. You know how to make a guy feel great."

"Jesus, you've lost more weight. Those cargos are about to slide off your ass. I thought you had bags under your eyes before, but now you have an entire luggage carousel."

"Seriously, did you go to charm school for all that?" Weir was beginning to doubt the wisdom of stepping into the Loft, much less sitting at the bar.

Sterling slapped a trifold paper menu in front of him.

"Soup today is split pea," Weir wrinkled his nose, "or chicken chili." His traitorous stomach chose that moment to rumble its approval. Sullenly, he snatched up the menu. Childish, yes—he had been in search of a decent meal, after all. But for some reason he hated being told to do things. Long ago in another life, his dad used to comment that the best way to get him to do something was to tell him to do the opposite. Oppositional personality disorder, his middle name.

Eventually he settled on the chili. When Sterling plopped the bowl down in front of him, he'd been staring into space for ten minutes. "Thanks." Sterling didn't move away until Weir picked up his spoon and began to eat. Weir rolled his eyes.

It turned out to be pleasant, sitting at the bar chatting with Sterling about nothing while he worked. A dribble of customers would come in, Sterling would serve them and then return to continue their conversation. Weir couldn't remember the last time he'd had a casual conversation. Even the New Year's party at Buck Swanfeldt's had been strained because of the "developing situation" at the time with the case he had been working on.

"So what are you, besides a suit?"

What a good question. "Not much these days," he answered, trying to recall what he used to do before he began his crazy journey as a federal investigator. "I used to surf a lot. I run."

"Oh, yeah. Like big surf?" Sterling looked mildly intrigued.

"Yeah, pretty big. I placed in some small tournaments back in the day. One season I had a sponsor. That was pretty cool. Nothing big, though. Running, too. I'm actually better at that."

"Like marathons?"

"Kinda. More endurance races, some people call it ultrarunning."

"What's the longest you've run?"

"I've done a 100k before." Qualifying for that race had been one of the hardest and easiest things he had ever done. There was one in New Zealand he planned on doing, someday, when he had the time again.

"How many miles is that?" He could see Sterling trying to do the math in his head.

"About sixty-five."

"That's... that's impressive. I have trouble going more than a couple miles." Sterling was doing the old-school bartender thing, polishing glasses while he stood there chatting. Weir glanced at his phone. He had been there for more than two hours. The bar area had emptied out, leaving just the two of them.

"It's not for everybody."

"Why do you do it?" Ah, the question everyone eventually

asked him. He had a stock answer, usually something along the lines of "just do it" or some shit like that.

"Running's free. Nobody can stop you but yourself. Throw on a pair of shoes and go as far as you can." Sterling stopped pretending to polish the wine glass in his hand, waiting for Weir to continue. "I didn't have the best home life. Well, that's not entirely true. I had a great home until I was five or so." He leaned back, away from the bar, and crossed his arms, then continued, focusing on the pattern of the wood grain, not Sterling. "My older sister was kidnapped. Or wandered off, no one knows, but she was never found. Things pretty much went to shit after that. I started running in fifth grade, for lots of reasons, but mostly because I could get away from my own head." Which was about the most he'd ever said to anyone, especially someone who was basically a stranger, blow job or not.

"That is all kinds of fucked up. Are you trying to con me for pity sex?"

Weir chuckled. Glancing up, he found himself trapped by Sterling's gaze. He shook his head at the guy. "Really?"

FIVE

"Really? I bare my soul and you think 'blow job'? Dude, that is classless."

Sterling could tell Weir wasn't upset. "I wouldn't say no to a blow job, just saying. I'm open to the idea if that's where you were headed," he teased. "You kinda owe me."

Dark brown eyes gleamed wickedly; it seemed Weir wasn't averse to the idea of a blow job either, now that it was out there in the universe.

He was still sitting at the bar hours later when Sterling flipped the CLOSED sign. What the hell was he thinking? Not only was he violating his "no customers" rule, he was violating his "no repeats" rule. It must be two-for-one night somewhere. He couldn't bring himself to care much. They were both having a good time, and it's not like the last time they had done this Weir had come back the next day begging him for more—or, worse, a phone number.

They were, in fact, two consenting adults, of the gay male persuasion, with an unspoken no-strings agreement. Another blow job did not mean they were in a relationship.

He flicked off the front lights, leaving only the safety lights on.

Chairs went up on the tables so the morning crew could sweep before opening. A *thunk* caught his attention, Weir had hopped up to help out. Nice. Ten minutes later they were back in the office.

"I gotta do the bank first."

"'Kay, I'll make myself comfortable on this awesome couch." Sterling caught the smirk Weir threw his way.

"We'll see about that," he murmured under his breath before he got to work counting the tills.

After stashing the day's receipts in the small safe he had in the corner, Sterling turned to face Weir. A thought crossed his mind.

"What is your first name, anyway?"

The smirk grew into a broad smile. "I guess that's for me to know and you to find out."

Sterling rolled his eyes. "I'll find out one way or another. Let's get down to business."

"Such a romantic." Weir stood up and motioned to the couch. "Sit."

Sterling sat, in much the same pose as Weir had a few weeks before, lazily slumped against the back of the couch, legs splayed in a kind of wild abandon. Weir kneeled on the rug, licked his lips, then reached out to tug Sterling's hips closer the edge of the couch.

"That's better." He unzipped Sterling's jeans. "Mmm, look at you."

Weir had zero gag reflex. He swallowed Sterling whole, all the way to the base. The single thought Sterling had before his brain shut down was he hoped Weir was getting enough oxygen.

It had been a while since he'd had a decent blow job, or any blow job. The wet heat of Weir's mouth, the rough tongue stroking him, the overall sensation of everything made it impossible for him to last long. Hell, thinking about it for the past few hours had made his jeans tight.

Never one for delayed gratification, Sterling let himself fall into the sensation of Weir's soft, hot mouth on him. Thinking all shift about the possibility of a blow job later had him in a semi-erect state even before they'd come back to the office.

Weir's cheeks hollowed while he sucked in more air and dragged his lips up Sterling's shaft, teasing his hot tongue into Sterling's slit before swallowing him again, letting Sterling fuck into his mouth and throat. The only warning Sterling had was a tingling sensation that exploded into his balls before he released down Weir's throat.

"Oh, fuck, fuck, fuck." Sterling threw an arm over his face while his hips jerked one more time.

Weir sat back with a grin, letting Sterling's cock slip out of his mouth, swallowing before wiping his glistening lips. "Not bad? It's been awhile, thought I might have lost my touch."

"Your touch is just fine," Sterling rasped. "Come 'ere."

Weir considered for a second before crawling onto the couch, straddling Sterling, knees on either side of his thighs, hands on the back of the couch. Weir's decadent bulge hovered directly in front of Sterling's face. He reached up and popped the button of the familiar cargo pants. Weir's fully erect cock was pressed against his thigh under a pair of sexy black knit boxer briefs. Sterling kind of wanted to stare for a moment, but Weir made a strangled sound, spurring him on.

Tugging down the cargos and then the briefs as far as he could, Sterling admired Weir's package. He pressed his nose into the clipped dark-blond hair surrounding it.

"Are you going to suck it or sniff it?"

Sterling looked up at Weir. His hair was longer than it had been when they first met, and it hung down, shadowing his face. His cheekbones were sharp in the dim light. The guy was too fucking skinny. "You got somewhere to be? Lemme enjoy myself."

Instead of replying, Weir leaned into Sterling, bringing himself even closer, the heat emanating from his body restoking Sterling's own. He took the hint, opening wide and taking him in as far as he was able, one hand at the base of Weir's erection to keep him from gagging and the other grasping a firm, round butt cheek. Weir must've been feeling pent up as well; it didn't take long, or much work on Sterling's part, before he felt Weir tremble under his hand. He sucked harder, hollowing his cheeks with effort. Keeping his fist in place, he palmed Weir's ass as hard as he could, slipping his fingers into his crack, reveling in the quiet gasp he heard before he was swallowing.

Sterling let Weir's softening dick slip out of his mouth, but Weir didn't move away. He slumped closer, resting his head on the back of the couch and Sterling's shoulder while he caught his breath. Sterling didn't mind. It was pleasant to have the heat of another body close. His usual hookups didn't allow time for any more physical contact than absolutely necessary.

After a little while Weir leaned back, extricating himself from their tangle. Cocking his head, he watched Sterling while tucking himself away and re-buttoning his cargos. Lips parted, he seemed about to say something. Shaking his head slightly, Weir finished tucking in his shirt, then checked his face in the small mirror hanging over the desk. His pocket buzzed, and he grimaced before pulling his phone out, tapping the screen, then slipping it back into his pocket.

"Sorry, I need to go."

"S'all right, I've got work to do."

Companionably they left the office together, Weir following Sterling to the front door. Minutes later he was gone, disappearing down the sidewalk into the darkness. Sterling wondered what he thought he was up to, shook his head, and headed back to the office to start monthly inventory.

* * *

FATIGUE WAS Sterling's companion when he stumbled home in the early hours of the morning, inventory having taken much longer than it should have. Someone was stealing liquor. Which goddamn pissed him off. He hated when he had to be the bad guy. Now he was going to have to be an asshole and threaten everyone with firing until somebody caved. True or not, he counted a lot of the staff as friends—maybe not friends he'd invite to breakfast on a regular basis, but still friends. He didn't want to fire anyone.

Home wasn't far, since he had managed to rent the small apartment above the retail space where the Loft was located. It wasn't the nicest place, small by the standards he had grown up with, but 500 square feet of his own space counted for something. It had been a long haul, but things were looking up.

The building had been constructed in the 1880s. Red brick, unusual for the region, just two stories, one exterior wall covered top to bottom with an original painted advertisement from the 1930s hailing the long-gone Kangaroo Café. The faded ad displayed a large tan kangaroo enjoying its morning cup of coffee while inexplicably reading the paper and wearing reading glasses. Sterling loved it, and hated seeing it fade year after year.

His apartment consisted of two-and-a-half rooms: main room-kitchenette and bathroom. He'd bought a large Asian-style rice-paper screen that stood between his bed and the rest of the room. He was single; it worked for him. He didn't see it changing. Two large windows looked down onto Steele Street, and another on the opposite wall had a great view of the alley. It could have been worse. He could have been directly across from the fish market.

When he had moved in, eight years earlier, he hadn't had much to bring with him. Over the last few years he had made the space more and more home-like. He liked supporting fellow local entrepreneurs and artists. Two small Gerald Klay prints hung on one wall. Now that the guy had died, Sterling would never be able to afford the real thing. Several other local artists' prints adorned his walls. A beautiful hand-thrown Japanese-style bowl he had picked up at the farmers market had a special place on the counter separating the kitchenette and the living room. The rest of his walls were covered with bookshelves, all of which were full to the point of being stacked two rows deep. Everyone had their own addiction.

Before stripping down and crawling into bed, he set his alarm for ten a.m. An errant image of Weir popped into his head. He found himself unaccountably curious about the younger man. Maybe it was the deep brown eyes, expressive yet wary. The few times he'd met him before Valentine's Day, Weir hadn't appealed. Now, while Sterling lay in bed trying to fall asleep, he had visions of a slender, athletic man with blond hair and an amazing mouth.

Even after the mutual blow jobs, all Sterling knew about Weir was that he had been a surfer, ran ridiculous distances, and his sister had disappeared when he was very young. With the long day, blow job, inventory woes all swirling in his head, it took Sterling much longer than he expected to fall asleep. Too soon an alarm was chiming in his ear.

SIX

The bathroom mirror, tactless thing, didn't lie. Weir looked like shit. The hellish schedule he had going was making him look like a ghoul. Sterling's remark about his cargos falling off his ass wasn't far from the truth. Remembering to eat had always been secondary, but when he was this wrapped up in a case it was inevitable that he forgot. It was mid-March; by October when Halloween rolled around he wouldn't need a costume, he would be a living skeleton.

Weir had been on the cock-clam assignment for what seemed like forever. The pace was insane. He was also still meeting with the vestiges of Adam's team left in Skagit to try and tie up the loose ends on that case and prop up the farce of his cover. They might have caught most of the pieces of shit involved in the human-trafficking ring, but a few had slithered away, taking vital information with them. His days were spent on the Matveev case, nights on the water chasing down leads, freezing his skinny ass off on the Skagit Bay.

Out on the water last night with Poole they'd again found nothing and nobody. He'd felt like a popsicle by the time he returned to his hotel room. The blow job from Sterling had been the highlight of his day. He'd fallen into a restless sleep for only about an hour before waking far too early, his brain still frustrated about the lack of leads, turning ideas over and over trying to find something that hadn't caught his attention before.

Weir hoped the smugglers made a mistake soon. He and Poole were searching for a needle in a haystack. Fuck, forget haystack, a grain of sand in the Sahara. Weir didn't even have Adam to bounce ideas off of anymore. Adam and his much-nicer boyfriend, Micah, had finally left for a long vacation in California. He was jealous of their trip south to sunshine.

Screw this. He needed to go for a real run. A long one to clear his head and keep the walls from closing in too close around him. He didn't think he could hit Sterling up every time he needed a little distraction. He'd struggled with anxiety attacks as a kid and teen. When his bio-dad had forgotten his existence for weeks he had been a fucking mess. Now, for the most part, it only bothered him when he didn't get enough exercise.

He dug his running clothes out of his still-mostly-packed suitcase and dressed quickly. Thankfully, he still had a protein bar stashed in the pocket of his jacket along with some high-carb gel snacks that helped keep him going when he hit the wall. He was good to go.

Out on the street he almost changed his mind. The heavy gray clouds were dark and ominous, but he wasn't going to let that stop him. Not today. He *needed* to feel the unrelenting pavement under his feet, the wind against his face, the fierce pump of his legs and lungs as he pushed himself as far as he could, then farther. The charge he got from pushing past the wall of exhaustion, tapping resources he didn't know he possessed, was addictive. Flying past the mental block of "I can't go any farther" was a high he could ride for miles. No thinking, no worry, only coasting, letting his body give his mind a break. Running was almost as good as sex, he fleetingly thought. Almost.

Pelting rain began about a mile into his run, as he was truly warming up. He didn't stop. Pounding past the rose garden, south along Old Charter, the scenic route that ran along the cliff tops of Skagit Bay, he was in his zone. Endorphins coursed through his system, keeping him going. He felt more alive than he had in months.

Weir had never run this part of the road before, although he had driven it several times as an alternative to I-5. It curved along Skagit Bay, offering tantalizing views of the frigid water and heavy waves crashing against enormous rocks far below. Wind-sculpted evergreens hunched eastward, forever battling the elements. Fascinated by the movement of the water, his heart and breathing in tune with the storm—the rain, the wind, even the crashing waves an extension of his own body—Weir kept running.

The last thing he remembered, before opening his eyes to the frantic deep-blue gaze of a stranger, was being enthralled by the sight of an enormous swell he knew would dwarf all the others he had seen that day. He slowed a little because he wanted to watch it crash against the shore.

"Don't move him," someone said.

"We have to do something." A second, lighter voice.

"His eyes are open."

Another concerned face pushed into view, but Weir didn't have the strength to keep his eyes open any longer. Darkness freed him from the agonizing pain.

SEVEN

It wasn't Sterling's alarm. It was some moron who didn't understand he had a very real need for sleep in order to function as an almost-pleasant human being. Rolling over, he snatched his phone from the bedside table. Why the fuck would Raven be calling him this early? She knew better. Plus, last he'd heard from her she was grounded, except for school and church.

Their ultraconservative parents hadn't learned much the first time around. Raven, fourteen years younger than Sterling, hadn't fallen far from the tree. Sterling's tree. If his youth had been a cautionary tale of how not to raise your gay child, hers was proving to be cautionary fact. Sterling had learned early on to nod and keep his head down. The less he rocked the boat, the less attention his parents paid to him.

Rocking the boat should be under Raven's name in the dictionary, although the connection to the trickster who stole the sun from its keeper and brought it to humans was pretty good, too. Their mother claimed Raven was named because of the color of her hair. Well, Sterling had that hair, too, and that didn't explain his ridiculous name.

His approach to growing up in the Bailey household had

worked until halfway through freshman year of high school when he had been outed by a so-called friend around the same time his mother had discovered she was pregnant with Raven. She'd been content to let her husband, his father, throw him out of the house. After all, she had a do-over child in her belly.

Sterling snorted. Raven had announced her plan to marry her best friend, Isabela, while in kindergarten. She not changed her mind over the years. Raven was the most stubborn person Sterling had ever met.

Their parents had tried to keep her away from him, but this had proved impossible. She had bonded with him like a baby duck with its mother the very first time she laid eyes on him. Sterling was never allowed back into the house to live, but he was allowed to visit his willful, beautiful younger sister. For her alone, he put up with their shit.

Over time he and his parents had come to an agreement of sorts. Sterling would be allowed a relationship with Raven if he never revealed how he had been treated when he had been outed. How for months he had lived on the streets of Seattle, making money the only way a fourteen-year-old boy with no access to his birth certificate or bank account could.

"Why are you calling me this early?" His voice was raspy and dry from sleep.

"Sterling, we need your help." Raven sounded breathless, panicked, and scared. Sterling immediately got out of bed and began looking for something to throw on. He could hear crashing waves and wind through the phone.

"What's wrong?"

"Okay, so I'm not at school."

Sterling groaned. Their parents were going to be fucking livid.

"Me and Pony were driving out on Charter. We found someone who is hurt. Hurt bad. We can't get in trouble, Sterling, the droids will ground me forever, and Pony's folks... This guy really needs help." Fuck, yeah, Pony's folks made their own parents look like PFLAG founding members.

Fifteen minutes later he pulled off Charter, parking next to his sister's little beater car. He had almost missed them because it was raining so hard his wipers were having trouble keeping up. Raven and Pony were standing guard over a sprawled form, trying to protect it from the rain. They'd laid their own jackets over a still figure to keep whoever it was warm and dry.

Before he left the warmth of his car he was dialing 911. No way was someone going to lie unmoving in the freezing rain like that and not need medical assistance.

They hadn't covered the man's face. Sterling stumbled over his words to the emergency dispatcher as recognition propelled him forward—the shock of tangled blond hair snarled in the thick mud, pine needles, and twigs around his head. At the very moment Sterling knelt down, Weir's eyes fluttered open, looking right at him.

"Jesus, Weir." Sterling swallowed down his fear. He didn't know where to look, to touch. "What the fuck happened?"

Weir stared at him for infinity, for a heartbeat, slurring, "Run," before his eyes slid closed again. Sterling wanted to prod him back awake but was afraid of what he couldn't see under the coats Raven and Pony had protected him with. He didn't want to injure him even more.

The sirens called from a long way away. Before they arrived, he rushed the teens off, promising to return their jackets later and demanding they make themselves available so he could find out what the hell they had been doing out driving in that storm. Threatening Raven with their parents if she stepped a single toe out of line.

Once the two were gone, he wanted them back. Against his own better judgment, he slid a hand under one of the coats to find Weir's cold one. It was probably only a reflex, but Sterling thought, maybe, Weir squeezed back.

Flashing lights *finally* appeared around the curve. Sterling stood, waving to get the medics' attention. He had no clue how Raven or Pony had seen Weir lying in the mud amongst the dead weeds and brambles along the side of the road.

For that matter, what the fuck had Weir been doing running out here? Why would any sane person be out in this storm? In his rush, Sterling had thrown on jeans, a T-shirt, his Doc Martens, and a raincoat that was past its prime. It was zipped against the weather, but he was still soaking wet from head to toe.

The ambulance rumbled off the road into the small parking area, and Sterling stepped aside to let them work. He felt helpless. He *was* helpless. A police cruiser rolled up a few minutes later. Two officers emerged. The taller one, K. Jorgensen according to his name tag, stepped over to ask Sterling what he knew about "the victim," while the other went to talk to the EMTs.

"I actually know him, he's—" Oh god, Sterling didn't know what the right thing to say was. He had the impression that Weir was working on a case, but he had no way of knowing for certain, especially with all that leave-for-work-in-the-middle-of-the-night skullduggery yesterday. Had it only been a few hours ago? Was he supposed to tell these guys Weir was a fed?

Sterling panicked. "He's... he's a regular at my bar." Jesus, how was he going to keep his sister out of this shitstorm? Their parents were already fed up with her. Sterling couldn't afford a second mouth to feed, much less fit her in his apartment.

In the end he made up something about heading toward Anacortes when he saw something out of the corner of his eye as he was driving, only realizing after he'd stopped that it was someone he knew. When the officer asked whose coats were covering Weir, Sterling told a half-truth, that they were his sister's and a friend's, and they'd been left in his car. The more complicated his lie became, the more he worried that the officer was suspicious.

It didn't help Sterling's state of mind when one of the EMTs, Roberts, strode over to the two of them to inform Jorgensen that the victim had no ID, no wallet, and no cell phone on his person. If Weir weren't so obviously badly injured, Sterling would have gone over there to shake some sense into him. What had he been thinking, running with no ID or cell phone? Remembering Weir's comment about getting away from his own brain, he wondered what he had been running from today.

After what felt like hours, the EMTs finished poking and prodding Weir. They loaded him onto a stretcher, strapped into a neck brace as well as a backboard. Sterling was unexpectedly agitated. A tide of uncomfortable emotion surged, threatening to drown him like one of the powerful waves crashing below. He needed to see Weir once more before the ambulance doors closed and he was swallowed by bureaucracy.

He grabbed Jorgensen by the arm. "Can I see him before he goes?"

The officer nodded his assent. Sterling dashed back to the ambulance, where they were getting ready to push the collapsible stretcher inside.

Weir's eyes were open again. It must hurt like a bitch to be jostled around. Sterling hadn't seen his injuries, but there was no doubt in his mind that things were broken—the angles had been all wrong.

"Hey." He looked into bottomless brown eyes. "Who do I call? They won't let me go with you."

"Adam," Weir slurred so quietly Sterling almost missed it. He was leaning in close enough that he saw Weir's eyes weren't only brown; there were tiny flecks of gold, confetti reflecting little flashes of light.

The rain, which had never let up, began to fall harder. The EMTs gently nudged Sterling aside so they could get Weir on his way to the hospital. The one sitting in back was pulling the doors shut when Sterling thought to ask, "What hospital?"

"St. Joe's, unless we hear otherwise."

Standing in the rain after the ambulance left the scene, Sterling tried to make sense of what had happened. The location wasn't one of the trickier spots for cars; there were other stretches that were unforgivingly narrow. A sheer cliff rising straight toward the cloud-covered sky on the east side of the road, only a flimsy steel guardrail separating drivers from the freezing, turbulent water of Skagit Bay to the west. Not here. Thank fucking god.

Pony and Raven had discovered Weir at the boundary of a scenic view turnoff. Tourists and Sunday drivers stopped at these spots on their way north or south between Skagit and the flats. There was plenty of room for both runner and vehicle where he had been found. Spinning in a slow circle, Sterling tried thinking like an investigator. Where had the car come from? Had the driver merely missed seeing Weir in the downpour?

Jorgensen and the other officer were efficiently taking pictures and measurements of the scene. Accident-scene tape was draped across the entrance so no one passing by would disturb the evidence, though not a single car had driven past while they worked. Sterling had no idea what he was doing standing there.

The thought of Weir being alone and afraid at the hospital spurred him into motion. After making sure the officers had the information they needed from him, he started his car for the drive back into Skagit. How was he supposed to get a hold of—he assumed—Adam Klay? He knew nothing about Weir. Did he have family who needed to be notified?

Pushing his car to its limit while praying to the gods of "Please don't let me get a speeding ticket," Sterling made it to St. Joe's in record time and rushed inside, only to realize that Weir had been taken in for treatment and he had no right to follow.

EIGHT

The ceaseless beeping was driving him fucking crazy, like an itch he couldn't reach, an irritating whisper of leaves against a windowpane, the irregular snap and buzz of electric lines in the heat. He would try to slip deeper into sleep and the beeping would begin again, get louder, change its pattern.

Weir couldn't stand it any longer. Twisting so he could turn off the alarm, he was hollowed out by an agonizing shock of pain through his entire body, halting any movement. The pain was so intense he whimpered, yet he still couldn't force his eyes open. Concluding he was dreaming as the pain's intensity faded, he attempted to will himself back to sleep.

"Oh no you don't. Not this time."

He knew that voice. He felt a cool hand on his left arm. The arm that didn't hurt.

"Open your eyes." Who was talking to him? Couldn't the asshole leave him alone already?

"I had to cancel my vacation for the second fucking time in three months, so you had better consider opening your eyes. I know you're in there," Adam Klay growled.

"Adam. You can't talk to him like that," Micah admonished his boyfriend. "Weir, Carroll, can you try and open your eyes? We're all very worried about you."

"Don't call him Carroll, he hates that."

Another voice. "His name is Carroll? Damn."

Who was that? "Sterling?" Weir rasped, but his mouth and throat were so dry the word only sounded like slush.

"Shhh. You're going to get us in trouble for bringing you into his room. They said only two visitors." Micah again.

"He said something." Sterling for certain. Something tugged at his memory, but he was too groggy to pin it down and the thought fled back to wherever it had come from.

"He probably said, 'Shut the fuck up, I am trying to sleep.'" Adam again. Did he practice being abrasive and rude in front of his bathroom mirror?

Weir tried lifting his other hand, to wave them away.

"G'way."

"Oh, I was right, he's telling us to go away. Not until you open your eyes for us, Ace."

Fuck, he hated that nickname. He was going to kick Adam's ass, soonish.

Weir's eyes didn't exactly fly open, but he was sufficiently irritated that he managed to drag his eyelids to a level where they allowed unwanted light in. He blinked. It hurt. Everything hurt.

Moving his head hurt, too, so he rolled his eyes around, trying to figure out where the three men in the room were. Adam and Micah both had chairs pulled up on his right, while Sterling, of all people, hovered somewhere to his left. That must be who had touched him when he tried to move. Why was he in a hospital room?

"Canceled vacation?" he managed to whisper before adding a pathetic, "Thirsty."

Through his lashes, he watched Micah get up and speak to someone outside the door. Minutes later, a nurse darted into the room with a large cup of ice. She made everyone go stand in the hallway while she checked and recorded his vital signs. She peppered him with questions, but he could only answer one or two of them and was too tired anyway. Yes, he knew his name, his birthday, and who the president was. As for what happened, he had no recollection beyond leaving his hotel to go for a run.

He was groggy and wanted to go back to sleep, but the nurse, Georgia, explained the police needed to question him about the incident. Oh, great. Fuck. He nodded to encourage her to go away. Hopefully everyone else would go away, too.

He had only met one of the SkPD officers who entered the room before, during the original case that brought both him and Adam to Skagit. Jack Summers. Weir loathed him. He was an asshole. Weir had hoped to find something on him when they conducted the ethics review of SkPD following the Matveev case, but he had been clean. Go figure.

Weir managed to answer a few of their questions before, like it or not, his damaged body decided it was time to return to dreamland. It was impossible to focus on their questions; their presence only increased his exhaustion. As his eyes were slipping closed, he heard Georgia inform them that that was enough; they would have to come back at a later time. It was nice to have her on his side.

* * *

IT WAS a relief when he pried his eyes open again an undetermined amount of time later and only Adam was in the room with him. He appeared to be sleeping, but when Weir made a pathetic sound he turned his head.

Seeing Weir awake, Adam stood, moving closer to the bed. "Ah, awake again. Are you planning on staying with us this time?"

"Du—" His voice crapped out. He cleared his throat and tried again. "Dude, why are you here?" On his best day Adam was barely civil, unless Micah was around. Micah had some kind of superpower that turned Adam to mush.

Adam gripped the rails along the side of the bed. "Ace, regardless of what you think, I actually do like you. I even respect you. When Joey called to let me know, of course we came back. Who else would be here?"

And thank you, Adam, for the sensitive reminder that Weir had no one. He turned his head away, not wanting Adam to see the emotion he couldn't hide. Whatever pain medications they'd pumped him full of left him feeling weak and vulnerable.

"Hey." Adam reached over, gently pulling Weir's chin so he could see his face. Weir wasn't strong enough to stop him. "Hey," he repeated.

Weir loathed the expression on his face. Pity. Weir hated pity. Adam was lucky. In the past few months not only had he fallen in love with a wonderful man, a nice half-brother (one he seemed to tolerate, at least) had crawled out of the woodwork, and he'd bonded with Ed Schultz and his daughter Sara. All in all, a little makeshift family created from his father's unfortunate death. Adam wasn't alone by any stretch of the imagination.

For months Weir had harbored a little crush on Adam, even when the guy acted like a complete tool. He'd known, though, as soon as he'd seen Adam and Micah together, that Adam was a goner. Weir was jealous, and man enough to admit it.

"Hey," Adam said a third time.

"'Hey' what? I'm not deaf."

"Christ, you're prickly today. What have they got you on? Demerol makes me a cranky asshole."

"Doesn't explain the rest of the time," Weir muttered.

Adam grinned, reaching to pull the chair he'd been sitting in closer to the bed. After making himself comfortable, he asked, "What happened? Do you remember? I want to hear it from you, not that caveman, Summers."

Weir gathered his scattered thoughts. "I decided to go for a run. I hadn't been going. I needed to get out. It was raining; I went anyway." Adam watched closely as he tried to put together a timeline of what happened. "What day is it? How long have I been here?"

"It's Thursday afternoon. Two days. They kept you sedated until last night. It was this morning when you woke up before." That sentence was way too complicated. Fuck, his head hurt.

A neuron trudged half-heartedly across his sore brain. Closing one eye, he tried to think. "Was Sterling here?" He had a vague memory of hearing his voice.

"Yeah, your boyfriend was here."

A wash of panic flooded his system. Boyfriend? Sterling wasn't his boyfriend. They had sucked each other off a couple times; that did not equal boyfriend. A boyfriend required more emotional investment than Weir was capable of.

"By the look on your face, although it's a bit hard to tell between the swelling and the bruising, I'd say you disagree? He seems to care, if that makes any difference."

Weir attempted to wave the comment away but ended up gasping from intense pain when he tried to move his right arm again. Finally he asked the question he most dreaded the answer to. "What's the damage?"

"Injuries?" Adam asked.

Weir nodded, very carefully.

"Regardless of what it's going to sound like, apparently you were very lucky."

"Not feeling lucky."

"Yeah, well, you're alive and annoyed with me, Ace. The short list is: fractured collarbone, right arm compound fracture, deeply bruised ribs. Your right femur, fractured. The orthopedic doc will be in soon to go over the details with you. Last I heard they were talking surgery as soon as the swelling goes down. Sounds like you may get some superhero metal stuff. There doesn't appear to be a spinal injury. Whoever hit you, they slowed coming around the curve, probably only going about thirty miles an hour. Maybe less." Adam did the finger-quote thing when he said "only."

"Fuck. Anything else?"

"We were hoping you could tell us."

"I don't remember anything except running, thinking about geoducks and why anyone would put something that ugly near their mouth. They look like giant cocks."

"You like cock."

Weir glared at him. "Not those cocks. Anyway, tell me more."

"Sterling *says* he found you at milepost seven near the scenic overlook turnout. Happened to be driving by, he *says*. There you were, lying on the ground like a rag doll. The car that hit you came from behind and was traveling fast enough to knock you into the guardrail—that's where the bruised ribs come from. It's lucky you weren't further down the road or you would have ended up in the surf. What the hell were you thinking, running in that weather?" Adam demanded.

"I was thinking I needed to go for a run before I went batshit crazy. I was thinking I needed to clear my head. I *wasn't* thinking I'd nearly be killed by some fucking asshole."

Weir felt tired again. He'd been hit by a car and left to die. It weighed him down. Images of Esther haunted him. Had she been run over and abandoned? Tossed in a ditch? Buried in a shallow grave? It was probably the medication, but still disturbing. Adam continued talking, while he shut his eyes and let himself drift away.

* * *

WHEN HE WOKE for the third time he was, unfortunately, truly awake. A Dr. Mortimer and a different nurse were in the room. It was still Thursday, early afternoon, they said.

"Mr. Weir?" The doctor was an older white guy, mid-fifties, with a shock of white hair and a stoop from being nearly seven feet tall, as far as Weir could estimate from lying flat on his back. He made a face at being called mister.

"Yeah?"

Long and short, he was going to be fitted for not one, but two metal plates. One in his arm and one in his thigh. His only question before being rolled to the operating room was, "Will I be able to run again?"

The nurse was sweet, a ginger-haired woman who smiled down at him, saying, "We certainly hope so."

NINE

"Look, he seems to like you."

Sterling squinted at the crazy man.

"Okay, *tolerate* might be a better word, but that says a lot. He's not an easy guy to get to know. He doesn't let his guard down very often." Adam sighed and ran his fingers through his hair. Definitely crazy.

"Why me?" He did *not* sound like a whiny bitch.

"For all the reasons I said. Plus, I am going on this goddamned vacation, but I can't if Weir is here alone. The hotel he's staying in isn't going to cut it. He doesn't have anybody to help him out, all right? Plus, stairs. It works out, too, because if you guys are around Micah will quit worrying about his psycho cat. It's the perfect solution. Also, I won't tell the SkPD that you weren't first at the scene."

Sterling gaped.

"Shut your mouth, you're gonna catch flies."

Sterling shut his mouth.

"So, am I calling Micah and letting him know it's a done deal, or what?"

"Fine. But this is ridiculous. We don't know each other."

"By the end of it both of you will have a new friend; isn't that sweet?"

Sterling wanted to strangle Adam. If the man weren't built like a brick shithouse, he might seriously consider it. He had a bar to take care of, a sister to keep an eye on, and other shit he was barely getting a handle on. "How do you know I wasn't first at the scene?"

Adam pinched the bridge of his nose. "Why am I constantly having to remind people that *I* am the one who is a federal investigator? Your story was a bit farfetched, plus I wondered about the two jackets. I had your phone records checked out. Don't worry, your sister is clear; it wasn't her car. You're both ruled out as suspects."

A weight Sterling had been struggling with lifted. He believed his sister would never purposefully do anything like that, a hit and run, but what if she'd panicked, left the scene, and then come back? Sterling had concocted all sorts of scenarios over the past few days, none of which looked good for Raven. He almost felt like he needed to apologize for suspecting she might be so careless.

Who was he kidding? Raven was a newly minted sixteen-year-old driving in terrible weather conditions. Pony was older, but that hardly made a difference. It was not beyond the scope of imagination that they were responsible for Weir's condition.

The last four days had taken their toll on Sterling. After following the ambulance to the hospital, he'd hadn't known what to do. With Weir somewhere on the other side of the automatic doors, hooked up to god only knew what kinds of tubes and bags of fluids, Sterling had felt helpless. Helplessness was not something he had experienced in many years. It was a feeling he detested.

"Fine."

"Whoop! I'm calling Micah right now." When Adam reached

over to fist-bump Sterling, he couldn't help recoiling. The guy was certifiable.

It was Joey James's fault that Sterling had claimed to be Weir's boyfriend.

He'd been desperate. Joey had approached him while he was cooling his heels and freaking out in the ER.

"Sterling, you came in asking for Weir, the guy who was found on the side of the road?"

"Kind of, yeah." He had forgotten that Joey worked in the ER. Joey and he had never been friends. Currently they were operating under a let-bygones-be-bygones sort of truce. Sterling hadn't been kind to Joey when they were in school together. He regretted that, but couldn't change it.

Joey looked at him closely, a little closer than Sterling was comfortable with. "So are you guys, um, seeing each other?" Joey irritated the shit out of Sterling. He was a very large personality crammed into a single, very petite, package. Also extremely persistent. Sterling wondered how Buck dealt with him on a daily basis. The guy was fucking exhausting. Joey and Buck's sweet New Year's kiss under the mistletoe bobbed to the surface of his memory, and Sterling lost his power to resist, because that kiss had been adorable.

"Kind of, okay. We hung out a couple times."

"Hung out." Joey had his hands on his hips.

"Fuck, you are irritating. Hung out, blow jobs, what the fuck else do you want to know?"

"Well," from Joey's tone of voice Sterling knew he would regret his outburst, "I was wondering if you want to be able to see him at some point, but for that you are going to have to be more than a 'blow-job friend.'"

And that was how Sterling went from "blow-job friend" to "boyfriend."

* * *

STERLING WAS CURRENTLY PLOTTING Joey's death. Joey had opened his big fucking mouth and told Adam that Sterling and Weir were an "item." Who the fuck was an "item" these days? It made him sound like he was in his seventies instead of his thirties. Sterling took a deep, calming breath. He needed to focus on the bar and its endless paperwork, not freak out about babysitting the child detective.

"Yo, Bailey, what this I hear about you and some girl? Carol?" Kent yelled over the small crowd in the Loft tonight.

Joey must have told Adam about the fake-boyfriend thing. Then a sort of insane tin-can fucking phone tag had ensued. Sterling could only imagine that Adam had mentioned something to Ed; Adam wasn't friendly enough with anyone else in Skagit who spread gossip. Ed must have told Sara, and from there it spread like a wildfire. Now the whole fucking city of Skagit thought he and the (admittedly very sexy) injured, not female, Weir, were an "item." ITEM. He had, happily, never been an item with anyone. Ever.

Ever.

He scowled across the short distance to where Kent was standing at the door, checking IDs. "Shut it. Have you met me?"

Kent looked like he wanted to press further, but Sterling narrowed his eyes at him, effectively ending the interrogation. Sterling went back to pouring drinks and thinking about Weir, wondering exactly how he had gotten himself into this mess. He managed quite nicely, thank you, avoiding relationships. Didn't want one, never pursued one, happily single. Suddenly he was expected to take care of someone? He shuddered.

It wasn't like he had been horribly scarred by a breakup or anything. Sure, his parents rejected him, but Sterling had landed on his feet. Eventually. The lesson learned had been, don't trust anyone, especially the ones you think have your back. He was making it on his own. His achievements were his alone, things no one could take from him. And he had plans.

He did not want, or need, a relationship to validate his existence.

There was no way this bizarre plan of Adam's was going to end well. He liked Weir enough. He *had* panicked at the scene of the accident, and later at the hospital. Any normal human being would have.

Maybe not every normal human being would have agreed to Joey's cockamamie pretend-boyfriend scheme in order to gain access to Weir's hospital room. But Sterling had needed to see with his own eyes that Weir could recover. He hadn't been able to rid himself of the gruesome image of Weir's broken body strewn across the mud and weeds, discarded like so much trash.

For a Saturday night it was damn slow. Sterling had his back to the door and was restocking the liquor lining the back bar, making a mental note that St. Patrick's Day had taken its toll on the supply and he needed to stock up on Irish whiskey. When he turned around, Adam and Micah were sitting at the bar. Adam was sporting an irritating grin. Sterling wanted to slap it off his face, except the agent surely had moves that would put Sterling in traction.

"Thanks so much for offering to house sit, Sterling," Micah gushed.

Sterling glared at Adam. The asshole didn't even have the grace to look ashamed of himself.

"It will make such a difference for Weir, too." Micah leaned closer over the bar top, whispering, "He doesn't have any family, so even if he could get home to California, he would have to go into assisted care for a few weeks, maybe longer. We came directly from the hospital. His surgery went well, but he has physical therapy and movement limitations. He's lucky he's in such good shape, although the doctor did mention he's underweight."

"Yeah, I bet he's thrilled you're sharing all this, Micah," Adam drawled.

"If Sterling is going to be helping him, he needs to know this stuff," Micah retorted.

Sterling groaned, rolling his eyes toward the ceiling and trying to dig up patience from somewhere. Micah was a seriously nice guy. Adam, he was going to vote off the island.

Micah looked from Adam to Sterling. "I've got the house ready. Weir can use my bedroom on the main floor. You'll have to take one of the second-floor ones, sorry. I've emptied them out as much as I could on short notice. We're planning on leaving tomorrow."

"Tomorrow?" Sterling choked out, his voice rising an octave. He hoped his sister appreciated his sacrifice. If he was going to be somebody's nanny, she better not plan on missing any school or fucking up in any other way until she was well over the age of eighteen.

"Clock's ticking. Warning, I have no idea how Weir is going to handle this… arrangement." Adam tapped the bar with his thumb and forefinger.

Sterling stopped fidgeting with the bar towels stacked underneath the drink station. "You haven't told him?"

"Time didn't seem quite right. He was in recovery, coming out of the anesthesia."

"Wait." Sterling finally clued in on what Micah had said a minute earlier. "He had surgery already?" Sterling hadn't known Weir was having surgery so soon. An unnamed emotion surged again. "He's okay?"

"Yep, got a couple metal plates that'll make it fun to go through airport security with him."

"Oh." He didn't know what to say, but the situation was becoming increasingly ludicrous.

* * *

THAT NIGHT, after he'd finally closed and locked the front door behind Kent, Sterling poured himself a drink. He rarely drank, since he worked at night and generally chose not to drink after his shift. Beer he still couldn't drink unless it was dark and smooth; it reminded him too much of what he did to get by those months when he'd been homeless and scared.

Finding the courage to blow a stranger in a filthy, stinking back alley had come at a steep price. Sterling had managed to steer clear of meth and the ever-present heroin while he was living on the street, but not cheap alcohol. An eighty-cent beer went a long way for a not-quite-fifteen-year-old lightweight, making it seem easier to put his mouth on a stranger's dick. Sex for money or food (or, very rarely, both); he refused to be ashamed of what he'd had to do to survive. Pushing those memories away where they belonged, Sterling straightened his shoulders and concentrated on the present.

He wasn't scared anymore, at least not scared of where he would sleep or if he had enough to eat. Now he was wary of a bedridden, surfer-dude federal agent who had to be six years younger than him. Sterling was curious about Weir, wondered about the story of his sister, his family—but not *that* curious.

Jesus Christ, what the hell was he doing, sitting here at the bar with a shot of bourbon, wondering about some guy he'd sucked off a couple times?

Shaking his head at himself, he rinsed out the glass before setting it in the glass washer and heading back to the office. He had work to do. Business proposals didn't write themselves. He'd been haunting the local bookstore, already dropped a couple hundred bucks trying to learn the vagaries of small-business ownership. There would be a meeting with the bank soon, He needed to be prepared.

TEN

"What? No!"

Weir was flabbergasted that Adam would go behind his back like this. He looked to Micah for support. Instead, he received a sheepish crook of the head.

"No way, Micah. You too?"

They'd stopped in to visit him on their way out of town. Informing him that Sterling would be taking him to Micah's house, where both of them would be staying. Together.

The fuck that was going to happen. No way was he going to allow himself to be taken care of like some invalid.

Fuck.

He *was* an invalid.

The physical therapist, Dana, had already been in to torture him. He'd had surgery less than twenty-four hours ago and they already wanted him up and walking, starting with four times a day across his hospital room. The whole thing sucked. He was in agony, and now he was being pawned off on some stranger he'd had bar sex with. Great, just great.

His arms were both killing him: the right from surgery, the left from bearing much of his body weight. He couldn't use a walker because of the surgery to insert a metal rod, correcting the compound fracture that had shattered his right radius. Likely when the car had hit him, he'd instinctively tried to stop the forward motion with his right arm.

He could only use a crutch with his left arm, which, while not broken, was covered with bruises and cuts from gravel and whatever else was on the ground where he had landed. He had road rash pretty much along his entire body, including his face.

As soon as he could walk the length of the hallway outside his room they would release him, Dana said. Merely walking across his room had been hell.

"You guys are leaving already?" Weir couldn't explain why he felt so abandoned. It had to be the medications. Like Adam said, they messed with a person.

Adam actually looked apologetic. "Yeah, Ace, we gotta go. I've been in contact with a few people, relatives, who knew my dad, and I can't keep changing the dates. I've already canceled once."

Weir understood, he did, but he didn't have to like it. "You're leaving me here, alone?" He was whining.

Micah piped up. "You won't be alone, Weir. That's why we arranged for Sterling to stay with you. He's agreed to pick you up when they discharge you and get you to my house. Which is great, because now I won't worry about Frankie being alone."

Right, Frankie, Micah's hideous twenty-pound cat. Last time Weir had been over, Frankie had proudly presented Micah with what was left of a baby bird, in the middle of the living room.

"Anything on the car that hit me?" He changed the subject, but Adam shot him a knowing glance. Weir gave him a "fuck you" glance back. He had no choice and Adam knew it.

"Nope. Nothing. When you're set up at Micah's I'm having Sammy come talk geoducks with you. I'd like to think this was an accident, but we might as well act like it isn't until we know better."

"Sammy?" Jesus Christ. Sammy Ferreira was the newest

member of Adam's team. Nice-enough guy, but he followed Weir around like a puppy, constantly asking him questions, wanting to "get to know" him. Sammy was in a contest to be nominated the nicest person on earth, maybe nicer than Micah. He helped old ladies cross the street, rescued abandoned puppies, climbed trees for stranded kittens.

"Yeah, Sammy. Get over your problem with him; he's an excellent agent and his skills complement yours. He is not replacing you, he's helping you."

Right. Adam had to go for the jugular. Figuring out what a frightened little boy Weir was on the inside, afraid he wasn't good enough. Because he hadn't been good enough, had he? He hadn't been even a close runner-up. Esther had been the golden child. When she disappeared, the family fell apart.

Christ, he needed to get off whatever drugs they had him on.

Dana swept in, ready to take him for his second painful walk of the day. Adam and Micah took that as an excellent time to leave. Adam said he would be in contact daily, and not to overdo it. Micah snorted at that, and Weir was reminded what a horrible patient Adam had been after being shot in the chest in December. A bad case of pot and kettle he had going on.

WEIR WAS in the hospital for another week. They would have let him go sooner, except they were concerned about him doing too much and reinjuring himself. During that week he, unfortunately, had a great deal of time to think. Very few people came to see him. Mohammad called a few times to check up on him, but that was it.

Joey popped his head in a few times, but that didn't count as a visit because he worked at the hospital. Joey was a nice guy, and Weir found himself liking him. He was irreverent, did not care what other people thought about him, and was naturally good-humored.

He didn't expect a visit from Thomas Poole. The detective arrived just after lunch one day. Merely walking into Weir's hospital room, Poole managed to suck all the extra space out of it. Weir kind of wanted to open a window so a little oxygen could flow inside. Even Dana, his chirpy and cheery physical therapist, took one look at Poole and judged him a lost cause before leaving to torture another patient.

"Weir." Poole stood at attention, with his hat and sunglasses still on, reminding Weir of a Canadian Mountie. Unreadable and inscrutable.

"Poole." The über-man greeting made Weir uncomfortable. He went by his last name out of self-preservation, not some inherent need to prove his masculinity.

"Glad to see you made it."

"Uh, yeah, me too." Why was Poole even here?

"No leads?"

"Not as far as I know. You'd have to check in with Klay, or the local PD."

"I'm sorry you got hurt." Was the man actually trying to comfort him? Someone should tell him to never, ever do that.

"Thanks. Looks like everything will heal, and now I have some superhero titanium."

There was an awkward pause while neither of them could come up with another topic to talk about. Weir cast about for something, anything, to break the silence. He came up empty.

"I'll be going. I just wanted to see how you were doing." With an even-more-awkward little bow, Poole departed as quickly as he had come.

* * *

WEIR WAS CONVINCED he was going mad, he was so bored. TV was making him insanely grumpy. The shared room they'd moved him to had TVs for each of the four inmates. The competing soundtracks of daytime soaps, Judge Judy, NASCAR, or whatever else was on, were mind-numbing. Joey had brought him some crossword puzzles and books, but he couldn't concentrate enough on them to read a single page or solve a clue.

Instead he brooded.

Sterling finally showed up the day before he was set to be released. Weir had managed to walk the length of the corridor twice without tipping over only a half-hour earlier. It hurt like fuck, but he did it, teeth clenched.

It irritated him that he felt a surge of pleasure when Sterling tapped on the privacy curtain. Weir wanted to be angry with him. He hadn't seen anyone except Joey, Dr. Mortimer, and the other caretakers since Adam and Micah had deserted him.

"I don't know why you're doing this, but you don't have to. We'll tell Adam something came up. I'll be fine on my own." Because also, Weir didn't want to be exposed to this guy. To *anyone*. It was hard enough feeling helpless in the hospital. If he could walk the length of the corridor, he would be fine at Micah's alone.

Sterling looked at him as if he had grown a second head, dark eyebrows shooting up and practically touching his hairline. "Are you fucking kidding me? No way am I going back on a promise to Adam."

Oh, that's how it was. A promise to Adam. Not about wanting to help Weir out. Nothing about helping a guy through a rough patch.

Oh god, he was completely psycho. One minute, mad because Sterling showed up to hash out details about his release, and the absolute very next, sad because it's a favor for Adam. He needed his head examined. Or a pillow shoved over his face.

"I stopped by to see if there was stuff you like, or whatever.

I'm heading to the grocery store. Looks like you're getting out of here by noon tomorrow, but I gotta work tonight so I'm going now. I know you like chicken chili, and that's about it."

Weir *could* actually feel worse. Not only was Sterling helping him out, it was on top of his job as a bartender. Shutting his eyes for a second, he tried to bring himself under control. After a deep breath, he opened them again. Sterling was still standing next to the bed waiting for an answer, one eyebrow raised.

"No red meat, no processed sugar, sprouted-grain bread," he mumbled. "Plain yogurt would be nice, too. Thanks." He didn't intend for his requests to sound ungrateful, but he was certain they did anyway.

Sterling nodded, pulling out his smartphone to make a few notes. "Anything else I should know? You allergic? Have a favorite brand of toilet paper, only drink imported goat's milk?"

"Fucker."

"Asshole."

Like that, they were on even footing. Weir was grateful. Sterling flipping him shit was better than any therapy. It was everyone else walking around on eggshells making him crazy. Clearly, Sterling wasn't going to let Weir's mood get to him.

"I'm dying for a salad. A real salad, not from a bag." Weir stuck his lower lip out tragically, milking the moment.

"A salad."

Weir blinked at him. "Macaroni and cheese. Homemade? I'm supposed to try to put on some weight."

"Fuck my life. Fine. Whatever. I'll be here by ten tomorrow morning so I can eavesdrop on whatever the doc has to say before you check out of this place."

With a quick salute, he was gone, and Weir was left wondering who Sterling really was underneath that goth exterior.

* * *

BEFORE BEING RELEASED the next morning, Weir was subjected to one more brutal physical therapy session. He almost shed actual tears, it hurt so much. But Dana was adamant that he had to increase the amount of weight he bore on his right leg every day, that this was the fastest, healthiest, and most effective way to promote new bone growth.

When Sterling showed up, Weir was so exhausted from the PT he had a hard time being excited about going home. Well, going to Micah's. Home was nebulous; even his condo near Hermosa Beach didn't feel like home. He was there so rarely, and then only for such short periods of time, that he had never done anything to it. Bed, couch, TV, a few pots and pans. Gaming system. A plastic plant a colleague had given him as a joke. That summed it up.

Looking around Micah's house, Weir recognized a real home. He saw signs that Adam was on his way to making it his home as well. A small collection of pictures featuring Micah's deceased family: his little sister Shona smiling with her friend Jessica in front of a huge wooden roller coaster, Micah's parents with their arms around each other at some professional function, looking happy. Added to these were a few photographs of Adam with his dad when he was very young. Micah must have found them and put them up, but Adam had let them stay there.

Weir had few memories of early childhood. He knew he had felt safe and happy. Most of his memories started the day his sister disappeared, every prior experience eclipsed by a single moment in time. He'd been asleep on the couch in his parents' living room. The TV was on the Disney Channel or Nickelodeon. He'd woken up and was lying there under his favorite blanket with his eyes closed, letting the mindless chatter of cartoon characters wash over him.

He remembered hearing his mother calling for Esther, her voice becoming more and more shrill. He'd gotten up to look, too. Sometimes he and Esther played hide-and-seek; Weir knew all the places she hid. As evening grew closer to full dark, his mother became frantic, demanding he turn off the TV so they could hear Esther if she answered their calls.

His dad came home from work to find the house in an uproar. Esther was three years older than Weir. He worshipped her, thought she knew everything, soaked up all the information she brought home from being in the second grade already. Sometimes Weir did her homework. It was fun; the homework he brought home from school was easy and boring.

Esther didn't come home that night, the next night, or ever again.

Weir sighed and continued clumping toward the couch. His leg and arm throbbed. He needed to sit down.

"Um, Micah fixed up his bedroom for you. So, no stairs," Sterling reminded him.

Yeah, Weir had managed to block that part out of his mind. Because he wanted to hang out in Micah and Adam's bed. Where they had sex. Lots of it. Sex he had unfortunately witnessed more than once. He shuddered at the memory.

"I'm tired of lying down," he whined.

"They said you still need to keep your leg elevated."

Irrational irritation surfaced. Barely managing to control it, Weir bit out, "I know. I was there, remember?" Okay, so maybe not such a good job controlling his temper. Sterling seemed to take it in stride. His twisted smile made a quick appearance before he moved next to Weir. Placing an arm around his waist, Sterling helped him to the couch, then carefully lifted Weir's leg onto one of the colorful throw pillows Micah had strewn about.

Leaning Weir's crutch against the wall next to the couch, Sterling proceeded to take the variety of medications the hospital had sent Weir home with and organize them on the side table. Without asking, he went into the kitchen, returning with a huge glass of water and some cheese and crackers. Only then did Weir realize how hungry he was.

Sheepishly, he accepted the food. "Thanks, sorry."

"No worries. Adam warned me you'd be a bastard." He grabbed one of the bottles of pills and shook out two, handing them to Weir. "Here, it's painkiller time. The doc said there's no reason to tough it out. Right now your body needs to heal, not be distracted by pain."

Yes, but the painkillers made him groggy. He frowned at the pills in his hand. Sterling wasn't giving him a choice, standing over him until Weir popped them in his mouth and took a big swig of water. He grimaced at the metallic taste of the pills.

"Have some cheese and crackers."

Before he fell asleep from pain and exhaustion, Weir managed to finish off most of the plate of food Sterling had brought out. Sterling spent the time bringing bags into the house from his car. Not only had he gone shopping, he'd gone to Weir's hotel and picked up his luggage.

Weir was starting to drift off when Sterling knelt down in front of him. Even though he had no desire for sex at the moment, it reminded Weir of their exploits in Sterling's office. Sterling must have thought the same thing, because he quirked that fucking eyebrow at him before speaking.

"Today is normally my day off, but I have to go in for a few hours. I'm sorry to have to leave you alone. Can I trust that you won't do anything stupid while I'm gone? When I get back we'll get you into the bedroom."

"Yeah, promise," Weir murmured.

The sound of the front door opening and then closing behind Sterling was the last thing he remembered for several hours.

ELEVEN

Where this newfound well of patience was coming from, Sterling
had no idea. Weir had been a complete jackass from the moment
Sterling arrived at St. Joe's to pick him up and take him to
Micah's. Weir'd been arguing with the physical therapist. She
threw Sterling a glance of relief when he entered the room, using
his arrival as an excuse to leave. Weir had argued with the orthopedic doctor who came to educate him on post-surgery care and
recovery. Every single instruction the doc had, Weir had questioned or barely tolerated, until Sterling had enough and politely
told the man (Weir, not the doc) to shut it.

Weir's mouth had opened and snapped back shut. He even
managed to keep it that way until he was officially cleared to
leave. Then he started again when the nurse brought a wheelchair
to transport him to the front entrance, where Sterling had left his
car in the visitor's lot. As if he could possibly walk that far.

Then he'd bitched about Sterling's car. Sterling admitted it
was a little too low to the ground and difficult for Weir to get his
leg into. But Jesus Christ, he was doing the guy a favor and all he
could do was bitch? Of course, after Weir had demolished the
plate of cheese and crackers Sterling had thrown together, before

thankfully falling asleep, Sterling figured out Weir had been hangry. The guy was a complete bitch queen when he needed food. Note to self.

Weir was far too skinny. He'd been skinny before the accident; now he was bordering on dangerously underweight. The doctor had taken Sterling aside while Weir had been arguing with the nurse and told him if Weir expected to heal well he needed to gain weight. Sterling was given strict instructions to get him to eat. Too bad Sterling could barely boil water.

Sterling was headed into what was bound to be an uncomfortable staff meeting. He hadn't wanted to schedule it for today, but had been left no choice. He'd waited as long as possible, to see if he was imagining things, but now he had to put a stop to it. Any sign of theft or unusual activity would give the bank pause, and he couldn't afford for that to happen. Not when he was so close to his dream.

Parking in front of the Loft instead of behind it, since he wasn't staying, he opened the front door and left it unlocked for the meeting. Inside he pulled a few tables together, grabbed some sodas out of the fridge, along with chips and salsa, and got ready for the staff to arrive. Might as well make them comfortable before the interrogation began.

Kent and Kevin arrived together, interesting. Sterling hadn't known they were friends, although he supposed it was none of his business. Mac, the quasi–kitchen manager, showed up next. Pretty much everybody else arrived at the same time: Jude, Sebastian, and Marco, the main serving staff, then Cameron and Danny, who mostly bussed and did dishes. Sometimes Cam helped Mac in the kitchen with prep. These were the core staff, and one of them was stealing.

Pulling a chair out and turning it around so he could sit in it backwards, he motioned for everybody to sit. All part of his plan to make them comfortable.

First, they went over schedules and some ideas Mac had for

the menu. Sterling wanted to change things up a bit. Everybody had burgers; he wanted the Loft to stand out a little more. He'd already worked on the beer list, adding more local breweries and artisan stuff. Sterling wasn't a fan himself, but out-of-towners liked their fancy beer. Even the gay ones.

"All right, we've done the easy part of this meeting." He looked over the staff one by one. "I hate to say this, because I like to think we're a kind of family here at the Loft, that I am a pretty decent judge of character... but somebody is stealing liquor." He raised his hand to keep people from chiming in right away. "So far it hasn't been a lot. But it has been enough for me to notice, since I'm usually the one who takes inventory. Last month four different bottles of a variety of liquor disappeared.

"Here's the deal: it stops now. This *one* time, I'm giving whoever is doing this a pass. You know what you took, and I want it replaced by the end of the week, Sunday close. No questions asked, whoever it is, however you choose to return it, is up to you. Am I clear?"

A chorus of muted yesses while everybody gave each other the side-eye, trying to be Agatha Christie and figure out who the culprit was. Ugh, Sterling hated this part of his job.

Before they left, he cornered Kent and Kevin. He was nearly positive it wasn't one of them.

"Guys." They stopped their meander toward the door. Kevin shoved his hands in his pockets, trying to hide that he had been reaching for Kent's hand. Aw. "I'm going to need some extra help for a while, maybe even a month. Can you two each take a couple more shifts?"

Kevin shrugged. "Yeah, I could use the money." His eyes widened, "But I'm not, I mean—" He broke off, muttering, "I'm not stealing, neither is Kent."

Sterling shook his head. He didn't think it was one of them, but he couldn't make any promises, either. "Look, I need some time off. This isn't the best time to take it, but I don't have a choice. We'll figure this out. If you guys could cover Thursday, Friday, and Saturday for a while, and one of you take Sunday and the other Wednesday. I'll pick up the slack with Monday and Tuesday."

They looked at each other, doing some sort of silent communication thing.

"No sex in the office," Sterling added for good measure. He was the only one who got to have sex in the office.

Seemed like he was too late with that warning, as he watched both of their faces turn bright red. Kevin's was harder to see, with his skin tone, but Sterling could see the telltale blush.

To Sterling's relief, they agreed to the extra hours. He didn't trust Weir not to do something stupid and reinjure himself before he was fully healed. Plus, he had physical therapy and other doctor appointments Sterling needed to make sure he got to. He had the sneaking suspicion that Weir would never set foot in a medical facility again if he didn't have an escort.

As he got back into his car, leaving Kevin and Kent to sort out who was going to work that night, his phone buzzed in his back pocket. Dragging it out, he saw a voice mail from his mother, of all people. He had a sinking feeling this was not going to be good. She only contacted him when she needed him to talk Raven off the ledge. He did not need this today, but he'd learned not to ignore these rare phone calls.

"Sterling." His mother's voice was clipped. A sure sign of anger or frustration.

"Sybil."

"Your sister skipped school today and is out with that... person... I banned her from association with." Good lord, his mother sounded like she had an actual stick up her ass. Taking a deep breath, he tried reason. It had never worked before, but what the hell, he might as well try.

"Which friend?" He knew full well Sybil meant Pony. Raven was nothing if not a passionately devoted friend. If Pony was in a bad situation, if they needed help or a shoulder to cry on, there was no stopping Raven.

"The horsey one."

"Pony."

"It doesn't matter. This was her last chance. Your father has had it with her. I have had it with her. We are making arrangements for boarding school. They can take her mid-April."

Sterling felt a sharp pain in his chest. He had to tighten his grip on his phone in order not to drop it. Fuck. They had used "boarding school" as a threat before but never followed through. Boarding school was code for pray-away-the-gay therapy.

"Why are you calling me if you've already decided?" Raven was an amazing person, his favorite person on earth. The only person he loved. There was no way this was happening if he could prevent it. How, he had no idea. His mother must have an ulterior motive behind calling him.

"She listens to you."

"She would listen to you if you respected her at all."

"We will not tolerate her lifestyle choice. The church is very clear about what an appropriate relationship is." They'd changed churches after he had come out; the one they had been going to turned out to be too liberal. He rolled his eyes.

"Sybil, I don't understand why you're calling me. I am a gay man, your own son, who you allowed to be banned from the only home I knew when you found out. Nothing has changed since then. I am still gay. It is not a choice, not a lifestyle. Your refusal to understand this is the root of all your issues with Raven."

"She listens to you." Her voice had gone low, a wheedling tone.

"She listens to me because I listen to her."

"Sterling, your father is adamant. She cannot stay in this house any longer."

A dam burst inside him, words he'd been saving up for screaming into the empty night rushing out before he could stop himself. "How can you stay with him? Why do you let him take your children away from you? Why is Stephen Bailey more important to you than your own children?"

Damn, damn, damn. Taking air in through his nose, he tamped down his anger. It wouldn't help.

Sybil didn't answer. Sterling didn't expect her to. He thought he knew why she stayed: fear of the unknown, fear of what would happen to her status in the community if she left him. And yet, when she called, Sterling answered and did her bidding because he lived in fear, too. Fear of what would happen to his amazing sister if she was forced onto the streets or, god forbid, into some sort of boarding school that focused on "behavioral therapy."

Raven was scary smart. Sterling was not embarrassed to admit she was much smarter than he was. That was the core problem. She understood exactly what her actions were going to mean for her. She didn't care. She was a passionate, incredibly intelligent, caring human being. Their parents had done her a disservice by keeping her in the public school system in Skagit. Now, however, it was far, far too late to send her away.

Conversion therapy over his dead body.

"She's sixteen, Sybil. It's great to know you managed to keep her in the house two more years than me. That's almost a 15 percent increase. Wow, I'm super impressed."

The rest of the staff not working that night were filing out of the bar. Seeing his car, Cameron looked curiously at him. Normally, of course, his car was around back because his apartment was upstairs, but he wasn't living there right now. Sterling needed to get moving. He didn't want Weir waking up and doing something stupid.

"What do you want?" he repeated. Goddammit, whatever she wanted, he was going to make her fucking ask for it. Starting the car, he pulled a U-turn from the curb, violating about ten traffic laws, including having his phone to his ear.

"She said she would go to school if she could stay with you."

In his five-hundred-square-foot apartment? What was his mother thinking? Sybil had no concept of how Sterling lived. She had never visited him, and he had never invited her. She chose to live in a bubble, safely padded by Stephen's money.

"Stephen agrees with this?"

There was no way his father would agree. They hadn't seen or spoken to each other in years, communicating only through Sybil or Raven, but Sterling knew he would never agree to have Raven stay in his home.

"He will. Please, Sterling. I don't want to send her away." She was actually whining.

Then fucking don't, he thought.

Honestly, he had no idea how the inner workings of his mother's brain operated, how she lived with herself.

"I'll talk to her." He'd let Raven stay with him, but he needed to figure out how that was going to work, since he was babysitting Weir at the moment. *Fuck. My. Life.*

Passing the bank on his way home, back to Micah's, he made a mental note to reschedule with them. He hoped they were understanding.

He parked in front of Micah's house and took a moment to collect himself before heading up the front steps and inside. There was no way he could do this without asking Micah first. Fuck, he hated airing his dirty laundry.

The living room was quiet. Weir was still passed out from the pain medications Sterling had plied him with. As the front door clicked shut behind Sterling, Weir's eyelids cracked open, and he tracked Sterling's movement across the room toward the kitchen before shutting them again. Once in the kitchen, Sterling allowed himself a minor freak-out. Elbows on the counter, he leaned in to rest his forehead against his hands. Fuck, fuck, fuck.

When he was done with his breakdown he called the newest number saved in his contacts. Micah answered on the second ring.

"Everything okay with Weir?" His voice was breathless, concerned.

"Yeah, no, sorry to worry you. He's here, currently tucked up safe on the couch. I'll badger him into your room soon enough. Listen, I, uh, have a favor to ask."

By the time he was done telling Micah the sordid story of his, and Raven's, family life—as little as he could get away with, but feeling like Micah deserved some sort of explanation—Sterling felt eviscerated all over again. He didn't share with many people, anyone really, what had happened to him as a young teen, but it couldn't happen to Raven. Sterling wouldn't let it.

The next call he made was to the girl herself. She answered right away; she'd been waiting for his call. Ten minutes later, he had a verbal agreement that she would stay with him and go to school every day. No skipping, no shenanigans. She would be there by five, as she had the Gay-Straight Alliance after-school club to attend before coming over. It drove him nuts that she would skip school but make sure she was at the GSA.

They would see how things went, if their dad calmed down. Raven was a junior. It was conceivable she was out forever. Sterling hoped not; that was a legacy they did not need to share. After ending the call, Sterling spent another few minutes gathering his thoughts. He about hit the fucking ceiling when he heard Weir's voice from directly behind him.

"Who were you talking to, dude? That sounded intense."

Whirling around, Sterling came face-to-face with Weir, who had retrieved his crutch and snuck into the fucking kitchen without Sterling hearing him. "Jesus Christ!"

Rumpled and sleepy, Weir looked good enough to eat.

Sterling was in a whole hell of a lot of hot, hot water.

TWELVE

The kitchen hadn't seemed that far when he had the bright idea of grabbing his crutch and shuffling that direction. The twelve-foot journey took Weir five minutes, most of it spent heaving himself up off the couch without injury.

He'd watched Sterling come into the house. Weir may have been on all sorts of medication, but even he could tell the guy was barely holding himself together. His eyes were wild and his face was tight. He looked a little unhinged.

By the time Weir dragged himself to the kitchen doorway, Sterling had finished his phone call and was leaning facedown on the kitchen countertop, his black-denim-covered ass on display. Weir was on pain meds, not dead; he could appreciate a very fine ass.

"Dude, who were you talking to? That sounded intense."

Sterling whirled around, staring at him like he was a ghost. "Jesus Christ."

Trying to appear as if he was casually leaning against the door-jamb rather than using it to keep himself from falling to the floor, Weir pressed on. "What was that about?"

Sterling rubbed his face, then ran his fingers through his

short, dark hair. Classic avoidance gesture. Damn, a bolt of pain streaked through Weir's leg, and he couldn't keep from grimacing.

"For fuck's sake, you need to be lying down."

He pouted. "I'm supposed to move around at regular intervals."

"With help," Sterling pointed out, moving to his side and taking the crutch from him. He replaced it with an arm around his waist, slinging Weir's good arm over his own shoulder and pressing his warm body against Weir's.

The meds must still have been doing something in his system, otherwise he never would have allowed himself to sink into the heat Sterling offered. They were almost the same height, and while Weir normally had more muscle mass, currently he and Sterling were probably the same weight. He liked how they fit together, liked that Sterling was lean instead of built.

Slowly Sterling turned him, heading down the short hallway toward Micah's room. Weir had to focus on putting one foot in front of the other, not on the warm body next to his. Sterling smelled good. Weir distracted himself trying to figure out what the scent was: aftershave, or shampoo? He hadn't decided by the time they arrived at the side of Micah's nice big bed. Weir was sweating buckets, and swearing internally, from the pain and effort. He tried not to think about the long road from barely shuffling to Micah's bedroom and a New Zealand ultramarathon.

The bed was welcoming.

At that point he wouldn't have cared if Micah and Adam had had sex in it five minutes ago. Sterling turned them both around again so he could ease them into a sitting position on the edge of the mattress. Carefully moving out from under Weir's arm, Sterling lifted Weir's injured leg up onto the bed while helping him lie back against the mass of pillows.

"I should have checked to see if you needed to use the bathroom."

"If I did, I wouldn't admit it right now. Or I'd ask for a gallon milk container." Lying back felt good.

Sterling left the room but was back in a minute with another glass of water and handful of pills. Weir choked them down, welcoming the slight dulling of pain they promised. "So, what were you talking about on the phone?" Medicated, not dead.

A hunted look crossed Sterling's face. Maybe no one else would have caught it, but Weir was an expert at reading faces. Sterling grimaced. "I hate drama, so you know."

Gently scooting Weir over a little, creating space to perch on the edge of the bed, Sterling took a deep breath before continuing. "I'd really like to avoid this whole conversation, but, um. I have a younger sister. Her name is Raven. Anyway, long story short, my ultraconservative parents, mostly our dad, are 'at the end of their ropes.' Our mom is merely his puppet. If I don't take her in, they are threatening to send her to," air quotes, "'a boarding school for troubled girls.'"

"How old is she?"

"Just turned sixteen."

"So, what's happening?" Weir had to shut his eyes again, which bothered him because he enjoyed looking at Sterling's face. He had nice eyes, a piercing blue ringed with something lighter, wolf-like. There were smile lines, too. His brain was focusing on all the wrong things.

"How old are you?' Weir accidentally wondered out loud.

Sterling chuckled. "Almost thirty-three, youngster. Anyway, the phone calls. The first was to Micah asking if it's okay that Raven stays here with us for now. The second was Raven, who will be here around five tonight."

"Is she like you?" He'd blame the meds for this entire conversation, but dammit, he had curiosity about Sterling he needed to slake.

"I guess. We look alike. She's wickedly smart, I'm not. Raven's got a different outlook on the world than I do, I suppose." There was a loose string on Sterling's knee he felt the need to pick at.

"Hmmm?"

"Yeah, well." Now he looked up at the ceiling. Everywhere but at Weir. The ceiling seemed to help. "When my parents found out I was gay they threw me out of the house, same ol' story and song."

"How old were you?"

His jeans were going to be reduced to a single strand of thread at this rate.

"Fourteen. Sybil found out she was pregnant with Raven, so she was getting a do-over kid anyhow."

Weir didn't have to ask to know Sterling was still haunted by his parents' actions. His own eyes were wet. Goddamn medication.

"They told everyone I'd gone to boarding school, which is ironic because they really would send Raven. I took the Greyhound to Seattle. None of my friends could help me. I basically lived on the street for six months. Raven is smarter than me; she'll go to boarding school if they make her, but I'm afraid it would break her or she'll run away and I'll never see her again."

Weir had no problem imagining a fourteen-year-old Sterling living on the streets of Seattle. It was a perk of the job: he didn't have to use his imagination. When people told him he "couldn't imagine," he really could. He could imagine worse. Much, much, worse.

"Hey." Sterling reached over and wiped his cheek, thumb rough and warm against his cheekbone. "What's this?"

Fucking goddamn medication. "Nothing, sorry." He turned his head away from the touch. It was too much. Another stupid tear escaped his eye before Weir could stop it.

"It was a long time ago, okay?" Sterling removed his hand, and irrationally, Weir missed it. "I survived to tell the tale."

Weir tried reassembling his mental barriers. Unfortunately,

his mouth and brain seemed to be working independently of each other.

"When I was in sixth grade, my dad was arrested for vehicular homicide. He was so drunk, even by the time police got to the scene, he had to be hospitalized to sober up. I guess he was in the hospital for days, detoxing. My mom had already left. She dropped me off at school one day when I was eight or nine and never came home. My dad looked for a while, but gave up and looked in the bottle instead." He was telling this story; fuck his life.

"I had no idea where he was. I figured, like my mom, he decided to leave me. I found out later he'd never updated our address, so no one knew to look for me, or where we lived if they had. That he even had a kid. He never said a word. I went to school, most days, but there was no money for food. I hid out in our tiny shit-hole of an apartment, living on dry cereal. Started sneaking into the lunchroom for free breakfast at school. I still hate French toast."

Now it was his turn to look at the ceiling. There was a hairline crack in the corner that looked like a lightning bolt.

"*Three weeks* before my dad remembered to tell the authorities he had a son. So, yeah. I had been going to school, living on nothing, no money and no idea who to call. I thought he'd left me, too. I expected it. He blamed me for my sister and then my mom leaving. Told me all the time, especially when he was drinking, how everything was my fault. I was resigned to getting kicked out, had a bag packed and everything for when the day came. There was a knock on the door one Saturday morning; I knew it was the apartment manager coming to evict me.

"I'm not sure who was more surprised, the officers on the other side of the door, or me. Long story short, I went into the foster-care system for a little while but ended up being taken in by Ben Tompkins, one of the responding officers. I worshiped him. The feds busted me hacking into banking websites for fun about a year later." Weir grinned. It felt crooked and sad. "Needless to say, instead of juvie I was given the choice to use my powers for good or, well... best to use them for good." Weir shut his eyes, because he didn't want to see the look of pity in Sterling's.

He never understood why Ben took him in. By the time Weir came along, Ben was a forty-five-year-old confirmed bachelor who lived for his job as a police officer. If he wasn't working, he was volunteering with a variety of youth groups and homeless shelters. He put in overtime providing security at events aimed toward at-risk communities. Weir had asked him once and all Ben had said was, he was paying it forward.

A cool hand cupped the right side of his neck and chin, thumb caressing his cheek, soothing him. It felt nice. The mattress dipped and rose again as Sterling stood to leave. Weir opened his eyes for a moment before sliding into dreams of his father and Ben Tompkins. Sometimes there was a shadow he thought was his sister, but he couldn't remember her face, and all the pictures of her were long gone.

THIRTEEN

Raven arrived just after five, as promised. Sterling installed her in the second upstairs bedroom, with strict instructions not to fuck up. They both knew what he meant. Sterling had given up a great deal of himself in order to be a part of Raven's life, to make sure she was safe and knew she was loved.

Maybe he had been the one who had impressed on her, not the other way around. When he finally met her he was so lonely and starved for unconditional affection that any handouts were welcome. Having a mini version of himself launch herself at him, nearly knocking him over in her enthusiasm, had broken through any protective barriers he might have put up.

Maybe it was because her affection had been pure, simple. After all, he owed his parents nothing. It wasn't them who found him and brought him back to Skagit. They never would have made the effort. If he had disappeared and never returned, neither one of them would have raised an eyebrow.

Ironically, one of the youth pastors from his parents' church found him. He'd been sitting with a group of other homeless kids on the "Ave" in Seattle's University District. A tribe of teens banded together for safety. Although even those kids stole from each other, and worse. Todd Cottrell had been minding his own business, strolling down the sidewalk one afternoon, and spotted Sterling sitting there with his hand out and a hand-lettered cardboard sign next to him.

Todd had done a double-take that would have been funny in any other, less tragic, situation. Sterling was dirty, no less filthy than the rest of the kids he was hanging around with. His dark hair was longer than it had ever been. He had even grown a few inches, but Todd still recognized him. He had recognized Todd, too, certain he would keep walking past their group like so many others had. Or stop to heckle them and scream invective, tell them they were going to hell. He hadn't meant for the spark of hope to flare inside him, that his parents had sent someone for him. Maybe Todd had seen the flare of hope, but he hadn't been sent by anyone.

Sterling still found it ironic that the church his parents had so fervently believed in was ultimately the one that brought him home to Skagit. Todd had pulled strings and called in favors to find Sterling a safe place to live. Todd had even visited Sterling's parents, trying to change their minds. His father's mind. In the end, in exchange for Sterling staying quiet about what they had done, he was given enough money to rent a tiny studio and access to his college fund when he graduated high school. He never touched the fund. It felt too much like a bribe, a way for his father to try and control him again. His parents had changed churches.

The deal infuriated Todd, but to Sterling it had felt like victory. The only place his father felt anything was with his wallet. Raven had come later. A whirlwind three-year-old who laid eyes on her brother for the first time while she and Sybil were out shopping. Sterling had been nearly eighteen, caught off guard by the sight of his mother and the sister he had never met. Sybil must have been off-balance too, because when Raven asked who he was she had responded with, "This is your brother, Sterling."

If Sybil chose to claim that Raven was so persistent and stubborn that she absolutely had to see Sterling once a week, well, Sterling wasn't strong enough to deny he missed having family. Missed being hugged and told he was a good boy. Missed lying on the couch watching TV and drawing in his sketchbook. Missed the illusion of being loved.

Raven learned early she had both her mom and her brother wrapped around her little finger. Which was why she was staying in Micah's upstairs guest room for the foreseeable future.

* * *

SO FAR SO GOOD.

Since Raven had moved in, things had gone surprisingly smoothly. They had found a routine that worked. She was up and off to school in the morning and home in the afternoon. If she stayed out, she called or texted Sterling to let him know. It had been years since Sterling had more than an evening or two off each week. Now he only worked two evenings, although he went in to do paperwork during the day and work on the business plan for the loan he was applying for.

The missing liquor had been returned. Not having to fire someone was a weight off his shoulders. His life felt oddly *regular*. Even Weir was behaving. Mostly he was sleeping, or bitching about being sleepy, or whining about physical therapy but going anyway. In Sterling's mind that was behaving.

Sterling was reluctantly learning to cook a few things while Weir sat at the kitchen table and directed. The three of them spent several evenings binge-watching TV shows Raven insisted they *had* to see. Sterling didn't own a TV, so any show was new to him. Weir confessed he was normally too busy and generally relaxed in different ways. Raven had not seen the accompanying eyebrow waggle, thankfully, or Sterling would have melted into the couch. He didn't need his sister anywhere near his sex life.

Weir and Raven tried to teach him how to play an online video game they were both into. Well, at least Weir knew which game Raven was talking about. Overlord, overmatch, overdrawn, something like that. The twentieth time Sterling died and they had to restart the game, he threw the controller onto the couch and declared himself done. He'd never really had any interest in video games before he'd been kicked out; afterward it had been a matter of survival. He had no bandwidth for that stuff.

Weir and Raven surprised him. With Weir being reserved and, by necessity, closed off about his work, Sterling hadn't expected the two of them to have much in common. Sterling loved his sister, but she could be hard to take. Opinionated, headstrong, and intelligent, she often talked above people, inadvertently making them feel less than adequate. She met her match in Weir.

The problem her teachers had with her was that she continued to be a straight-A student. One who skipped, slept in class, argued facts… and was usually right, would never concede a point. After all, why should she? It had to drive them crazy: to have her miss class, but still ace the tests? Needless to say, she was not popular.

He returned from the Loft one afternoon, having spent several hours doing receipts and catching up on the books, to find them both in Micah's bedroom. Raven was sitting cross-legged on the bed with her laptop open. They were good-naturedly arguing about something, Sterling didn't know what. Weir grabbed her laptop and spun it around so it faced him, typed rapidly—gibberish, as far as Sterling knew—hit enter, and spun it back around.

"See? That's what you were missing. You have to be way more careful. It's one thing to remember everything you see, but that doesn't help when what you were looking at was wrong in the first place. Admit it, I was right."

Raven looked chagrined. She stared down at the screen, dark

brows furrowed like the wings of the bird she was named after, trying to find something there to prove Weir wrong.

"Fine, you were right. What else can you teach me?"

The memory of what Weir had confessed to him the first afternoon out of the hospital floated back to him. Neither one of them noticed him standing in the doorway. The identical guilty looks on their faces when he interjected, "Hell, no," should have amused him. But they didn't. "No way. Are you teaching my sister how to hack? She's in enough trouble as it is."

Weir raised a palm and hurried to explain. "Uh, no, she's already got the basics down." Seeming to realize that didn't sound any better, Weir tried again. "I mean, she already knew this stuff. And I've given her the fed lecture. But seriously, Sterling, her brains are wasted here. Did you know she has an eidetic memory?"

"What?"

"Used to be called photographic memory, but that doesn't really exist. Eidetic memory means Raven has an extraordinary ability to remember facts. That's what got us started on coding. I swear that's all we were doing, working on code."

"How'd you figure it out?" Sterling had wondered about his sister's amazing recall.

"I gave her complicated lines of code, with errors I inserted into them, and she replicated them... exactly."

Boy, he looked smug. Raven looked both pissed and pleased, which ended up making her look constipated.

"Come on, gimme a break, I'm not going to lead her to a life of crime."

"No," Sterling responded, "she's fully capable of heading that way herself."

"Hey!" Raven objected. Weir snickered and leaned back into the pillows.

Raven hopped off the bed and came around to give Sterling a tight hug. "Thank you, big brother, for letting me stay with you."

He leaned back from her hug, looking down at her face, so much like his own. "What have you done now?" This kind of distraction was reserved for when she knew she had crossed a line.

"I didn't skip school!" Sterling looked at her, eyebrows raised. "They sent me home. I argued with Mrs. Patterson, and she sent me to the office again. Ms. McMillian said I had been trouble enough and told me to sign myself out and leave." Raven looked hurt and leaned back into him, hugging him tighter.

Why were the school administrators such Luddites? Why couldn't they see what Sterling did? That his sister was a vibrant, passionate young woman who was going places. She would leave Skagit in the dust. When she was successful they would all want to claim her; Sterling hoped she told them to go to hell.

"What were you arguing about?"

"Animal welfare." Ah yes, her Achilles heel.

He gave her another squeeze and tugged her thick, long dark braid before steering her out of the room. He turned back to Weir, who looked better every day. The worst of his bruises had faded to a yellow-green tinge. The scrapes and nicks from the road rash were no longer red and irritated-looking. The bags under his eyes had completely disappeared.

"I really wasn't teaching her anything she didn't already know."

Sterling sighed, "I know. Sorry. I'm glad you get along." He'd been worried she would drive Weir crazy.

"No, man, she's pretty cool."

The SkPD came by a few times to follow up on Weir's accident, but it was pretty clear they had no leads. The last time Weir had pissed them off. Sterling would be surprised if they returned anytime soon.

And so it went for a few more days. Sterling was impressed that the makeshift household was holding up under the pressure of a housebound federal agent and an impulsive teenager. He should have known better.

* * *

RAVEN'S CAR was in front of the house when he got back from a trip to the grocery store. He'd hurried back after getting a dropped call from Weir. He *never* called Sterling. And now Raven was home on an afternoon when she wasn't expected. He was going to kill her if she'd managed to finally get expelled from school.

Heaving the grocery bags out of the back of his car, he walked as quickly as he could toward the house. The front door was slightly ajar, which also freaked him out. Skagit wasn't exactly Detroit or St. Louis, but people shouldn't leave their front doors open where anyone could walk in.

"Hello?" he called out. "Why's the door open?" Only the creaky silence of the house answered him. He dropped the bags on the floor, starting to panic a little. "Hello?" he called louder, "Where are you guys?"

"Sterling! I think he broke something!" Raven shrieked from upstairs.

Sterling's life flashed before his eyes. Literally. The sound of his sister's hysterical voice had him taking the stairs in three bounds, his heart in his throat.

Weir was lying in a crumpled heap at the top of the stairs, Raven standing in the doorway to her room, hands covering her face.

"Jesus fuck, what happened?" Falling to his knees next to Weir, heart pounding hard enough to break his rib cage, Sterling reached out a shaky hand to brush the too-long hair off Weir's face. Gingerly, he ran his hands down Weir's chest and along his right leg. "Motherfucker, what the fucking hell was he thinking coming up here? Jesus Christ, Raven, where's your phone? Call 911. God fucking dammit!"

Raven was suspiciously quiet, not moving to get her phone. Weir's shoulders started shaking. Sterling glanced at her, then over at Weir again. Open, *laughing* brown eyes were watching him.

"April Fool!" they yelled, before collapsing into giggles.

FOURTEEN

After the April Fool's joke—which was really fucking funny—he and Sterling were a little rocky for a day or so, but he seemed to have been forgiven now. It had been a brilliant prank, and one day Sterling would admit it.

Three days later, Sterling had the closing shift at the Loft. He chauffeured Weir to his physical therapy and back before leaving for the rest of the day. Weir finally felt like he was making real progress. At his last appointment Dr. Mortimer had said his leg was healing well, that he was lucky it had been a simple fracture and not something worse. His arm was taking longer, but that had been a pretty nasty compound fracture, so a longer recovery time was expected.

On the way out of St. Joe's they had run into Joey, who, of course, had been effusive and exclaimed over how improved Weir looked. Weir figured the last time Joey had seen him he had been pretty banged up, but still it was nice to hear. He'd definitely noticed a chill in the air between Joey and Sterling and wondered out loud what that was about. When he asked Sterling on the way to his car, he had muttered something about "ancient history."

Injured or not, he was getting restless. It had been three

weeks since he had looked at his files. He pulled out his work laptop and logged on to see what was happening with the cases he had been working on. Sammy Ferreira immediately noticed his presence online.

- S. FERREIRA: I'm gonna tell on you.
- C. WEIR: Knock it off, kid. I'm checking in.
- S. FERREIRA: Not supposed to.
- C. WEIR: Fill me in, otherwise I'll find another way.
- S. FERREIRA: That doesn't sound like a threat at all. Also, not a kid. Older than you.

Was he really having this conversation? In an arena where the exchange would be saved for at least ninety days? He groaned. In the end, he convinced Sammy to come over to Micah's and bring him up to speed. Sammy hadn't had much more luck with the geoduck angle than Weir. Moreover, much to Poole's dismay—not to mention Sammy's—Sammy had lost his dinner all over the cabin of Poole's precious boat.

AS FOR THE MATVEEV CASE, they had lost the money trail in the Cayman Islands. Weir hated it when they lost the money trail. The problem, as always, was rules. Once he had committed to work for the government, he had protocol he was required to follow. Rules weren't exactly meant to be broken, but Weir generally approached them more as guidelines. Guidelines had more wiggle room. Unfortunately, international banking institutions didn't like it when he poked around in their private information. They acted like he was lifting their proverbial skirts. In his experience, those skirts were usually hiding something the general public would be furious about.

They had no leads on who had sent Weir to the hospital. No clue if it was an accident or related to one of his cases. SkPD didn't even know what kind of car hit him. The rain had been heavy, all traces of the car erased by the time anyone thought about tire tracks. The first SkPD on the scene had taken pictures, but nothing was of much help.

He'd been so focused on Sammy and the details of the cases that he didn't realize it was after seven p.m. until his stomach rumbled. Sammy packed his things and left, promising to let Weir know if anything happened.

Raven wasn't home yet. They usually ate dinner together when Sterling was at work. She had pinky-promised Sterling she would be home every day and check in if she was going to be late. He texted her, asking when she was getting home.

Twenty minutes passed with no answer.

Sterling was going to flip his lid. He would have told Weir if Raven had plans to be late. Weir briefly considered waiting longer, but Sterling was going to freak out as it was. It was kind of adorable how protective Sterling was of his sister.

Oddly enough, Weir had mostly enjoyed the past couple of weeks. Maybe not the healing-from-being-hit-by-a-car part, but the rest. He had never spent enough time around someone, or someones, to learn their habits, their likes and dislikes. He could look at Sterling now, when he walked in the door in the early morning, and tell whether he'd a good night or if customers had been assholes. He knew when the guy was cranky by how he held his shoulders.

He'd learned that Sterling was a terrible cook. Like certifiably awful. The attempt at mac and cheese would have been funny if Sterling hadn't been so sensitive about it. Even though he refused to admit it, the pasta had been cooked for just a few minutes. It had been like trying to eat cardboard. No amount of cheese in the world would make that taste better. Weir would have eaten it without saying anything, but Raven opened her big mouth. Sterling had snatched the plates from them and dumped everything into the trash before picking up his phone and ordering pizza. It was a little like being a family.

Before his bio family went to hell he'd had a pretty nice life, although he didn't have much memory of it. More like a shadowy black-and-white film that played in his head, the details becoming less clear as the years passed. Life with his dad had been a lesson in learning to live with ghosts. His mom, his sister, the family they had once been, haunted his father. Eventually Carroll Weir Sr. had lost his way completely.

Drunken rants in the evenings accusing Weir of being a fuck-up, of being the reason his sister disappeared and his mother left. In the mornings, if he wasn't too hungover, there would be tearful apologies. The apologies were worse than the rants. A person could only say "Sorry" so many times before it became meaningless.

Living with Ben had given Weir some better memories, but their time as a family had been cut short. After Ben died Weir was on his own again, and that was how it had remained, until now.

Sterling was skittish, but around his sister he allowed himself to relax a little. Weir learned that he couldn't function before coffee. That early was ten a.m. He had a terrible diet, living primarily on sliced sandwich meat and potato chips. Weir was reasonably sure he hadn't ever seen a vegetable pass Sterling's lips except when they ate dinner together. Sterling tried cooking things off Weir's menu, which was really nice, though always an adventure.

Sterling clearly loved his sister, and Weir admired him for going to the lengths he had to protect her. Privately, Weir thought Sterling could use a little TLC himself; Raven was spoiled rotten. They hadn't brought up their late-night activities at the bar again. Their history could have made things uncomfortable, but somehow Sterling made it simple. It was easy to enjoy his company and not worry about expectations, his or Sterling's. He didn't think either of them had any.

The fact of the matter was, Weir *liked* Sterling. He was surprisingly okay with that. At least when it was only the three of them and their pretend family unit. Having Sterling in the same house and liking him was kind of weird, but it also allowed Weir to see the parts of Sterling that were hidden from most other people. It was a secret all his own.

Dragging in a lungful of air, he tapped in Sterling's cell number. It rang a few times before going to voice mail. Weir decided not to leave a message. Sterling would call back anyway.

His phone rang about ten minutes later.

"Hey, you called? It's been weirdly busy in here tonight. I thought everyone would be saving their energy for the weekend, but apparently they're all in training for Friday." Sterling sounded frazzled but happy.

"Yeah, um." Fuck. "Hey, Raven isn't home yet. I texted her but she hasn't answered."

"Goddammit. Fuck. I'll be right there. Gotta find someone to close for me. I'll text you."

"Yeah, okay," Weir replied, but Sterling had already clicked off the call.

* * *

WEIR MANEUVERED himself into the kitchen before Sterling arrived home. He tried texting Raven again, but she continued ignoring his messages. He fervently hoped she was ignoring them. Sterling pounded up the front steps and burst into the house. The cat, which had snuck downstairs to complain about its empty tummy, fled in the face of Sterling's anger and fear for his sister.

"I tried Pony, too. No answer there, either." Sterling pulled off his coat and flung it over one of the kitchen chairs.

Pony was Raven's friend. Weir had not met them, but Raven talked about them all the time. Raven had appointed herself

Pony's protector. From the sound of it, they lived in a very toxic household with no way to escape, no other safe family or friends.

"Have you tried their hangouts? Do you know where Raven goes when she isn't grounded for the rest of her life?" he asked. Weir had been through this. Sterling needed to focus, not panic.

"No. Shit. Okay." Sterling started to grab his coat back off the chair.

"Hey, wait." Weir stood gingerly, using the chair for support. "We need a plan, not to go running around. Think about it. What resources do you have here in town? Who knows her and would help you find her? Do we call your parents? Most likely this is nothing; she forgot or lost her phone or something."

Sterling looked at him like he was crazy. Weir understood. There was virtually no way Raven would go against Sterling's wishes. His requirements for her to stay with them were very clear, and she had agreed to them.

"Take a deep breath and let's think clearly. Approach this as logically as we can." Weir tugged Sterling's chin toward him with his injured hand. The rough stubble felt delicious under his fingertips. "Look at me." Sterling did, and Weir saw the panic and fear welling in his eyes, threatening to overwhelm him. "We will find her. She's a smart girl. We both know something has happened, because she promised, but we will find her." How he could put such strength and conviction behind those words, when he had never been able to find even a trace of his own sister, Weir had no idea.

Leaning closer, he pressed his forehead against Sterling's; let their breaths and heartbeats mingle. He felt it when Sterling relaxed. Instead of pulling away as Weir expected, Sterling pressed his cold lips to Weir's warm ones.

They had never kissed before. This quiet press of lips was terrifyingly intimate, and unnerving. The kiss didn't last long, nothing more than a moment's assurance, a promise, a suggestion between them. Unthinking, Weir let go of the chair he was propped up with, touching his lips as if to reassure himself it had happened. Sterling caught him when he lost his balance, grinning through his stress.

"Whoa there, cowboy, don't get too excited."

"Fuck off," Weir grumped. Again, Sterling had taken an awkward moment and made it no big deal. "Let's find your sister."

First they made phone calls. A lot of phone calls. As it was after eight at night on a Tuesday, they were able to reach most folks. None of whom had seen or spoken with Raven over the past few days. Finally, Sterling tracked down Sara Schultz to see if she had heard anything through her grapevine. Nope. She promised to keep an ear out, though, and suggested that Sterling check in with Brandon Campbell, as he seemed to have a finger on the troubled pulse of Skagit.

Weir respected Brandon. He was a guy who put his money where his mouth was. More evenings than not, he could be found driving around in his van handing out food and sundries to the homeless people who refused shelter or who had nowhere to go when the single shelter in Skagit was full. He knew where the homeless teens hung out. He had, inadvertently, been an enormous resource on Adam's case earlier in the year.

"Sure, I know who your sister is. I haven't seen her, though, or heard anything. Wasn't out long today because Stephanie has the flu. In fact, I just got back." Sterling had his phone on speaker so Weir could hear, too.

"Weir here. Is there any place you'd recommend looking first? If we were to go looking?"

"I don't know why she would go to any of those places," Sterling interrupted. "She's not homeless."

"It's a place to start," Weir argued.

"Hey, guys, let me check in with Stephanie, then I'll head back out. These kids trust me. They might not tell you anything at all.

Even if they know Raven, they don't know you. And you fall into the 'adult' category."

They haggled a little while, but Sterling really had no choice except to agree to Brandon's plan.

"We should check upstairs and see if there is unusual stuff missing from her room. Maybe she packed ahead of time?"

Sterling rushed upstairs while Weir organized his thoughts. It wasn't the same thing as his own sister. Raven was older and wiser. Still, there was a frisson of anxiety forming in his gut. Where *was* she? Why would she do something like this to Sterling when he had done everything in his power to protect her from their parents?

"Nothing seems like it's missing," Sterling shouted back down the stairs. "Her laptop, but she always takes that. School bag, all the normal stuff." His voice grew louder as he bounded back down the stairs. "Now what?"

FIFTEEN

Sterling hadn't planned on sleeping. Once Brandon called back to say he had found nothing, Sterling contacted his mother. Sybil had been no help, answering his questions with a strange forced cheerfulness instead of her usual sharp, barbed speech. He thought maybe she was trying to hide the conversation from his father. Still, she told him nothing.

Weir said he should call the police. Sterling wanted to wait until the morning. If she was just fucking off, he wanted to try and get to her before his parents. The police probably wouldn't do anything that night anyway. A sixteen-year-old girl with her own car, a known habit of running off... she could be anywhere.

He shifted on the bed. Weir had convinced him to lie down in his, Micah's, room, instead of the couch. Weir was peacefully asleep. Sterling took a moment to really look at him. Weir looked closer to his actual age when he was relaxed into sleep: smooth skin, a dusting of freckles across his nose, a small scar on his temple, his blond hair a tangled mess.

A remarkably vulnerable person hid beneath the smart-talking federal investigator Weir showed the rest of the world. Sterling would be a liar if he didn't admit to the quiet part of himself that he felt protective of this facet of Weir that seemed to be his alone. He hadn't thought he would come to enjoy Weir's company, but he had and he did. Sterling had been self-sufficient for so long it had been difficult to imagine sharing life space with anyone, so he had quit trying. Also, Weir was great with Raven, which, while not a deal breaker, he appreciated. Most guys he hooked up with had no interest in Sterling's personal life. Which, he supposed, had been the point of hooking up in the first place.

They hadn't fooled around, except for yesterday's kiss, since the two nights in his office at the Loft. Sterling had never spent the entire night with another man before. He had never trusted a hookup enough to allow himself to sleep with them. It was bam-bam, don't let the door hit your ass on the way out. Or hit his own ass, since he controlled things by never letting them come to his place. Even though they were both dressed, and Sterling was on top of the covers wrapped in a spare blanket, it was oddly comfortable. Something a couple would do.

Weir slept on his back with his good arm over his head resting against the pillow, neck exposed, pale lashes delicate against his cheeks. He looked good. He had gained a few pounds and no longer appeared like he'd spent a week in the wilderness with only a granola bar. From what Sterling knew, the guy might actually do something like that. Sterling shuddered. The woods were for bears, and not the fun kind of bears, either.

"I can hear you thinking." Weir's voice startled him, and he blushed because... He had no fucking idea why, but he blushed. He'd been caught ogling Weir while he was asleep and vulnerable. Gah, bears. Sterling rubbed his face with his hand, trying to pretend he was getting the sleep out of his eyes. When he looked back, Weir was smirking at him. Asshole.

His sister was missing and he was blushing over a guy in bed? Sterling's brain was more messed up than he had realized. With a groan, Weir sat up, abs flexing under his T-shirt. Sterling rolled his mental eyes at himself for noticing how sexy Weir was, even after sleeping in his clothes with a mending leg and arm. Maybe Sterling should think about getting laid. The only problem with that was, when he thought about getting laid, Weir popped into his head.

"What's the plan this morning?" Weir asked, his voice husky from sleep. They'd only managed a few hours. Sterling had been too wound up. Which was how Weir had eventually convinced him to lie down on his bed instead of the couch, claiming he was keeping Weir up with his muttering and restlessness. He'd surprised himself by dropping off within minutes.

"I don't know." The helplessness he'd felt last night flooded back. His own memories of living on the streets haunted him, waking and sleeping. The thought that his baby sister, as fierce and smart as she was, could possibly be sleeping out on the streets, cold and hungry… he could not go there.

"Would you please stop with the worst-case-scenario stuff you've got going on in your head? It's not going to help find her. You need to clear your head and really think. Think about where she could be, and why."

Okay. "Okay." He could do this.

Weir grabbed his hand and squeezed it. "How about if I make a couple phone calls to the team. See if maybe Sammy can come up with something, a different angle?"

Looking down at their clasped hands, Sterling took strength. He could do this. They would find Raven.

* * *

BY MIDMORNING, Sterling was a mess.

They'd stopped by the high school. He hadn't set foot inside the building for fifteen years, and he'd planned on keeping it that way. Weir stayed in the car. Although the administration was aware he was more Raven's parent than Sybil or Stephen, they were not allowed to tell him anything.

Pony's mother slammed the door in his face.

The kids holed up in one of the abandoned warehouses in Old Town didn't know anything, but asked if Sterling could give them some money.

Sterling gave them twenty bucks.

Weir called him a sucker, nicely, when he got back to the car.

By afternoon, Sterling was certifiable.

They had been to every coffee shop or drive-through in the city. The amount of caffeine they had ingested, well… no sleep for the wicked.

They'd visited both public libraries, St. Joe's as well as the hospital associated with the university, and stopped by the teen center.

There was no sign of her.

Finally, Weir asked, "What's going on with Pony? Raven never said. Claimed it was their story to tell."

"Pony is one of Raven's special projects. I don't mean that in a bad way. I mean as soon as Raven figured out that they had no support at home, no one in their court for who they really were, she took it on herself to be there for them. They've known each other since seventh grade. Pony came out as trans last year, and their parents did everything but dig a shallow grave for them."

Weir sighed.

"Yeah." Sterling agreed.

"I'm hungry." Weir was borderline whiny, but Sterling realized that, aside from coffee, he hadn't fed his patient all day. What a great caretaker he was proving to be.

Because it was one of the few spots they hadn't stopped by already, Sterling took him to Patty's. In honesty, Sterling hated the restaurant/dime store. It was fucking creepy, with weird headless or torso-less mannequins and decades-old stock mixed in with the scattered tables diners sat at eating their scrambled eggs and hash. But Weir was hungry, so they stopped at the creepiest café in Skagit.

"This place is awesome. How come I never knew about it before?" Trust Weir to find Patty's interesting. They sat down at a table toward the back. Weir propped his injured leg up on a spare chair. Sterling snagged one of the plastic menus off the table, knowing what he was going to get but looking anyway. Yep, two eggs over medium, bacon, and fruit.

The waitress stopped by with the coffee pot and an order pad. God, he hated their stupid uniforms like nothing else. The owner had overdosed on *Brady Bunch* reruns and made his female wait staff wear an outfit identical to Alice's, down to the white apron and sensible shoes.

Sterling placed his order, then gaped as Weir ordered enough to feed five hungry men, with plenty of red meat, processed sugar, *and* a side of biscuits and gravy.

"What? I'm a growing boy, you starved me all day," Weir said, full of innocent indignation, his eyes flashing with amusement at Sterling's reaction.

As they chatted, waiting for their food, Sterling looked around the café. Not that he really *wanted* to focus on the weird décor. It was more of a compulsion. His eyes widened when he noticed a familiar hoodie hanging on a hook on the wall near the kitchen. Raven had been here recently and left her favorite gaming hoodie behind. The fuck. He nearly launched himself out of his seat to get to it, but something held him back. Gathering himself, he gestured surreptitiously toward the hoodie. Weir turned, pretending to take in all the monstrosities, and raised his eyebrows at Sterling, mouthing, "What?"

Sterling leaned across the small table. No way was all the food they ordered—Weir ordered—going to fit. "That black hoodie? It's Raven's, I'm sure of it. It's her favorite. No way would she accidentally leave it here."

"Okay." Weir's gaze sharpened, taking note of the environment and the people around them.

Luckily, or not, the waitress reappeared just then with

armloads of food, the many plates taking up every square inch of the small table. Instead of wolfing down his food as Sterling expected, Weir merely picked at a few things before leaning back in the chair, crossing his good arm over the special sling his right arm was wrapped in.

"Why aren't you eating?" Sterling was not letting him get away with not eating. What was Weir's thing with food, anyway?

"Leg hurts. Why haven't you asked about the sweatshirt?"

The black hoodie hung there, mocking Sterling with its nonchalant appearance. If he asked, he might not like the answer. It could be the worst answer, even if he didn't know what that was yet.

"Excuse me, miss?" Weir called to the waitress. "My friend and I are keeping an eye out for his sister. We think that could be her sweatshirt over there. Could you tell me how long it's been here?" He had pulled out his most charming SoCal smile, dimples popping. It was eye-catching in spite of the residual bruising and the healing scrapes across his face. The woman didn't have any idea what had hit her. She literally blinked a few times before answering.

"Uh, well, two girls were in here yesterday afternoon. One was crying and the other one was trying to comfort her. An older man came in and began talking to them—one was shaking her head—and then he started to cause a real scene. I had to ask him to leave. I mean, we're tolerant, but he was using terrible language. He grabbed the crying girl and tried to make her to go with him. Kenji came out from the kitchen, you can ask him what happened." A Japanese American man appeared behind the waitress. Sterling had been so intent on her story he hadn't seen him approach.

"I asked the kids if they needed help, but they said no," Kenji said, "and the man said to back off, this was family business. They all left together."

"What did the older man look like?" Weir asked.

"My height, so 5'9" or so, skinny, brown hair, bowl cut."

Weir looked at Sterling.

"Not my dad, he has a stylist." A terrible feeling was growing in the pit of his stomach. Much longer and weather forecasters would be naming it Storm Raven. There was an off chance Raven could have forgotten her sweatshirt in the heat of the moment, but she would have come back for it if she could, the second she realized it was gone.

"Can we take the sweatshirt? I'm sure Sterling's sister will be glad to see it," Weir said. "And can we get the check?"

Sterling eyed the mostly full plates still sitting on the table. "Eat." Weir glared at him before sullenly picking up his fork.

Kenji handed him the sweatshirt. "Good luck, dude." Sterling wasn't sure if he meant looking for Raven or dealing with a surly federal agent.

THEIR MOOD WAS EVEN MORE SUBDUED once they managed to get back to Sterling's car. It was obvious Weir's leg really was bothering him, his face wan in the fading afternoon light. This was the first day since the accident he had been out and about for more than physical therapy and maybe a coffee at the Booking Room. On the upside, he'd polished off almost all the food he'd ordered.

"Who do you want to talk to first? Pony's family or yours?"

Pony's mom had slammed the door in his face earlier. His mother had been weird, even for her, over the phone. Sybil was going to be the weak link in whatever was going on. The sick, sick feeling Sterling had been attempting to squash returned. It was too much to hope now that Raven had gone on an unsanctioned trip to Seattle or was at a friend's.

Images assaulted him, sound clips, mostly from that horrifying documentary *Jesus Camp* he had watched a few years ago. His beautiful, willful sister... not even someone as strong as her could withstand something like that. Those "rehab" programs were still out there. Not as easy to find as they had been even a few years ago, but if you knew the right catch phrase, had the right connections, a person could be sent away against their will to be "reprogrammed." They would beat the gay right out of them.

Even though he had just gotten into the car, he quickly reopened the door. Leaning out into the street, he lost everything in his stomach. He collapsed back against the driver's seat when his stomach was empty, wiping his mouth with his sleeve. Gross.

A light touch to the side of his face brought him from his morbid thoughts.

"Hey." Dark, nearly bottomless eyes looked deep into his, calming him. "Federal investigator, remember? Can you drive us home, to Micah's?"

SIXTEEN

Weir had to stop making promises he had no idea if he could keep. It wasn't as if he hadn't worked several missing-children cases since he had qualified for Mohammad's team. He'd been involved in one as recently as last fall when he and Adam were assigned to Rochelle Heid's disappearance. It had ended "well" only inasmuch as her remains had been found and the piece of shit that abducted and killed her apprehended.

Missing children had informed his choice to commit to the feds in the first place. He would never see his sister again. Even if she was alive, he didn't remember what she looked like. How would he know if she passed him in the street? Regardless of the age difference between him and Sterling, he was the professional. He needed to start acting like it.

The drive back to Micah's was long and quiet. Weir could literally feel Sterling pulling himself together, grabbing the sharp ends of himself and tucking them back inside where they belonged. Finally, Micah's house appeared in the distance. To Weir's dismay, he needed Sterling's help getting out of the car and back inside. He had definitely overdone it today, not that he would admit that.

"Overdid it, huh?"

"Fuck you."

Gently, Sterling helped Weir lower himself onto the couch before going into the kitchen, where Weir heard him rinsing his mouth and spitting into the sink. Grateful for the moment's privacy, Weir groaned in relief at being off his feet with his leg elevated. He knew he was improving, but it seemed to be at a snail's pace.

Sterling was a complicated man. These moments when he exposed his nurturing side were surprising. It seemed to come naturally to him, though.

When Sterling returned, taking a seat beside Weir, Weir tried to return the favor. "You have good instincts, you're doing the right things. We need to bring in the big guns now. Report Raven missing. Maybe it won't go anywhere, but you need to try. You should report Pony, too, I think." Reporting was complicated when kids were involved. They *needed* to figure out where Raven was.

While Sterling called his mother again, Weir wondered about Raven's phone. It hadn't been at the diner. Only her hoodie. Their recent calls had gone straight to voice mail. That meant it was turned off or out of power. There were ways to find out what cell tower a phone had pinged off last, or at least it could be narrowed down to a geographic area.

He also wondered what the hell had prompted him to convince Sterling to sleep in his bed last night. At the time he'd assured himself it was his natural sense of altruism: the guy needed sleep. He wouldn't be any help to Raven if he stayed up all night worrying and pacing. On the other hand, Weir had gravitated to the human warmth of Sterling beside him, following Sterling into sleep like it was the most natural thing in the world.

A knock on the front door startled Weir from his thoughts. Who would come to their, Micah's, door? Shit, he kept getting caught up mistaking this house for his home.

Sterling was on his cell phone in the kitchen arguing with Sybil, who from the sound of things was vacillating between cooperation and obstruction. She wanted to find her daughter but didn't want to be involved? What kind of mother was she? He grabbed his crutch, hobbling to the door as a second, louder, knock sounded.

Fumbling with the stupid crutch, Weir opened the door to find a group of bedraggled teenagers huddled on the front porch. They all stared at him.

"You aren't Raven's brother," one of them blurted out.

"No... he's on the phone." They looked expectantly at him, like cartoon baby birds with their mouths half open. "You guys want to come in?"

Dumb question. Three of them all but pushed him down in their haste to come inside. The fourth, a skinny kid with long dark dreadlocks, moved a little slower, limping. Weir saw the kid's left foot was encased in one of those soft orthopedic boots. All of them were soaking wet. The rain, which had held off all day, was pelting down. It looked like a small lake was forming up the street where the storm drain was blocked with leaves and other debris.

He shut the door and gingerly clumped after them as they straggled into the living room, trailing behind them the murky scent of rain and damp clothing. The bemused expression on Sterling's face when he poked his head out of the kitchen to see what the uproar was made Weir chuckle. He'd forgotten how much noise teenagers made.

His own teenage years had been filled with adult responsibility. He had no frame of reference for a "normal" teenage experience. Ben had done his best, but by his own admission the man had been a confirmed bachelor. Weir's outlet, other than computers and running, had been the beach. It still was. While Weir was in high school, Ben had left Walnut Creek and they moved south to San Luis Obispo. Weir figured out the bus system, and every day after school he took the #10 to freedom.

It had been too late to try and make friends with all the entitled-asshole kids in his new school who had known each other since pre-K. They took one look at him, with his ill-cut multi-shades of blond hair and freckles, and he was instantly classified as an outcast. His brain didn't help, either. He'd open his mouth and people would look at him like he was crazy. Who *was* this smart-ass kid? He was a nobody who came in and was immediately top of the class.

At the beach, no one cared. It was a bunch of anonymous surfer dudes in wet suits with boards they could make fly.

Weir had been hanging out at one spot on the beach for a couple of weeks near a board-rental shack, watching and trying to learn. One day, some idiot tourist was bitching about the waves and the crappy board and the instructor's inability to do anything right.

He listened to the jerk rant for a minute before deciding enough was enough. Inserting himself into the "discussion," Weir proceeded to give the guy a laundry list of exactly what he was doing wrong: too stiff, angles all wrong, no core strength, and also a jerk because he wouldn't listen to the instructor.

Instead of punching Weir, like he probably deserved, the guy challenged him to get on the board if he was so smart. Weir proved he *was* smart that day and never looked back. One second standing on the same board the other guy couldn't find his own two feet on and Weir knew he was where he belonged. He didn't stand long that day, but longer than Mr. Midwest.

Every day after that, if he could manage it, he took the bus to the same beach. He tracked down a surfboard at a garage sale and convinced Ben to let him buy it. The board came home, and Weir was in heaven. Weir lasted half a year at the high school before he tested for early entrance into USC. Never looked back.

Ben Tompkins had been silenced when Weir was seventeen,

still in college. A domestic violence call gone sideways. It had taken Weir months to pick himself up off the ground. The thing— the only thing, besides the blue expanse of the Pacific Ocean— that kept him going was knowing that Ben wouldn't want him to give up.

Weir was damned tired of putting himself back together.

"Uh, hi?" Sterling asked.

"Hi, Mr. Bailey." Sterling physically recoiled at being referred to by that name. Weir turned his laugh into a fake groan as he lowered himself back down onto the couch.

"No, no. Please, it's Sterling. You're Raven's friends?" Tandem nodding. They all started talking at once before Sterling asked them to have a seat and maybe take turns.

A petite girl with short dark-blonde hair and a mouth full of braces was Alex. The beanpole of a kid wearing a knit beanie half-covering unruly dark hair falling to the shoulders of their soaking denim jacket was Drew, possibly second in command to Alex. The other two appeared to be along for moral support.

Lee (Leigh?) was tall, at least 5'8", with wild, curly blonde hair also half-heartedly tucked into a beanie. The ends of her hair were bright pink, and the Doc Martens she was wearing made her appear even taller than she was. Maybe she was along for protection, not moral support. The kid with the dreadlocks and boot was Marcus. He plopped down on the couch next to Weir. Drew and Alex squished together on Marcus's other side. Lee lurked at the far end of the couch, hands in the pockets of her black hoodie, ignoring Sterling's invitation to sit.

Alex and Drew started talking at the same time. Alex glared and Drew snapped their mouth shut.

"Okay, so, we're from the GSA, the Gay-Straight Alliance at school."

"Yeah," Drew confirmed, nodding.

"Raven and Pony weren't at school today, and they didn't come to GSA. We're worried," Alex looked at her friends, and they all nodded, "that Pony's family did something bad. They've been scared for a while that they would send them away to 'boarding school.'"

"Yeah, *boarding school*," Drew muttered, scorn dripping from the very words.

Lee and Marcus muttered under their breath. It really did feel like the gay teen mafia of Skagit were lounging in Micah's living room.

"So anyway, Raven had a plan—" Alex started.

"—but we think Pony's family found out—" Lee interjected, from her side of the room.

"—yeah and took Pony—" Drew added.

"Whoa, slow down," Sterling said, holding out his hands and motioning for them to stop. Remarkably, they all did.

"So, what happened to you?" Marcus asked Weir, startling him out of his dark thoughts about conversion camp and what happened to kids who were sent to those kinds of places.

"Marcus! Focus," Alex snapped.

Weir leaned closer. "I'll tell you later," he whispered.

Alex glared at him. Weir had the urge to roll his eyes, but managed not to.

"We think Pony's family forced them to one of those conversion places."

"Okay, how is Raven involved?" Sterling asked, his voice low and intent.

"She was helping Pony with a plan, but we know your parents had threatened her, too. What if they both had to go to *conversion*?" Alex's eyes grew wide with horror; she emphasized the word like a person would *axe murderer* or *serial killer*.

"I just got off the phone with our mother. She swears she has no idea where Raven is. She is beside herself with worry."

Weir thought that was a bit of a stretch. He doubted Sybil Bailey had ever been beside herself with worry over anything worse than a hangnail.

"What about your dad?" Drew asked.

Weir could see all the carefully folded pieces of himself Sterling had tucked away when they returned from their day starting to fray again. His pupils dilated, and his knee was bouncing like crazy. Weir wanted to grab his thigh and remind him he wasn't alone in this, but Sterling was too far away. Both literally and figuratively. His expression told Weir he absolutely believed his dad would do something heinous like send his daughter to conversion therapy.

Lee spoke up again. "We think we know where."

"This place in Sedona," Marcus added.

"Arizona?" Sterling asked.

"Yeah, it's like horse conversion camp. They ride for Jesus."

"Raven hates horses." Sterling was slipping beyond devastated. Weir needed to take the wheel of this conversation before Sterling broke down.

"How do you guys know this?" Weir surprised them with his question. It seemed they'd forgotten he was part of the conversation.

"Pony overheard their mom and dad talking and found a brochure or something at home. They were going to run away. Pony was going to run away," Alex clarified.

A few more questions and, they appeared to have exhausted the teens' factual knowledge about what Pony's parents might have orchestrated. Instead they were content to hang out and speculate wildly on the fate of their friends. Sterling looked a hair's breadth from breaking down. Weir glanced at the clock on the mantel. It was almost nine at night. "Don't you guys have school tomorrow?" he asked. They collectively looked guiltily at both men.

Frankie chose that moment to stalk into the living room. He appeared to be personally affronted that there were *strangers* in *his* house, sitting on *his* couch. The battered orange cat weighed in at about twenty pounds, had a chunk missing out of one ear, and his tail looked like it had been mauled by a hand mixer. After surveying the room full of people (all watching with varying degrees of fascination, wondering what the beast was up to) he padded over the couch and jumped into Marcus's lap.

"Awww," the chorus sounded. Weir groaned. That fucking cat. Marcus seemed pleased by Frankie's choice, if the ear scratch the cat was receiving was any indication.

Marcus leaned back to Weir. "Mariah Carey high kick," he whispered. "In roller skates, while I was performing on amateur night at Escape." Escape was an all-ages dance club in Everett.

"What?" What did Mariah Carey have to do with anything?

"That's how I broke my ankle, in three places. Had to have emergency surgery. Did you, uh, get bashed?"

Ohhhh.

"Nah, hit by a car when I was out running. Fractured femur and collar bone, compound fracture in my arm. I had surgery, too. Got some nifty metal plates." Weir had made a new friend. Huh.

"Salty. Hit by a car? You must be the guy Pony and Raven found."

Weir swiveled his head around in time to see Sterling wipe the guilty expression from his face. Weir didn't remember much from the accident scene. Perhaps he and Sterling needed to have a little chat.

While Sterling went to let the teens out, Weir considered his plan of action. He was pretty sure unless he took drastic measures Sterling was going to be twitchy and pacing until the sun rose. He stretched his arms over his head and got a whiff of himself. Problem solved.

SEVENTEEN

When Sterling returned from saying goodbye to Raven's friends, Weir lurked on the couch, seemingly harmless. The cat disappeared back up the stairs. Sterling had waited for a minute at the front door while the four teens piled into an older-model Ford Taurus and sedately drove off, navigating the small lake that had formed in the street. Weir seemed to have spent those few minutes plotting something.

Sleep would be impossible. His body and mind were twitchy from stress. He couldn't halt the terrifying images his brain was providing him, of Raven and Pony being forcibly converted to the "Christian path."

"I'm going to drive out to my parents' house," he said. They lived in a snooty gated community south of town. This time of night he could be there in fifteen minutes. He had never lived in that house; Stephen and Sybil had built it and moved there after he had been kicked out.

"No. You're not."

Sterling swung around to stare at Weir. "You going to stop me?"

"Sterling." Weir's voice carried a warning. Or a promise, he wasn't sure. "It is almost ten p.m. If the kids are right about why Raven and Pony are MIA, there isn't anything we can do about it tonight. I know you don't want to hear this, but she is under eighteen and you are not her guardian, right?"

Sterling nodded.

"If your parents decided to send her away, our hands are tied." Sterling opened his mouth, Weir raised his hand to stop him from interrupting. "Our only hope is to get through to one of your parents. Your mom?"

Sterling nodded again.

"Okay. In the morning you can deal with her. In the meantime, I pulled in a favor. Hopefully tomorrow we'll know what cell tower Raven's phone last pinged off of. It could help."

Sterling wasn't sure how, but sure, any information would be good.

"Also," Weir pinned him with his eyes, "how come I didn't know Raven was first at the scene?"

Sterling shifted uncomfortably. The feeling of being interrogated was disconcerting. "Adam knows."

"Adam knows," Weir repeated flatly.

"She was skipping school with Pony. They found you and called me for help. They didn't know who you were or anything. I was trying to make sure our parents didn't find out." And now didn't *he* feel like he'd been called into the principal's office? "Adam said he looked into it, and it wasn't her car that hit you."

"I never thought it was." Weir shook his head, seeming to brush away a thought. "You need to get some sleep."

"I don't think I can." He couldn't stop thinking, worrying.

"Here's what's going to happen. You're going to take a shower. You stink."

"What?"

"You stink like fear and sweat. Mostly fear. After your shower, you are going to help me take a shower, because I stink, too." Weir grinned wickedly.

Seriously? Sterling frowned. Not that he hadn't enjoyed their encounters at the bar, but still, his sister was missing.

"I have a broken leg, I'm not dead. Also, twenty-six. I've got needs, old man. You go first and I'll get myself ready."

As selfish as it surely was, the images his brain provided him of a hard, wet Weir threatened to short it out in an entirely pleasant/erotic way, shoving worry for Raven to the recesses of his mind—for now.

Wait. "Old man? Fuck you."

"One day you may be so lucky. Get a move on." Weir shooed him in the direction of the bathroom.

"We're not having shower sex when you have broken bones," he shouted over his shoulder as he did Weir's bidding. What was wrong with him?

Sterling tried not to hurry his shower. The warm water cascading over his shoulders and back felt so good he ended up taking at least eight whole minutes, maybe ten. After hastily drying himself off, he wrapped the towel around his waist and returned to the living room and found a mostly naked Weir reclined on the couch.

The sight of him, battered and semi-bruised, but still beautiful —still alive, and breathing the same air as Sterling—moved him more than he expected. He was feeling emotional from all the shit going on. The resurgent awareness that his sister was missing, possibly alone and frightened, almost stopped him from going to Weir, but he knew the man was right. There was nothing else to do tonight. Tomorrow, first thing, he would confront his mother face-to-face.

There was something else he wanted to be face-to-face with at the moment. Weir still had the sling on and the soft wrap cast on his leg, but he had managed to cover the almost-healed incision on his thigh with plastic wrap so it wouldn't get wet. Other than that, he was wonderfully naked. Wonderfully. Naked.

As he bent over to lift Weir from the couch, his poorly tucked towel loosened, slipping onto the floor.

"Much better," Weir commented. "Far too much clothing."

Together they limped to the bathroom, where Sterling propped Weir against the wall while he removed the soft cast. He turned the shower on and waited until the temperature was perfect before helping Weir into the spray.

"Fuck, this feels good. Fuck, fuck, I could come from this alone." It sounded like the washcloth baths Weir had been giving himself were lacking in quality. Sterling admired Weir's body. He may have been injured, but that didn't hide the top physical condition he had been in before the accident. Sinewy runner's muscles, pale skin but darker than Sterling's own, a slight dusting of blond hair trickling down from his chest to his groin.

Tossing caution aside, Sterling climbed into the small shower enclosure along with Weir. They hadn't thought this through. If Weir lost his balance it would be disastrous. Sterling slipped into place in front of him, chest to chest. Sterling was slightly taller than Weir, a fact he had not realized until that moment. Even injured and disheveled, Weir had an imposing air.

"Put your arms around my neck. I'll soap you up." Said no sane person ever when they were suddenly horny and wanting something really badly. He did manage to soap Weir up, mostly. And himself, again. And fuck. His mission was not helped by the little noises Weir made when Sterling ran the bar of soap down his back to the top of his ass, hinting. The whimpers killed him. Slayed him. Weir's face was tucked into Sterling's neck; the sounds he made reverberated along Sterling's skin. His neck was an erogenous zone. He had never known. He was beginning to suspect his whole body was an erogenous zone where Weir was concerned.

Sterling was hard. Weir had a semi. There was no way anything was happening in the shower.

Someday.

When Weir was as clean as possible under the very hard circumstances, Sterling turned off the water and grabbed a fresh towel to dry them both off. Weir's eyelids were half-mast. Sterling wondered what was going on in his head.

Ten minutes later they had traded the wet sling for a dry one, removed the plastic wrap, and replaced the soft cast. Weir was sprawled across the middle of the bed. Had to be record time. They were still naked, and Sterling had no idea how they were going to do this. Or what they were doing.

"Hey." Weir grabbed Sterling's hand as he fussed over something fussable. "I, uh, probably can't fuck, but I think we could manage a sixty-nine. Put some pillows behind my back to prop me up on my good side."

"Fucking genius."

"And federal investigator."

"And smartass." But Sterling quickly went to work with the pillows and blankets. If Weir was offering, he was not refusing.

Weir's penis had softened while Sterling figured out logistics. "You sure?"

"Yes, goddammit!"

All right then. Positioning himself on his own side facing Weir's cock, which was making a strong comeback, Sterling pressed his nose into Weir's groin, inhaling his scent, musk and clean man. One hand on the base of Weir's erection, the other on his very squeezable ass cheek, he licked down and back up, enjoying the helpless sounds Weir was making, until Weir sucked Sterling's cock into his hot, wet mouth and Sterling almost came. He hoped the noises he made around Weir's dick in his mouth were appreciative enough. Jesus Christ, he needed to focus.

It turned into a game of who could last the longest, or maybe who could make the other come first; Sterling wasn't sure. He loved the heat of Weir's mouth on him, kept finding himself drifting mindlessly into the sensation, almost coming before snapping out of it and getting back to business. Weir's cock was gorgeous, nice and long but not a monster. Sterling's gag reflex, which he was embarrassed by because he loved sucking cock, seemed to be getting a little better. He still had to have a hand at the base, controlling how far he took it down, but he wasn't freaking out. He needed more practice.

There was saliva everywhere. The sharp taste of Weir's precome on his tongue spurred him to suck harder. The erection in his hand grew impossibly harder; slipping his free hand further around, he ghosted a finger along Weir's taint to his balls, a light touch intended to tease. Weir stiffened and moaned, trying to keep sucking Sterling's cock, but lost control, shooting come into Sterling's waiting mouth. Sterling smiled around Weir's dick. *And we have a winner!*

Sterling was on the edge. He often got off on his partner's reactions, and tonight was no different. As soon as Weir took his pole back into his mouth, Sterling started to come. He couldn't stop himself, and he didn't try; he let the tension of the day flow out of his cock along with a gallon of come.

Sterling lay there for a minute, gathering the parts of himself that had shattered across the room. So much glitter. He ended up drifting off, his head resting against Weir's good thigh for maybe a half hour before he collected enough of himself to manage a coherent thought. Finally, when he reached a place where he could probably put one foot in front of the other, he rolled over to heave himself up.

"Stay?" Weir whispered into the dark.

He did. Before he made himself comfortable, Sterling gently helped Weir move so he wasn't lying across the middle of the bed and cleaned both of them up. For the second night in a row, the second time in his life, Sterling stayed the night in bed with another man.

. . .

THE NEXT MORNING he woke to find himself under the covers and wrapped around Weir like English ivy, Weir's good arm keeping him firmly in place.

They had fallen asleep naked. Weir's morning wood was prodding his hip. Sterling slid his hand down Weir's chest and wrapped his fingers around it, tugging it to full hardness. Weir *mmmm*ed. Sterling had no idea if he was fully awake or not, but he didn't object to Sterling's touch. Soon enough, Weir's hips jerked and warm come spilled over Sterling's fist. It didn't take more than two or three pulls on his own hard cock before he added his come to Weir's.

Weir gripped the hair at the back of Sterling's head. Looking up, Sterling was surprised by warm lips pressing against his own. He opened his mouth for Weir's tongue, inviting him in. Sterling sucked Weir's tongue into his mouth, licked and bit those plump lips, wanting more, a lot more, than he ever had. Weir groaned and shifted so they were chest to chest. Disregarding the come drying between them, he pressed his mouth harder against Sterling's, devouring him. The hand that had been in Sterling's hair had drifted downward; now a finger was sliding with some regularity between his ass cheeks, teasing. Sterling wanted to be teased, devoured, eaten, fucked.

As if he had read his mind, Weir whispered against Sterling's mouth, "I want to fuck you so badly. I want…" Before Sterling could form a coherent reply, Weir was kissing him again, rubbing their revived cocks against each other and stroking his fingers as far between Sterling's ass cheeks as he could. Mindful of Weir's injuries, Sterling let himself rut against his good side. Together they set a wicked pace, ensuring neither would last. Sterling didn't try to stop himself this time either. He let the electricity of orgasm flow through him. At the last moment he grabbed the back of Weir's head, bringing him closer, wanting no space between them. Ripping his mouth away from Weir's, he buried his face in Weir's neck, biting and sucking as he came with an unexpected, urgent passion.

"Now we've made a real mess." Weir's husky voice rolled over him while he lay in his third orgasmic haze in less than twenty-four hours. Sterling wondered if he meant the drying come on the sheets or whatever was happening between the two of them.

After a shower that was not nearly as fun as the one the night before, Sterling dressed in his standard black uniform, preparing himself to face the people who had never once in his life had his back; had in fact betrayed him at the most basic level. Stephen and Sybil had never been good parents, not even before they knew he was gay. They were the worst kind of parents because they only wanted to raise a child exactly like themselves.

Well, neither Sterling nor Raven were the children they wanted. How tragic for them.

As Weir had pointed out, his mother was the weak point. If they were going to learn anything about Raven's whereabouts, it would be through her. Grabbing his car keys and wallet, he headed for the door. Better to face the dragon first thing.

"Wait," Weir commanded from behind him. "I'm going with you."

Sterling almost couldn't believe his eyes. Weir had showered, too. Now he was dressed in an unbuttoned dark-gray suit, the tailored shirt underneath the jacket also unbuttoned. Still managed to shout "federal investigator." A little the worse for wear, but fed nonetheless. Nice. A twitch of desire shivered across Sterling's skin. He had been unaware of having a suit kink until that moment.

Weir cocked an eyebrow. "You like?"

Hell fucking yes. He cleared his throat before replying. "Yeah, you look good. Even with that sling ruining the lines." Sterling stepped forward and buttoned the shirt, which was a darker gray than the suit. He tucked the unused jacket sleeve into a pocket and left the jacket open. Weir had managed to get the rest of himself respectable, even socks. Sterling knelt to tie his leather oxfords.

"Don't start anything," Sterling growled before Weir could say or do anything that sidetracked the morning's errand.

Weir chuckled, which was as good as starting something.

EIGHTEEN

The Bailey residence was… appalling. One of those fake Southern Antebellum-style mansions, possibly influenced by too many viewings of *Gone with the Wind* while drinking, that had no business anywhere close to the Pacific Northwest. Even the property had been infused with a plantation-like air, with a carriage house and a few other matching outbuildings used for god knew what. Weir wondered if there were household help, but quickly decided he didn't want to know.

To make matters worse, the Bailey house wasn't the only one in the area with a nod to false Southern heritage. The gated community had several of the monstrosities. Sterling had the gate code from prior visits to see Raven, so they arrived somewhat stealthily. Sterling's practical little car chugged up the pretentious driveway where he parked next a gleaming Lexus and a Tesla, both of which looked freshly washed and waxed.

Sterling came around to help Weir out of the car. As quickly as he was recovering, his right arm was still weak, and his fancy crutch was in the back seat. Dana had said he would be able to run again—maybe not ultramarathons, but long runs for certain.

The sense of relief he had felt when she said those words was so strong he almost cried.

Once out of the car and certain he was stable, he joined Sterling for the journey to the front door. Even though he hadn't known Sterling for very long, he could tell by the set of his shoulders and the grim line of his mouth that the man was ready for war.

His first impression that Sterling judged and found the rest of the world lacking had been replaced by the understanding that Sterling held his true self aloof out of self-preservation. Sterling was most comfortable feeling separate from the crowd; it had become his safe place. It made sense that Sterling was a bartender. Bartending allowed for a very controlled sort of interaction with people.

They were both pretty fucked up, that was the truth. At least Weir had had Ben. Ben was gone now, but in the short time they were a family he had made a big impact on Weir. Ben had been a person who cared, and who did the right thing because that was the way he was built. His actions had always reflected his words. Ben had made sure Weir went to therapy, helped him to understand that what happened to his bio-family was not his fault—even if Weir didn't always believe that.

Becoming an investigator had been part of his journey as well. Helping victims and their families find closure healed him a little, too. Selfish? A bit, but it worked for him.

"Are we knocking, or do you have a key?"

Sterling shot him a look that said everything. There was no chance either of his parents would give him a key. If Weir weren't halfway through recovery he would be tempted to do something stupid like kick the door in.

The door opened before Sterling had a chance to knock, and a petite, fiftyish woman stood before them. It was impossible to miss the resemblance. The black hair and pale skin, as well as the shape of her face. She dressed in all black, like Sterling did.

"What are you doing here?" she hissed, her face twisting in disgust.

"Lovely to see you as well, Sybil. And you know perfectly well why we are here. Where is she?"

Weir leaned forward, pulling his badge out of his pocket and flipping it open so Mrs. Bailey could read it.

"Carroll Weir, ma'am, federal investigator. I'd like to ask you a few questions." He'd ask forgiveness later if the boss found out.

Two pairs of intense blue eyes blinked at him in shock. Tucking his badge back into the inner pocket of his jacket, he motioned inside. "May we come in? My leg still bothers me sometimes."

Finally noticing Weir was using a crutch and she was overlooking her hostess duties, Mrs. Bailey waved them in. The foyer was immense, thirty feet high, gleaming under the transient April sunshine. She led the way toward another room, her high heels clicking against the marble tile, the sound echoing across the open space.

"Your leg really bothering you?" Sterling whispered. Weir shook his head. He had taken the risk that Mrs. Bailey wouldn't want an injured officer of the law collapsing on her massive front porch. What would the neighbors think?

On second thought, in this neighborhood, they would probably rally to hide the body.

Mrs. Bailey didn't offer, but Weir sat anyway. His leg was tired, not sore as he had implied. It didn't hurt to make himself comfortable when she probably hoped to get rid of them quickly.

The room she'd led them to was a library. There were hundreds of books lining the walls. At a glance, most of them looked to have been ordered from the same catalogue. The spines were somber hues of brown and black, with a few dark-red bindings strewn amongst them. In a far corner, several shelves harbored brightly colored mass-market titles. Weir couldn't see what the titles were from where he was sitting, but he bet that was someone's personal collection.

"I assume you know why we are here?"

She wrung her hands, trying to come up with a reason that didn't include her missing daughter.

"Do you know where Raven is, Mrs. Bailey?"

Her eyes, so like both of her children's, stared at him with something akin to horror and, Weir thought, a touch of fear. Sybil's gaze skittered away, ending up somewhere over his left shoulder.

"Surely, as her mother, you understand that Sterling, to whom you gave the task of watching over her for the past few weeks, would be concerned when Raven did not return to…" He stuttered to a stop, having no idea whether Mrs. Bailey knew where her daughter had been living: in a house owned by a gay man, currently inhabited by two different gay men. "Where she was staying," he finished lamely.

Sybil's body language was conflicted. She was wringing her hands, that was unconscious. It was the lack of eye contact that bothered him. He'd only been in the field for a little over a year, but families of missing people looked you in the eye earnestly. They *wanted* you to find their wife, daughter, sister. In his limited experience the missing had all been female.

"He promised he wouldn't do anything."

"Who promised? Your husband?" He refused to call Stephen Bailey a father. The man had failed both of his children.

Sybil nodded. "As long as Raven behaved."

"Behaved." The word sounded depraved, dirty, bestial.

"Behaved." Her hands fluttered. He and Sterling were supposed to understand the inherent definition of *behaved*. Weir was pressing her to say the words out loud.

Sterling opened his mouth, and Weir held up a hand to silence him. Sybil Bailey needed to hear how her words sounded out loud. How they echoed across the cold marble tile, vicious promises piling up like dead leaves, invisible against the cream-colored walls of her prison. He wondered what malicious words already poisoned this room.

Her gaze drifted back from over his shoulder, and he saw her surrender. She couldn't say the words. Whether it was because of him or that her son was standing there as witness, Weir didn't know. This time he let Sterling speak.

"Sybil, Mom, what do you know? Where is Raven?"

Sybil sat on an uncomfortable-looking Louis XV–style chair with pink-and-gold upholstery. The thing was hideous but matched the unfortunate décor. "Stephen threatened to send Raven to boarding school." Looking down at her hands, she continued, "My husband has very strong beliefs about how people should be... be together."

Weir nodded to keep her talking.

"Raven refused to give up her lifestyle. That school club she went to, she continued to go there over her father's command. But he promised me," this time she did look him in the eye with the earnestness he had come to expect, "promised me he wouldn't send her away."

"Where is your husband, Mrs. Bailey? I'm surprised he isn't here with you today." He was surprised she had let them inside the house, much less met with them without her overbearing husband present. From what little Sterling had shared with him, Stephen Bailey was a bully as well as a bigot.

Again, she looked everywhere but his face. Her hands fluttered restlessly, and she shifted in her uncomfortable chair. "He had a business meeting."

"Does he know Raven is missing?"

"Raven is not missing!" She almost shouted the words.

"If Raven isn't missing, Mrs. Bailey, where is she?"

Unexpectedly, she leaned toward Sterling, hissing, "Why did you bring the police here? We don't need the police."

"Mrs. Bailey. What are you not telling us?" Something was

going on in this house, something that had Sybil Bailey lying her ass off. The tension rolling off Sterling was palpable. They needed straight answers, not this bullshit runaround. Normally, Weir didn't have trouble with his temper. Compared to Adam, he was a paragon of patience.

A door opened and closed. Footsteps sounded in the foyer, and a man called out, "Sybil?" Before she could respond, Mr. Bailey entered the room, coming to a stop when he saw Weir and Sterling with his wife.

"What is that faggot doing in my house?" Stephen Bailey had an unfortunately nasal voice; it grated on Weir's nerves instantly.

Weir stood, pulling his badge out of his jacket pocket again. "Two faggots, Mr. Bailey, but I'm a federal faggot so you have to be polite to me or I'll have you arrested for obstructing an investigation so quickly you won't know your ass from a hole in the wall." He limped closer to Mr. Bailey. "You know, in prison they don't care who you are."

An ugly vein bulged along the side of Mr. Bailey's forehead, his face flushing an unhealthy scarlet. Bailey looked nothing like his son, or his son nothing like him. Lucky Sterling. Weir was trying to see what part of himself Bailey had donated to Sterling, but nothing jumped out at him. It was as if Sterling and Raven had popped fully formed from Mrs. Bailey's forehead, like Athena.

"Why are the police here?" Storming over to where his wife sat, Bailey grabbed her thin shoulder with a tight grip. "Why... did... you... call... them?" Each word was ground out separately.

"I didn't—"

Stephen shook her violently, making her head rock backward. Weir started to move, but Sterling was way ahead of him.

"What the fuck is wrong with you? Get your hands off her." Sterling knocked Bailey's hand off Mrs. Bailey's shoulder, inserting himself between her and her husband. Mrs. Bailey blinked, in shock, Weir thought; they were both shocked. She, probably because someone she had epically failed as a parent was protecting her. Bailey, because his "faggot" son was standing up to him.

Bailey lifted a hand; whether for a slap or punch, Weir didn't know.

"If you so much as touch him, I will have you arrested for assault." For a charged moment Bailey considered ignoring Weir. He saw it in the man's eyes. Then Bailey stepped back, conceding to Weir's power.

"Who is going to tell me what is going on?" Weir asked. As glib as he had been, telling Sterling they would find his sister, a very, very, bad feeling was beginning to claw its way into his chest. He could see that Sterling was starting to feel the same thing. This was no simple case of Raven running off or being sent away to "boarding school."

In the end, after Stephen Bailey spent a little more time posturing and essentially pissing a circle around his wife, the story emerged.

The night before, a package had been delivered to the house. Mrs. Bailey assumed it was for her husband so had waited for him to return. When Mr. Bailey opened it, he found a picture of Raven, a lock of dark hair, and a demand for several million dollars or they would never see their daughter again... although first they would see little parts of her, like fingers. As well as all the usual stuff: don't call the police or she will be dead and you will never know what happened to her. Standard kidnapping ransom note.

"Now you're here—you've ruined everything. I've spent hours trying to round up funds." Bailey dragged both hands through his salt-and-pepper hair. Definitely not a bowl cut. As Sterling had said, Bailey senior had his hair cut somewhere fancy.

"First of all, I came here as Sterling's friend. I am a federal investigator, though; this badge is not fake. *Now*, I am here as an investigator. Second, do you have this kind of money, Mr. Bailey?"

"I can get it. I don't have it lying around in a safe, if that is what you are wondering." Weir did wonder. Skagit wasn't a big city, but there seemed to be a lot of money floating around.

The kidnappers said they would be back in touch in three days, which meant Weir had about sixty hours left and a lot of work to do. So far, the Baileys were being cooperative. The entire conversation didn't last much longer than a half hour. Weir took the note and the padded envelope it had arrived in, hoping he would be able to glean some information from them.

As they all headed toward the front door, Sterling hung back a moment, murmuring to Mrs. Bailey. She answered and he nodded, then hurried to catch up with Weir.

On the doorstep, Weir turned around and asked the question that had been troubling him since they had found out about the ransom demand. "Mr. Bailey, I understand you were considering sending your daughter to conversion therapy. Why would you want to spend millions of dollars to get her back? If the way she is is so abhorrent to you, why would you bother?"

Bailey slammed the door in their faces.

"That went well, I think," Weir remarked.

Sterling glanced at him, sharp eyebrows raised in astonishment, while they navigated the steps down toward the parking area. He kept a hold on Weir's arm to keep him from stumbling. Perversely, Weir enjoyed the warmth of Sterling's palm heating his skin in front of the Bailey mansion. He hoped Mr. Bailey was watching them leave from a front window. Leaning closer, he turned so he could brush a kiss across Sterling's cheek.

"You are a menace." But Sterling didn't move away from him until they reached the car.

NINETEEN

"A federal faggot?" Sterling's mind was reeling. Of all the words that had been said inside that house, those stood out.

"It had to be said. I've been waiting to say it for years. It felt gooood." Weir chuckled.

"You're twenty-five, how long is 'years'?"

"Twenty-six. My birthday was last week."

Sterling whipped his head around to look at Weir. "What? Why didn't you say anything?"

"Dude, eyes on the road. I've never celebrated my birthday. Why start now?"

Sterling had a love-hate relationship with his birthday, especially since he turned thirty, but at least he acknowledged it. He usually spent it at work. Mac would make some obnoxious special named after Sterling, and there would be cake. He'd forbidden them from singing "Happy Birthday" ever again. Threatened them all with firing, in fact. They laughed and sang anyway.

"Quit worrying about my birthday. Get us home in one piece so I can call Adam and Mohammad."

"Is that a good idea?" Maybe he'd read too many thrillers, but it seemed like getting authorities involved always went sideways.

"Yeah, it's a good idea. Adam's been involved in one of these before."

Sterling was hit by another sideways thought. "Uh, what are you going to do when they get back? Micah and Adam?"

"The hotel will have a room. Same place I was before. Why, you offering?"

Weir's phone buzzed before Sterling could answer, and he found himself listening to one half of a conversation: Weir filling Adam in on what had happened, a lot of nodding and uh-huhs, before he clicked off. Sterling spent the intervening moments freaking out about whether or not he should offer to put Weir up at his apartment. Despite the fact that it was two stories up, had no elevator, and was only five hundred square feet.

They arrived at Micah's as the call ended, and Weir seemed to have forgotten Sterling's question. Thank god. He did not need to add drama to the drama. The focus right now was figuring out where Raven was and getting her back.

"Adam's going to send Sammy Ferreira around to talk to the folks at Patty's. See if he can get any more information out of them. We have to hope your parents are going to cooperate and not fuck everything up by going rogue on us. It's still early days."

"I think Stephen knows more than he is saying." Sterling didn't know *why* he thought that, but he did.

"Yeah, I think so, too. Sammy's good. He'll check in after he's talked to them."

This time it was Sterling's phone buzzing. He glanced at the screen. "I've got to take this." It was the bank. They needed him to come in and go over some details of the loan he was applying for. That didn't sound terribly ominous, and he agreed to be there in an hour.

Weir cocked his head at him. Weir had no idea Sterling was

trying to buy the Loft. That he had been saving and planning for years, that this meeting could make or break his dream.

* * *

HE PARKED in the lot between two monster pickup trucks and tried to calm his nerves before heading inside. Both trucks were splattered with mud. One had mud flaps adorned with the silhouette of a naked big-breasted woman; the other prominently displayed a rainbow sticker in the back window. Chuckling, Sterling opened the door to the bank and went in.

It was difficult for him to distinguish whether his nerves were from the situation with his sister or at finally finding out if he had successfully jumped through all the hoops for the small business loan application he had begun last fall.

The current owner of the Loft had moved to Seattle several years ago and floated the idea of Sterling buying him out when he could. Rick Daniels trusted Sterling, leaving him in charge except for the few times he dropped in on his way to Vancouver. As long as the books were balancing, Rick was happy. Rick was a good friend. Sterling often wished he hadn't moved away, but he had, and now Sterling had a chance to fly on his own. He wiped his sweaty palms on his jeans.

Sterling had worked his ass off to get to where he was now. He had enough savings and business experience to qualify for the loan he needed for full ownership. He wiped his clammy palms on his jeans again before shaking the hand of the bank representative who called him into his cubicle.

"WHAT?" Sterling was shattered. And furious. And wanted to hit something.

"At this time, we are unable to approve the loan you have applied for." Vijay Mandyjam, the bank's small business loan officer, repeated himself slowly, like Sterling was an idiot for not understanding in the first place. He'd been nervous coming in, sure, but he hadn't been prepared for rejection.

"Why?" His voice came out reedy, fucking pathetic. Vijay, as he had asked to be called when Sterling sat down, seemed to realize that Sterling was very close to the end of his rope.

"Mr. Bailey, Sterling, the documents are all here in this file. I suggest you take it home with you and review them." Vijay had kind brown eyes—nothing like Weir's, though, which seemed to hold promise and hope. "I suggest you check your credit report. If there are errors, have them corrected, and then the bank may reconsider its position."

Rather than argue, Sterling allowed Vijay to hand him the file and escort him out of his cube. He stood for a moment in the bank lobby trying to get his bearings, embarrassed to discover he had not been at all prepared to be turned down. That all the hard work and sacrifice had come to nothing. Saving money by living in a shoebox and taking a minimal salary so he could put the difference back into the bar had been worthless effort.

Back outside, he hazily noticed that both pickups had gone, leaving his car alone in the tiny parking lot. His car was listing oddly to the left. He walked over to it and saw that he had a flat tire. Not a slightly flat tire, but one so flat the rim was sitting on the pavement. Was the universe trying to tell him something? Should he drive to the nearest cliff and fling himself off it?

The spare was flat as well, and even if it hadn't been, Sterling couldn't have changed it because the jack was missing. Tossing the file of fucking bad luck onto the passenger seat, he called the only person he felt like talking to.

"How'd your appointment go?" Sterling hadn't told Weir what it was for, only that he'd had to leave.

"Not good. Look, I have a flat tire. I'll be a while." He was pinching the bridge of his nose, keeping away an epic headache or maybe tears. Something was brewing at the back of his skull, threatening like a slow-moving thunderstorm. No way to stop it, just prepare for when it finally arrived.

"Call Triple A?" No, because Sterling didn't have Triple A. Which right now seemed all kinds of fucked up. "Where are you?" Sterling read off the bank's address from the front doors. "Gimme a sec, I'll call someone for you."

Not that Sterling wasn't perfectly able to call someone himself, but it was a nice gesture on Weir's part, and Sterling wasn't sure he was up to any more phone conversation. Weir hung up. A few minutes later Sterling got a text saying someone would be there soon.

Fifteen minutes later, when the big tow truck with "Swanfeldt's Auto and Body" emblazoned across the doors rumbled down the street, Sterling wanted to smack himself. Weir had called Joey James's boyfriend. He groaned before plastering a smile on his face and getting out of the car to greet Buck. Buck was an awesome guy. Sterling liked him, but he and Joey had kind of a rocky history, and now Sterling was going to owe Buck a favor.

Buck maneuvered his big truck into place before getting out and greeting Sterling. Buck was a big, good-looking guy. Sterling had had no idea he was gay until Joey'd started hanging around. Buck had left the truck door open, and Sterling could hear the strains of some oldie-but-goody playing from the radio.

"Thanks for helping out, Buck. I owe you one."

Buck smiled. "Nah, I'm always happy to help a friend."

Standing up from where he'd been crouched by the flat tire, Buck tucked his hands into his pockets. "I could be wrong here, but I think your tire was slashed. You making enemies these days?"

If Buck only knew. Because the answer to that was probably a resounding, "Yes."

Quickly and efficiently, Buck loaded up Sterling's car and towed it back to his shop. Sterling sat next to him, wondering how this day had gone from unexpected but wonderfully quick and dirty sex that morning to a complete shitstorm. Somebody was fucking with him, and he was going to find out who it was.

"Leave your car here, take Sheila." Buck pointed at a beat-up GTI sitting in the corner of the parking area and tossed Sterling a set of keys. "I'll check what kind of deals are going, see what we can do about getting you rolling again without busting the budget. I'll call ya in the morning, all right?"

"Thanks, Buck. You, uh, really are going above and beyond."

Buck grinned at him again, a megawatt smile that about blinded him with its intensity. "Like I said, for friends it's never a problem." Sterling stood for a second watching Buck stride back into his kingdom before shaking himself out of his weird bubble to get into Sheila and head back to Micah's house. Back to Weir.

By the time Sterling returned to the house it was late afternoon. The day felt like it had gone on forever. He was wound up, overstimulated, pissed off, grieving the bank's decision, afraid for his sister (who, honestly, he had put to the back of his mind since Vijay Mandyjam had ruined his day)... basically a complete wreck.

Weir met him at the door. He'd changed from his suit into a pair of ratty cotton sweatpants and a vintage Butthole Surfers T-shirt. The sweats were so worn they were practically see-through, and he was going commando *again*. The sweats weren't terribly tight, but the outline of Weir's cock was as plain as day. Sterling groaned silently. Mostly silently.

Staring pointedly at the shirt with both eyebrows raised, he waited for an explanation. Weir looked down at his chest, chuckling.

"*So* many possible meanings. I found it in a thrift store in LA, used to wear it around to embarrass Ben. Not a big fan of the band, though. I'm more of a Maroon 5 kind of guy," he said as he headed back into the kitchen.

"Hey, you're not using your crutch."

"Therapist says I don't have to at home anymore. Whoop."

Sterling got caught up watching the muscular flex of Weir's ass under the barely there layer of cotton covering it, and wasn't sure how long it was before he realized Weir had stopped talking and was looking at him over his shoulder, amusement dancing in his eyes.

"Uh…" he cleared his throat. "Uh, that's great," he finished lamely. For the love of all that was holy, what in the fucking hell was his problem? "I'm going to go change." He needed to get out of Weir's vicinity before he did something really stupid, like kiss the man because he was happy to see him, or tell him that out of this thoroughly shitty day, Weir was the only shiny part. On his way upstairs, to the room he hadn't slept in for two nights, he reminded himself he didn't do relationships, that he wasn't looking for one.

If he *were* looking for a relationship it wouldn't be with a man six years younger than him. Because six years made such a big fucking difference. Or because he was a fed. Or currently lived in California. He snorted at his own ridiculousness. How many excuses was he going to hide behind?

The point was, it didn't matter. He didn't do relationships. Ever. The proof was in the pudding, as one of his long-dead grandparents used to say, and the pudding was telling Sterling the house of cards he and Weir had built over the past few days was going to come crashing down.

TWENTY

Weir waited for Sterling to come back downstairs, debating the best course of action. Share what Sammy had learned while he was out first? Or fuck him first, and then share? He'd probably take the news better if he was fucked first. On the other hand, telling him the news after would ruin the excellent side effects of being fucked.

If Sterling preferred, he could fuck Weir. Either way, it was happening tonight. Part one of his plan, wear the sleep pants that displayed more than they hid: already in play.

Buck had called before Sterling got there and told Weir about the tire being slashed, so not a random flat. He didn't know what had happened at Sterling's appointment, but from Sterling's body language he didn't think the news had been good. Going out on a limb (federal investigator, after all), he was assuming it was bank business, seeing as that was the address he'd given Weir for the tow truck.

Part two of his plan called for a little cheating. He was going to ply Sterling with homemade dinner and alcohol. How the man could run a bar/restaurant and not know how to cook, Weir had no idea. Weir had learned to cook from Ben. Ben had been a firm believer in being able to get around in a kitchen.

When Ben had been home they'd watched cooking shows and then tried to recreate the dishes. There had been some hilarious fails, usually involving Ben winging it when they'd been out of an essential ingredient. Weir chuckled at the memory of pancakes made with mayonnaise because they were out of eggs, and mayo was basically eggs, right? God, they had been disgusting.

This evening, Weir was making homemade Bolognese, breaking his rule of no red meat again, with a green goddess–style salad and several bottles of red wine on the side. He'd paid a ridiculous amount to have the stuff delivered from the organic grocery on the other side of town. The sauce was starting to come together, the scent of it wafting out from the kitchen to the rest of the house, when he finally heard Sterling coming back downstairs.

"That smells incredible," Sterling said as he came into the kitchen, having changed into a plain T-shirt and flannel pajama bottoms with—Weir peered closer—lightning bolts and wands on them. He couldn't help but smile. "Spaghetti?"

"Cretin, spaghetti is the type of pasta. This is Bolognese sauce, which we will be having with fresh linguini, because I like it better than spaghetti."

THEY SAT NEXT to each other at the kitchen table to eat. Weir made certain that Sterling's wine glass was always topped off. The man was wound tight. As they quietly ate their way through the pasta and salad, he began to relax somewhat. Weir really wanted to ask what had happened at the bank but restrained himself. Sterling would tell him when, or if, he was ready.

"That was amazing, thanks," Sterling said after scooping the last of the pasta into his mouth, his lips decadently lush, glistening from the sauce.

Weir leaned closer. "You got a little on your cheek." Using his thumb, he wiped the offending sauce away. Before he could bring his hand back, Sterling grabbed his wrist and licked the microscopic amount off the tip, then sucked Weir's thumb between his lips. Most of the air in Weir's lungs escaped in an involuntary groan.

Tugging harder, Sterling guided Weir onto his lap, the chair clattering to the floor behind him. They both huffed a laugh, but neither stopped what they were doing to right it. Warm lips brushed against his neck, a tongue traced his Adam's apple, teeth gently nibbled his earlobe. The angle he was sitting at on Sterling's lap had their erections pressed together; it was incredible. Weir knew he could almost come from that, but he wanted this to last longer than a rut in the kitchen.

He almost didn't hear the whispered words, "What are we doing?" He didn't have the answer to that, so he said nothing, instead wrapping his arms around Sterling's neck and kissing his beautiful mouth, demanding that he open his lips and let Weir inside. His mouth was hot and tasted of red wine and pasta sauce. Fuck, if Weir didn't stop this now, they were going to end up on the kitchen floor. He didn't think his leg was ready for that.

Reluctantly, he pulled away. "Couch?"

Sterling was as dazed as he was, pupils blown wide, lips slick. Weir didn't doubt he looked much the same.

"Yeah, okay." He blinked slowly, like he was trying to process. Weir snickered and grabbed his hand, which was snaking its way under the hem of Weir's T-shirt. "Come on."

By the time they reached the couch, Weir had gotten his shirt off and was trying to decide if losing the sweats would be too much. Glancing at Sterling, he about swallowed his tongue. He had his shirt off, too. Weir couldn't stop staring at his chest. His pecs were nicely dusted with dark hair, enough to rub his face in, which continued down his stomach before compressing into a trail disappearing beneath the waistband of those ridiculous pj's.

Sterling must have thought he was judging the pants. "Raven gave them to me."

"They're adorable, but that's not what I was looking at." He leered to make his point perfectly clear. It was adorable how Sterling's cheeks turned pink.

Taking the initiative, Weir scooted back on the couch, his head against the armrest, bringing Sterling down on top of him. Careful to keep his right side against the back of the couch, he lowered his left leg to the floor so they wouldn't tumble off.

"Okay?" Sterling asked, concern radiating from his eyes. "I don't want to hurt you."

"Okay. No more talking." For now, anyway. He felt a niggle of guilt, but a few hours wasn't going to change anything.

Sterling allowed his full weight to press Weir into the couch before licking the line of Weir's lips, requesting entrance. Weir opened, letting him in. There was no way of telling how long they kissed. It was mind-blowing, flickers of electricity passing back and forth between their lips, not enough to shock but enough to send a series of jolts down his spine to his balls. The sensation of skin on skin, Sterling's hairy chest rubbing against his own smoother one, helped distract him from the grind of Sterling's hips against his own.

He wanted to wrap his legs around Sterling, but was afraid they'd roll off the couch. Sterling changed the game by sliding down a little, latching onto Weir's very sensitive nipple, nipping and licking at it while twisting the other perfectly. Weir's erection hardened further, and he returned the favor by pressing up into Sterling. Jesus. Sterling's waistband slid down a little, exposing the tip of his incredible, bare, very hard cock, which smeared precome on their abs.

Dragging Sterling back up so he could kiss him more, Weir stuck his hand down the back of those wizard pj's to massage Sterling's ass while sucking on a plump lower lip. He was close, but goddammit, he wanted... "Wait." Breathing hard, he pushed Sterling away. "I want you to fuck me."

The look in Sterling's eyes was feral and ravenous. Weir felt like a meal when Sterling hadn't eaten in years. "Fuck, yes," he groaned.

Weir dug around under the throw pillow and grabbed the supplies he'd stashed there earlier. Sterling didn't even ask; he snatched the bottle of lube and condom before practically ripping off his pants. Weir lifted his own hips so Sterling could slide his sweats down. Skin, skin, skin, it felt so fucking good. He really could come from the sensation of their skin sliding together, the smell of their precome and sweat.

Sterling tucked the pillow under his hips and gently pulled Weir's ass up onto his thighs, careful of his bad leg. "You are fucking gorgeous—shit, look at you."

Finally, he quit talking and began to massage Weir's entrance with his thumb. He pushed it a little way in, and they both groaned. "Fuck, you are tight."

"Gimme more." Sweat was dripping down his forehead as he willed himself to relax and accept Sterling's finger. It had been a while since he had bottomed. Sterling fucking refused to hurry. Weir kept trying to force his fingers further up inside, but Sterling smiled wickedly and kept torturing him. Fucking *finally*, he twisted his fingers around, finding the magic spot. Weir moaned so loudly passersby could probably hear him from the street. He did not care.

"Please, please, please..." and other utter nonsense spewed from his lips; he'd be embarrassed if he thought Sterling would remember any of it. When Sterling removed his fingers, Weir felt a loss. He wanted more. He wanted fingers, lips, a big fucking cock. Sterling rolled on the condom and tugged Weir closer again, pressing himself against Weir's hole. Weir bore down like a pro, taking him as far as he could in one movement. It fucking hurt.

"Whoa there, cowboy, this isn't a race."

"Says you," Weir panted. "Get fucking in me, I need to come."

Demonstrating his wiry strength, Sterling grabbed his hips again and held them tight while he pushed the rest of the way in. Weir was so wonderfully full. He moaned and panted, trying to pull Sterling closer because he needed to kiss those obscene lips. Sterling moaned, too, and began moving faster, dragging his thick cock across Weir's prostate. Every. Single. Time. Sterling leaned closer, shoving Weir's left leg up as high as he could, kissing him, tonguing his mouth.

Sweat pooled between them, despite the cool spring evening. They were both roaring furnaces. Weir's hands slipped from their grip on Sterling's shoulders; he really did almost tumble them off the couch. Laughing into his mouth, Sterling held him tighter, pounded into him harder, kept sucking Weir's tongue practically down his throat.

His orgasm managed to take him by surprise. Which, of course, was ridiculous, but one moment he had been reveling in the overfull sensation of having a cock up his ass, jamming against his prostate, and then, boom, Sterling let go of his hips to grab his cock, and that was all he needed. Clenching around Sterling, he came hard enough to bring tears to his eyes. Literally. He tried to brush them off as sweat—hopefully that was what Sterling would think—but real tears leaked out, leaving him vulnerable and exposed. Sterling's face was still buried in his neck, thank god, so he threw his arm over his face to hide himself. Fucking hell.

Night had fallen while they were busy. The room was shrouded in darkness, the only light coming from the kitchen. Sterling groaned and gently pulled out, tying up the condom before heading to the bathroom. Weir continued to lie there in a stupor.

Sterling brought a warm washcloth with him when he returned, cleaning off Weir's stomach before making him move enough so Sterling could fit behind him and be the big spoon.

During all of this, neither one of them spoke. There was a quilt across the back of the couch, and Sterling pulled it over them, draping an arm across Weir's chest. Weir felt it when Sterling drifted off, the rhythmic rise and fall of his chest soothing against his back. He couldn't fall asleep, though. The tears Sterling hadn't asked about, his confused heart at war with his brain, fought the rest he sorely needed.

WEIR DRIFTED off at some point, because when the front door opened with a rattle he startled awake. Whoever came in had keys. Weir only knew of one person, okay, two persons, who had keys to Micah's house other than himself, Raven, and Sterling. Sterling sat up with a start, and the quilt fell to the floor as Micah and Adam walked into the living room. They got quite an eyeful before Weir snatched the coverlet back up from the floor and they had the sense to turn their backs.

Micah was giggling. Giggling. Adam had a hand over his eyes even though he was facing the other direction. Sterling was breathing so hard Weir thought he might hyperventilate. Weir put a hand to Sterling's chest, trying to soothe him.

"It's okay, this is a kind of karmic bitch payback for these yahoos having sex all over the place when they first got together."

"Not helping," Sterling muttered.

"No, really, this is good for Adam. Now he can feel my suffering."

Sterling tried to pull the quilt tighter around them, but ended up exposing his ass. Again.

"Quit squirming."

"For fuck's sake, would you two *please* go get dressed?" Adam grumped before he stomped into the kitchen. "Jesus Christ, I texted and called, Weir, what the hell?"

Micah followed Adam into the kitchen, laughing so hard tears were running down his face. "I told you we should wait until tomorrow."

"And there's a big fucking mess in here." Weir heard Adam righting the chair they had knocked over earlier.

Ten minutes later they were both back in their clothing, *with* underwear this time. Sterling added a black hoodie, and Weir managed to get one of his USC hoodies on, even though his arm ached. He kept snickering to himself over Adam's reaction. Served him right, after all the times he had walked in on the two of them making out, or worse.

He met Sterling at the bottom of the stairs. It was obvious he did not find this as funny as Weir did. His expression was closed off, much like it had been when they first met. Weir sighed and tucked his hands into the pockets of his sweatshirt.

"So, you guys, huh?" Adam asked as they trailed into the kitchen, which someone, likely Micah, had quickly cleaned.

"You know, just because we fucked doesn't mean anything," Sterling bit out.

Huh. Okay, that hurt. It wasn't as if Weir was thinking the guy would get down on his knees with a diamond ring, but he thought he rated higher than "just a fuck." The sensation of being iced, *glaciered*, out was not one he enjoyed. On that note, he walked around to sit on the other side of Micah, forcing Sterling to sit next to Adam.

"I hadn't told Sterling yet about what Sammy dug up. Was getting around to it."

"If by 'around to it' you mean fucking on our couch first—"

"Adam, shut it." Micah broke in across the beginning of his diatribe, scowling at his partner.

"Why are you back?" Not that Weir didn't appreciate Adam's help with the situation, but he'd thought they were going to be gone another week.

"Apparently I can't leave this one-horse town without a crime wave breaking out."

"What he means is, we were done in California and he couldn't wait to get home," Micah added.

"Met the Klay side of the family." Adam ran his hands through his hair, making it look like he'd been caught in a windstorm. "Only one of them isn't batshit crazy. Luckily, we met her early on and she warned us not to stay long. Filled me in on some shit I would rather have never known. So, yeah, Micah's right, I'm glad to be back."

Sterling watched the exchange with a stony expression, not saying anything. Weir couldn't read him for once.

The long and short, or long-long, of it was, Sammy had followed up at Patty's diner. Based on additional discussions with the wait staff and patrons, the man who had taken the girls had been identified as Darren Potts, Pony's paternal uncle. Sammy discovered that Potts was deep in gambling debt. Tribal casinos littered Skagit County, and Potts had spent money, too much money, in all of them. He had an outstanding debt of over fifty thousand dollars to a money man who went by the name of Charlie Herb.

Sammy had tracked Charlie down. He'd called in the debt over a month ago. Hadn't seen the money yet, and Potts only had a few more days to come up with it before Charlie was placing a lien on everything the man owned, as well as alerting his ex-wife.

It wasn't hard to connect the dots and deduce that Potts thought he could use Raven to get the money he needed. Everyone in town knew the Baileys had money. Sammy figured Potts found out Pony and Raven were friends and took advantage of them being at the café. Frighteningly, Charlie Herb's deadline was tomorrow evening, and the Baileys had not come up with the two million dollars. Nice padding Potts was adding there. You know, in case he ran into trouble again.

Darren Potts. The name rang a bell. Weir had seen it at some point recently. Getting hit by a car and nearly dying had really done a number on him. Breathing deeply, he let the name swirl in the back of his mind. He'd remember. When Sammy had mentioned it, he'd intended on checking his case notes. Sterling's slashed tire and general needing-to-be-fucked demeanor had him putting Potts on a shelf.

He let out an involuntary snigger. Sterling glared at him.

"Where are they?" This was the first thing Sterling had said since sitting down.

"We don't know. We're hoping he'll lead us to them tomorrow."

"He has both of them?"

"The Schneider house has been under surveillance since you called in yesterday. At this point, while the Schneiders are not cooperating fully, we have no evidence Pony is in the home."

"Are my parents cooperating?"

"They are now." Adam grinned wolfishly. Weir wondered what evidence of repugnant behavior Adam had dug up to ensure Stephen Bailey's cooperation. Weir would have searched himself, if he had thought of it.

TWENTY-ONE

Sterling's head was going to explode. Weir was calmly sitting and discussing shit with Adam after they had been busted sleeping naked. After fucking. On. His. Couch. Even if it was technically Micah's couch, it still freaked Sterling out. Then there was the fact that that POS Darren Potts had his hands on Raven. And his own niece, most probably.

Darren and Sterling had a history. One involving Darren being a bully who made fourteen-year-old Sterling's life a living hell. Darren, in fact, was the person who was responsible for him being outed to his parents. Darren wasn't responsible for his parents' reaction, but he started the ball rolling. Darren was still a cowardly piece of shit, and Sterling was going to rip his throat out. He wasn't a ninety-pound fourteen-year-old anymore.

The chances of Darren being terribly original in where he had taken the girls was minimal. Sterling figured he had a 90 percent chance of being right. The 10 percent was because Darren was, at his core, a stupid man, and possibly had them stashed at his own home. Sterling didn't think so, though.

"Hey, guys, rather than playing musical beds, Adam and I will sleep upstairs in the other spare room."

Micah's announcement caused a conversation that would have been hilarious had Sterling not been so wound up. Micah prevailed, but it was after eleven before he and Adam finally tromped up the stairs. Sterling insisted on changing the sheets and moving Raven's stuff out of the way. Adam griped, but Micah seemed to have him in hand.

No. He hadn't thought that. Please, let them not have sex tonight. He didn't think he could deal with it. Didn't matter, he wouldn't be there to hear it. Aside from having plans to find Darren Potts, he also had a perfectly good apartment of his own a few minutes away. One where he could be alone with his thoughts. Thoughts he needed to unwind from the tangled web they had become. At the center was a crazy man named Carroll Weir.

While he waited for everyone to go to sleep, Sterling paced around the small bedroom, packing the belongings he had brought with him. He considered stripping the bed and tossing the sheets in the laundry. On the other hand, he didn't want to alert anyone to his departure.

After midnight, the house fell into a deep quiet. Everyone was asleep. Sterling listened to the creaks and groans of the old house as it, too, settled for the night. Thank god, he hadn't heard any sex sounds from Adam and Micah's room. Tossing his backpack over his shoulder and grabbing his duffel bag, Sterling made his way silently downstairs and outside to Sheila.

It was pitch-dark, of course, but it wasn't raining. In fact, the sky was mostly clear. Sterling saw peek-a-boo stars for the first time in months. Taking a breath, he got behind the wheel, debating for a moment before deciding that Darren had almost certainly taken Raven and Pony to the old ranger station at Olympic View State Park. It was a rite of passage for groups of teens to break into the old stone building during the off-season for drinking, drugs, or sex. Or all three. He'd seen Darren there plenty of times before his parents had kicked him out.

The streets were empty, streetlights semi-hazy in the cool night air. He loved this time of night. It was one of the many reasons he was suited to be a bartender. As soon as he took care of this business with Darren, he would turn his attention to what the fuck was going on at the bank. He made a mental note to call Vijay.

In the meantime, he needed to focus on Raven and Pony. Sterling had turned right from Micah's street onto Steele when a voice from behind him asked, "So, where are we going?" It was a good fucking thing there were no other cars on that stretch of road, because he swerved into the oncoming lane before straightening out.

"Jesus Christ, Weir, what the ever-loving fuck are you doing in the back of the fucking car?" He emphasized his expletive-laden rant by pulling over to the curb and stopping with a jerk that had Weir nearly sliding off the back seat into the footwell. The fucker had been lying down in the back seat, and Sterling had been so lost in thought he hadn't clued in that there was someone in the car with him.

"I'm getting out of the back and coming around to sit in front. My leg is killing me. If you so much as think for one second about driving off without me… just don't," Weir growled.

Sterling did consider it, but the thought of having to explain himself to Adam or Micah stopped him cold. For all his bitching, Sterling knew that Adam liked and respected Weir. If he left Weir on the side of the road, Sterling would find himself on the wrong end of not one but two pissed-off federal agents.

The passenger door opened, and Weir dropped into the seat with a groan. "What took you so long? I've been waiting for over an hour."

Sterling scowled at him. "I was being sneaky, waiting for everyone in the house to go to sleep. I thought."

"You were so totally unsneaky. Adam and I were on to you immediately."

"Wait. Adam knows?" Could this night, this entire fucked-up day, get weirder?

"Hell, yeah. We've been texting back and forth since you all headed upstairs. Dude, you do not have a poker face. As soon as Darren Potts's name came up, we knew. Hang here for a minute, Sammy and Adam are coming with." God, he sounded smug.

Sure enough, within a few minutes a nondescript gray sedan pulled up behind them. Sterling could see the silhouettes of two men in it.

"Where are we headed? I'll text them." Weir looked at him knowingly and wagged an index finger. Sterling had a nearly overwhelming urge to kiss that fucking look right off his face. From Weir's expression, he wasn't opposed to that idea.

"When we get back, baby, when we get back." Weir was a fucking menace. Sterling had a hard-on in the middle of trying to rescue his sister.

"Olympic View State Park, the old ranger station at the south end. It's been closed for years. The state doesn't have the funds to retrofit it or something. Great place to get in trouble in the summer. This time of year, it's usually vacant."

Weir tapped at his phone, then motioned for Sterling to get going. Asshole.

* * *

THE COLOSSAL STONE building harked back to the 1930s and FDR's New Deal. In its heyday it must have been gorgeous. Huge river rocks supported the foundation and rose halfway up the outside walls. Where the rock stopped, workers had fitted logs together, Lincoln Log–style, up to the eaves. The passage of time had not been kind, though. The roof was in disrepair, windows had been broken out by vandals (such as himself fifteen years ago), and the foundation had eventually settled oddly, making the building look like it was sitting back on its ass. Too much longer and there would be no way to save it. Last Sterling knew, there was a community fundraiser to try and save the place, but they were far short of the necessary funds.

Sheila's engine ticked into the inky night while they sat quietly in the car. There were no other cars in the small turnout area about a half-mile from the ranger station. Ironically, they were only about a mile south on Old Charter from where Weir had very nearly died. When Sterling pointed it out to him as they passed by, Weir only nodded, commenting that he didn't really remember anything from the incident.

* * *

"HERE'S THE DEAL." Weir's voice startled him from his thoughts. "We are going to patiently wait here while Adam and Ferreira do a little recon to see if Potts and the girls are inside."

Sterling sputtered, lunging for the door handle before Weir could stop him. Weir was prepared, though, and Sterling was driving an unfamiliar car. Before he had an idea what was happening, Weir had grabbed Sterling's right wrist and snapped a handcuff snugly around it, the other bracelet already attached to Weir. Sterling tugged futilely for a moment, even though he knew it was a lost cause.

"Problem solved. Besides, you wouldn't want me to be out here by myself, would you?"

Sterling thought it was pretty fucking amazing that he managed to remain dead silent, yet still communicate his absolute and complete fury at being forced to stay in the car.

"We could always make out."

Sterling didn't acknowledge him, didn't bother looking at him. Didn't want to think about warm lips that were almost always quirked up a little on one side like there was a joke but he was the only one in on it. Didn't want to look into dark-brown eyes that held a lot more understanding than anyone's his age should. He wondered how Weir managed it, searching for other families' lost ones without having found his own. He wondered if he had ever looked for his mother.

"So, that's a no?" Weir managed to sound a little pouty. "It could be a while."

"You are a fucking asshole," he huffed.

"Yeah, I know. You know I really like Raven, too? It's been nice spending time with her. I'm worried, too. But neither of us are the best people to go in there right now. If they're there, Adam will get the job done."

"I really hate you right now." He didn't.

"I know."

Sterling didn't hate Weir at all. Every time he thought he could turn his back, return to the way things had been before Weir had fallen into his life, something happened to prove him wrong. He'd stopped caring about the age difference. Weir's personality and life experience more than made up for any age gap. There was no going back, only going forward.

"Why do you go by Weir? No nicknames, or anything?"

"Adam calls me 'Ace.' If you do, I'll kill you in your sleep. No, never any nicknames. Didn't stick around schools enough to earn one. Carroll was my dad's name, too. He didn't call me Carroll, either. Usually it was 'Hey you,' or he'd get pathetically drunk and call me Esther, which was always wonderful."

"I can't believe you handcuffed me."

"Would you have stayed in the car if I'd told you the plan?" Weir turned so he was sideways in his seat, his arm resting across the console, watching Sterling. No, he wouldn't have stayed. He would have ignored Weir and burst into the building with his figurative guns blazing.

"Plus, maybe I've discovered a kinky side to myself," Weir mused with that stupid smile.

The handcuffs gave Sterling an easy excuse to twine his fingers with Weir's while they waited. The silence was comfortable. Weir's hand was warm and solid, an anchor. He absently stroked the back of Weir's hand with his thumb, letting the tide of unnamed emotion flow back and forth between them.

Weir broke the silence. "I may have discovered a flaw in my plan."

"Which plan is that?"

"One plan at a time, dude. Uh," he chuckled and lifted their joined wrists, "the key is in my jeans pocket, and the angle is bad for my arm. So one of us can crawl across the console, or you're going to have to get it for me. From my pocket."

"From your pocket?" Sterling repeated. "You are ridiculous."

"You like me." Weir huffed.

Weir was right, Sterling did like him. More than liked him, and he had never allowed himself that before. For another person. What he felt for his sister was different. It wasn't terrifying. It didn't make Sterling feel raw and exposed, a dog rolling on its back, belly up.

The darkness made it easier for Sterling to get the words out. Tightening his grip on Weir's hand, like he was about to jump out of an airplane, he said, "I do like you, Weir, you know that. I more than like you. I'm not sure what to do about it. It's confusing and frightening. I've never been with someone before, for more than sex—"

In the gloom, he saw Weir's mouth gape. Slowly he closed it, and a tentative smile appeared, not the quirky one Sterling was beginning to understand he used to keep people at arm's length. Keeping his eyes locked on Sterling's, he leaned in. Sterling met him halfway, their kiss gentle and sweet, a promise. Sterling wanted to deepen it, make it more, but Weir pulled away, taking a deep breath.

"Let's not get too distracted; we really do need that key. I don't think crawling over the console is a good plan. So hurry up and stick your hand down my pants."

TWENTY-TWO

"I think I can multitask." Sterling pushed farther over the cup holder and parking brake, pressing his lips against Weir's, warm tongue sliding across and requesting entrance. Weir couldn't help himself; he opened, letting Sterling in, reveling in the taste and feel of him, how his tongue swept across the roof of his mouth, making him shiver. Fuck, he was in trouble.

A hand, Sterling's hand, maneuvered its way into his right front pocket. Before he snagged the key, he took the time to stroke Weir's quickly hardening cock through the thin cloth.

Weir jerked his mouth away. "Jesus Christ, Sterling."

"Told you, multitasking." Triumphantly he held up the little silver key.

"What the fuck are you two doing?" Adam's voice boomed across the vacant parking area.

BY THE TIME the two of them stopped laughing hysterically and Weir got the cuffs off both of their wrists, Sammy had appeared as well, morphing out of the darkness like some kind of ninja. He looked questioningly toward Adam.

"Don't ask. I do not want to know what these clowns were up to. We're out here because Sterling's sister has been kidnapped, Weir, not so you can play pocket pool and act out your kinky bondage fantasy."

Weir opened his mouth to retort, but Adam beat him to it. "Shut it." He couldn't help smiling, though.

Adam and Sammy piled into Sheila's back seat. Weir had the absurd thought that they were in a clown car, but managed not to say anything. He did snicker, earning the classic Klay glare.

Looking over at Sterling, he saw that his mood had relapsed to anxious and worried. Weir hoped Adam had some good news. Unfortunately, Adam was wearing a grimmer-than-normal expression.

Sammy spoke first. "I was able to get inside; evidence points to it being inhabited. Tire tracks and footprints everywhere. There's a propane camp stove, an empty cooler, sleeping bag, trash, but the kids are not in the building."

"The upside is we can get a team out here in the next few hours, while it's still dark, to go over the scene before Potts knows we are on to him. Sterling..." Adam's voice lowered, became kind, a transformation Weir had seen before, yet it always surprised him. "You know Potts. Tell us about him."

"I don't know him that well," Sterling muttered.

"You know him better than the rest of us here. Give us some history. Somewhere we can start with this guy. How are you connected?"

Sterling barked out a bitter laugh. Weir didn't like the look on his face. "History. We have history. For starters, he outed me to my family when I was fourteen, which led to them throwing me out of the house. Don't feel sorry for me; it was a long time ago, and I'm not the only one it's ever happened to." They were holding hands again. Weir squeezed the hand curved around his own.

"I've had as little to do with him as possible since then. Don't know what he does for a living. We don't run in the same social circles; he doesn't come into my bar. Because, 'faggot.'" He paused, thinking. The car stayed quiet, no one wanting to interrupt. Weir could hear the ever-present wind blowing through the trees, early birds beginning to wake and sing their morning songs. "A few years ago there was some kind of scandal with his name attached to it. I know he's divorced now. You may need to ask the local historian—and by that I mean Ed Schultz. There's not a lot in this town gets past him."

Adam was quiet for a moment before speaking. Even in the dark, Weir could see the wheels turning. "All right, you two head back to the house."

Weir didn't argue, but Sterling sputtered with outrage, letting go of his hand and twisting further around to glare at Adam.

"Don't argue with me. This is dangerous. I don't need to be worrying about you"—he pointed to Sterling—"going off half-cocked, or"—pointing at Weir—"Ace here fucking up his leg or arm again because he's trying to keep you from doing something stupid."

"Fine," Sterling growled after a moment, "but I'm not happy about it."

"Good thing I don't give a fuck what you're happy about right now."

For crying out loud. Vacation didn't seem to have mellowed Adam out a bit.

"You." Adam pointed to Weir again. "Do some research, do your computer thing. Figure out everything you can on Darren Potts. Ferreira and I will take this part from here."

* * *

BEST-LAID PLANS AND ALL, was what Weir was thinking hours later. The only sleep they'd had was before Adam and Micah had surprised them on the couch. He smiled at the memory. No sleep and far too much coffee since they'd returned. He'd tried to make Sterling sleep, or at least rest, but that was not happening. Weir instead shamelessly played up how much his leg and arm ached in order to make sure Sterling didn't run off to play cowboy.

It had backfired magnificently. Sterling kept asking did he need anything, was he thirsty, hungry, hot, cold, tired, stiff? Weir was seriously considering knocking him unconscious with the crutch Sterling had brought out from the bedroom and insisted he use.

Darren Potts was a piece of work, that was certain. Getting his personal information had been child's play, something Weir could have done in his early teens. The guy had debts, some legitimate: mortgage, car payment, credit cards. Plus others that were less simple to define. Cash advances on all five of his credit cards in the last few months, with interest rates that were outrageous and compounded daily. His credit score was somewhere around 400. No legit bank would lend him money anymore.

He spent most of his time at the casino south of town, gambling. Besides the outstanding debt to Charlie Herb, modern-day loan shark, the state was after him for back child support. Yet he was shoving everything into the slot machines. Slots took credit cards these days, which made it easier to drain the account, and Potts was there *every day*. Except he hadn't been for the past week, according to his debit card.

In the meantime, his kid (Weir would love to have someone explain to him why any woman would let this guy close to her private parts) was suffering.

Money dribbled into his accounts from a variety of sources. As far as Weir could see, he hadn't had a regular paycheck for several years. Jobs were odd and infrequent. The most recent W-2 Weir found was issued by Northern Star, a Canadian fishing company. He dug around in the Skagit Tribune archives for a record of the story Sterling had remembered.

Five years ago, Northern Star had been permanently banned

from the US for illegally harvesting shellfish. Weir had researched them and another, larger, company when he first took the geoduck case, but he hadn't been able to find a link between then and now. Except here was Darren Potts, who used to work for them, desperate for money and obviously willing to go the extra mile to get it. Had he seen Potts's name before? In Krystad's notes?

He was lost in thought, trying to figure out the links between an old poaching job big enough that biologists and Fish and Wildlife had noticed, gambling debts, Darren Potts, and Raven, when Sterling's voice startled him out of his thoughts.

"All right, that's enough. You've been staring at that thing for four hours."

He had? He looked at the clock. He had. Dragging his hand down his face, he tried to loosen up his stiff neck. He had kinks all over; his body snapped and popped as he stretched.

"Adam called. You need to call him back." Sterling was literally vibrating with tension.

Picking up his cell phone, he saw that he had missed a very recent call. He'd been so far down the Darren Potts rabbit hole he hadn't heard it ring.

Adam picked up immediately.

"I've got the call on speaker, pretend Sterling isn't listening."

"Yeah, all right. Potts has gone to ground. No one has come in or out since we've been here. Been on the line with Stephen Bailey to set up a money drop." There was a big sigh on the other end of the line. "Fuck, Sterling, your dad is an asshole. I had to *encourage* him to cooperate. This is his own kid!"

"Family ties have never been strong for my dad. Not if it costs money or his precious reputation."

"Sending your sister to 'boarding school' would cost a bundle."

"True, but he thinks that is money well spent. If she returns not gay, he sees that as a win."

"I don't see how this has gone from forced conversion to kidnapping. It's so random," Weir interjected. Ludicrous was what he thought. If this were a movie he would be asking for his money back right about now.

Sterling began to pace around the living room. "The whole situation is surreal."

"We should look up the GSA mob again. Maybe they know something but don't realize it." Weir tapped his laptop to keep it from going to sleep. Where were Raven and Pony? The cell-phone trace had only shown that Raven's phone hadn't left Skagit before the battery was drained or it had been turned off.

"Potts is not smart. We were in high school together, remember?" Clearly, Sterling was off on his own tangent. He had a point, though.

Adam's tinny voice blasted out of the phone speakers. "Focus. Jesus fucking Christ, the two of you need to focus, focus, focus, and what the fucking hell is the GSA mob?"

Weir *was* focusing. He was following the money trail. One of the first lessons in any investigation: who would have the most to gain? He'd been monitoring Potts's bank account, which had updated seconds ago and now showed a pending debit from the casino forty miles south.

TWENTY-THREE

Sterling was not remotely amused that Adam and Weir had united in their insistence that he stay far away from the casino and let Adam and Sammy do their jobs. The fact that Weir was still staring at his laptop screen instead of distracting him—and the fact that he couldn't stop thinking about all the ways Weir could distract him—only added to his irritation.

"Sterling?" Weir's voice sounded... cautious. "Why were you at the bank the other day?"

He sighed, sweeping aside his irritation for the moment. He wasn't the point right now. "I'm buying—was trying to buy—the bar. It was supposed to be a done deal, but they sent me away with my tail between my legs. Then my fucking tire was slashed. It's been a bad week."

"Don't be angry..."

Cue anger. It surged through him hot and fast, molten glass sliding down his spine. "What?" He went to peer over Weir's shoulder, but he had no idea what he was looking at.

"The bar is doing well?"

"Yeah. Great, really. Even though I've been away, the guys are handling it. It's all bank."

"So, um, why is there no money?"

"What?" he asked stupidly. "There's plenty of money. Even if there wasn't, I still have most of the principal from the trust my grandparents left. In fact, it's part of the collateral for the bar."

Weir spun his laptop around so Sterling had a better view. He sat heavily on the kitchen chair, not trusting his legs.

There was *no* money.

Weir clicked rapidly through his banking details, as well as the main account for the bar. Fuck, there was barely enough to cover the upcoming payroll. Sterling had him back out of the account and reenter his information to make sure. His fingers curled into tight fists, fingernails digging painfully into his palms. The money he had been saving for years, even the college fund he had barely touched, was drained. Gone.

Stephen had to be responsible; no one else had access or knowledge.

Sterling had lived in absolute shitholes to save money, ate only ramen or beans and rice for months, for *years*. For fuck's sake, he wore all black because it was cheaper and easier to have all his clothing match. Sterling's stomach, already sensitive from the stress of the past few days, was ready to revolt.

He didn't have to think hard about where it had gone. Or to figure out that this had something to do with why Darren Potts had shown up demanding two million dollars in ransom.

His fucking father had stolen his life. Again.

This explained the weirdness at the bank the other day.

"That fucker." He wanted to punch something, someone. Someone named Stephen Bailey who was the biggest mother-fucker—who had not only betrayed him as a parent but now, now he was stealing his very soul. Fuck that. He spun in a slow circle, looking for something, anything to punch, pent-up anger roiling at the tips of his fingers, just waiting for a spark to release it.

A hand landed gently on the back of his neck. Weir was standing next to him. God, he hadn't even been aware of him moving. Weir squeezed, hard enough to get Sterling's attention, before relaxing his grip and dropping his hand to Sterling's waist. "This, this is why *I'm* here. Why Adam *and* I are here. This is what we are really fucking good at, okay? Let us do this." Weir turned so they were chest to chest. "I need a few minutes. I'm going to do something Adam will be pissed about, so I gotta do it before he gets here."

"Do what?"

Neither one of them had noticed Micah standing in the kitchen doorway. He'd wisely locked himself away most of the morning, steering clear of Sterling's volatile mood.

They must have had identical guilty looks on their faces when they spun around at the sound of his voice. Weir stumbled, off-balance on his weak leg, and Sterling caught him. Weir flailed a little before relaxing against him. "Nothing." His voice was so innocent not even an idiot like Potts would fall for it.

"Fine. I'm going back upstairs, but not without coffee."

Weir hustled back to the kitchen table, turning his laptop around so it wasn't visible to anyone not sitting next to him. The keyboard started clicking madly, and Sterling knew he was lost to them for the moment. Christ, his eyes practically glazed over.

"So," Micah said while he expertly frothed milk, "you guys?"

Sterling groaned.

"There is no 'us guys.' It's just," he waved a futile hand, "just something that happened."

"Huh." The steaming milk reached the magic temperature where it pierced the sound barrier. Micah pulled it away from the steam wand, swirling it a bit before loading up the shots of espresso. Sterling watched with fascination. Micah had coffee making down to an art. It was almost as good as watching the sushi guys at the grocery store.

First the shot went into the mug, then the steamed milk, and Micah performed a fancy move at the end before handing the cup over to Sterling.

"Here, this one's yours." He smirked.

Sterling looked down at the mug. Micah had managed to artfully draw a heart in the foam, smack on the top of his drink.

Without comment, Micah put together his own latte and disappeared back upstairs, leaving Sterling staring at the heart, wondering what the hell was happening to his life.

"Ha!" Weir declared. "Got it."

Sterling put the offending coffee aside and went to sit by Weir. "Got what?"

"The money. I think." Weir scratched his cheek. "Well, part of it, anyway."

Sterling still had no idea what he was looking at. It seemed like just line after line of numbers. Code?

Weir squinted at the screen. "Soooo, your dad."

Sterling growled, deep in his chest.

"Okay, gotcha, *Stephen* is way overcommitted. He's got money going out that he doesn't have. A lot of money. That gruesome house, for one thing. Also several business loans, and a lot of cash has disappeared recently." He clicked around some more, screens flashing by at a ridiculous speed. "I can't say exactly where your money has gone; they did something tricky with it. It disappeared somewhere in the fucking Caymans. I'm telling you, if I ever visit there, I am going to seriously fuck up their shit. Fucking international banking regulations." He trailed off as something caught his attention.

The Cayman Islands? Money laundering? The fuck? Sterling knew he should be freaking out, *was* freaking out, but the sheer scope of it all was kind of taking the air out of his sails. And where the fuck was Raven?

"I bet Raven and Pony are pawns in this whole thing," Weir muttered, as if he was reading Sterling's mind. "Maybe… hmmm… he's kind of stealing from himself. He's using Raven to steal money from himself. I think. After first stealing from you. Some of it goes to the fuckwad he recruited to do the deed, but he gets most of it back, right? And probably he's thinking then he'll disappear somewhere exotic. These guys have no imagination. Just once I'd like someone like him to choose somewhere like Akron or Fargo as a destination. We need to get a search warrant for, uh, their property. I mean, even someone as dumb as Darren Potts wouldn't go to a casino when he had hostages to keep track of, right? He'd stash them somewhere safe?"

The front door banged open, scaring the crap out of both of them. Their nerves were shot to hell. Weir slammed his laptop shut. Sterling moved to the kitchen doorway in time to watch Adam and Sammy tumble across the threshold, laughing like maniacs. Adam had a hold of Sammy's shoulder, keeping him from face-planting on the living-room floor. Micah heard them too, appearing at the top of the stairs where he took in the situation with a shake of his head. Adam dropped onto the couch with a thud.

"Did you see the look on his face?" Adam was wheezing, he was laughing so hard. "I have never felt like I was on that show, *Cops*, before. I guess, normally, the caliber of criminal we're after has more than one brain cell to rub together."

Sammy was practically having a seizure. Sterling went back into the kitchen to pour him a glass of water. He handed Sammy the water while Adam wiped his eyes and tried to get himself under control.

Micah let out a big sigh as he came down the stairs. He was smiling, though. "All right, you two, what happened? What's so funny? Sterling's been waiting on pins and needles for you to get back."

"Okay, yeah." Adam took a big gulp of air. "I apologize, Sterling."

"So, Adam and I walk into the casino," Sammy began. "We'd called ahead, security knew exactly who we were after. Hardly had to describe him, they're like, 'Yeah, yeah, slots.' We get there and Potts is sitting at the far end of a long row of slot machines, sliding his credit card as often as he can. Adam must have been doing that thing where his presence precedes him, because we were about halfway down the aisle when Potts looks up and sees us coming. The guy didn't hesitate, he *knew* we were there for him. He bolts out of the chair and runs the other direction. Adam and I look at each other—are we in a buddy-cop movie? Is there a hidden camera around?" Sammy chuckled, his eyes still damp from laughter.

"Just then, one of the servers comes around the corner with a tray of drinks," Adam said.

They were all quiet for a moment, imaginations running wild. There was a brief pause. Then, "Wait, it gets better," Sammy continued. "The drinks and tray explode everywhere. The server is at most five feet tall and probably weighs, like, a hundred pounds, but she's been around the block. She is strong, fast, and mad as hell. Potts is trying to get around her, but she's blocking his exit stage right, dancing back and forth like a prizefighter. Shrieking and swearing at him, telling him he's going to pay, threatening to cut off his balls. Potts pushes her down and just runs. She's like the Energizer bunny, though; pops right back up and takes off after him. Still screaming. Security is behind us, but Potts and the girl are way ahead."

Adam picked up the thread. "Potts heads toward an emergency exit; we can hear the server screaming at him across the casino floor. So we're racing past the tables and crap, but not really worried about losing Potts. There's some kind of water feature—we hear a big splash, and when we come around the corner he's shoved the girl into it. Whoa, if she was mad before… Anyway, security grabbed her and got her out, but I think one of them has bruised balls."

"We get outside, and for about ten seconds we both worry we did lose him. The back of the building is pretty typical: huge trash containers, employee parking, stacks of empty pallets, fifty-gallon drums of cooking oil—or whatever it is they store in those things.

We're looking around, and then all of a sudden there's this *gurgle* sound and Potts shoots up out of one of the trash containers... his face..." Sammy collapsed into giggles again.

"He'd jumped into one of the containers," Adam said. "But there were rats in it. They did not appreciate the intrusion, or the competition. We're hoping he's up to date with his shots. He starts to run *toward* Sammy and me, like we're going to save him from the rat hanging off his ass. *Hell fucking no.* Luckily, by this time backup had arrived. The new guy got to cuff him."

"What about the rat?" Weir asked. Trust Weir to ask about the rat.

"The rat knew when to cut its losses. It had dropped off by then, but Potts kept jumping around like it was right behind him. Fucking Christ, the guy was only in there for a minute, but he stank. Security made the mistake of letting go of the woman; she came barreling out to ream him some more, but even she was put off by the stench." Adam stood and clapped Sammy on the shoulder. "Good job, but seriously, fucking *rats*?"

Once again silence fell while they all replayed the visual.

Sammy had finally stopped laughing and caught his breath. "Okay, so, Potts hasn't said anything yet, except to claim he has no idea where Pony and Raven are, that this was all Stephen Bailey's idea. The fact that he said that without us prompting him... what a fucking idiot. I think they're close by, or Potts wouldn't be in the area. Agents are questioning him as we speak."

Adam wrinkled his nose. "Ugh, I stink from being near that loser. When I get out of the shower, we'll talk about your father."

Funny, Sterling had not thought once about what would happen to either one of his parents. They had dug this circle of hell for themselves. He was not going to help them out of it.

When Adam got out of the shower, though, he and Sammy were called downtown, leaving Sterling to his own devices, because Weir was back on his computer and lost to the world.

TWENTY-FOUR

He knew where they were.

He *knew* he wasn't wrong.

The right thing to do would be to call Adam and Sammy and let them take care of it. But Weir's ego demanded that he be the one. He wanted to prove something to Sterling: that he was smart, and capable, and also a hero.

The man in question had gone upstairs. Weir didn't know why, but it gave him time to log off his laptop and head to his bedroom, where he rummaged in the closet for a suit. It was odd to have to push aside other clothing to get to the suits and dress shirts he normally wore every day.

Admittedly, the few he'd brought with him had been in pretty heavy rotation before his injury. Deciding on the slate gray/blue suit and a white dress shirt with just a hint of blue, Weir proceeded to transform himself into a federal agent. After making sure his badge and weapon were in their appropriate places, he went back out into the living room.

His rental car had long been returned, and he probably shouldn't drive yet, so there was no way around asking Sterling to take him out to the Bailey homestead.

"Where do you think you're going?" Sterling demanded as he, too, came into the living room.

"Your parents'. I need you to drive."

Yesterday—had it been just yesterday? Yesterday, when they had arrived at the faux Tara, Weir had been focused on Sterling and the upcoming confrontation with Mrs. Bailey above everything else... but he had noted the cars sitting in the driveway.

Why, when you had very expensive cars and a custom-built garage, would you leave those cars outside? Spring in Skagit came with no guarantee of pleasant weather. In Weir's experience it rained more days than not.

The answer was, you *didn't* leave those cars outside unless something else was in your garage. Something you didn't want anyone else to see.

Sterling didn't question him. Grim-faced, he grabbed his wallet and the keys to Sheila off the kitchen counter and made for the front door.

The drive was silent. Weir stared out the window, watching the dark-green evergreens and newly budded deciduous trees flash by. Some early dogwood and magnolias were already blooming. Against the dark clouds, they provided a kind of hope.

The gate code hadn't been changed since the day before. Sterling punched it in, then waited impatiently for the ornate metal gate to slide open.

"Park by the carriage house," Weir instructed. If things went sideways, he needed them all to be able to leave quickly. He wondered how much trouble he was going to be in for this, before deciding he didn't care.

Sterling quickly turned off the engine and set the parking brake. Even before they got out of the car, Weir saw the front door of the main house opening.

"Hurry up. Get inside, see if they are okay."

Again, no questions. Sterling left the car and went for the side entry of the fancy garage. Weir watched him twist the handle, and realized it was locked. As quickly as possible, Weir joined him at the door. Taking out his service piece, he moved Sterling aside. Using the butt of his weapon, he struck the cheap handle several times. The metal-on-metal clash echoed across the yard.

"Now try."

The whole process had taken about thirty seconds. Looking over his shoulder, Weir saw a red-faced Stephen Bailey running toward them from the house. Sybil Bailey stood on the porch, arms crossed over her chest, watching. What was wrong with her?

"Get away from there, faggots!" Stephen screamed. The man needed to broaden his vocabulary.

The door popped open.

"Go on, see if they're okay. I'll hold him off."

Sterling disappeared inside.

Weir turned to face Stephen Bailey.

Blocking the door, Weir pulled out his badge and flashed it before Bailey got any closer.

Unhinged was a perfect description. Deranged came to mind, too. Stephen Bailey wasn't a particularly big man, but he was off the rails, and if Bailey tried anything physical Weir knew he was at a disadvantage because of his leg.

His phone buzzed. He automatically reached for it at the same time Stephen pulled a small handgun from the back of his pants. People watched way too many movies.

"Whoa, you point that at me, you are changing the game. Put the gun down," Weir said calmly. He'd only had a gun pointed at him once before outside of training, and he didn't like it any better this time around.

Behind him he could hear voices, both male and female. Sterling talking to Pony and his sister. He couldn't understand the words, but from Sterling's tone he didn't think they were hurt.

Stephen raised the snub-nosed handgun. Guns were not Weir's thing. Mostly, he would prefer not to carry one, but it wasn't a choice he was allowed, so he dutifully strapped his service weapon on whenever he was out on a call. Like today.

A tiny blur raced down the slope from the porch to the garage. He wished she hadn't.

Stephen had no idea what hit him when his tiny wife slammed into him from behind. Her approach had been silent, her angle wicked. Using her small size to her benefit, she rammed into Stephen, hitting him in the small of the back at full speed and sending him catapulting forward.

Time slowed down, a thing Weir had only ever read about before. Stephen's finger reflexively tightening on the trigger caused the weapon to fire. With no suppressor, the 145-decibel report of a bullet exiting the barrel of a gun carried across the property.

Too late to shout a warning.

The shot resounded out across the flats. Stephen Bailey was facedown on the grass, his wife shrieking, punching his back, and getting up to kick him while he lay there stunned, his gun arm stretched out in front of him, his face in the mud. A strangled sound came from behind Weir. He whipped around, nearly losing his balance, and saw Sterling down as well, holding his shoulder, blood seeping out between his fingers, staining his sweatshirt and the ground beneath him. Raven, still wearing the clothes Weir had last seen her in, went into hysterics.

"He fucking shot me!" Sterling's face lost all color. "It fucking hurts," he whispered. His heartbreaking expression of betrayal was nearly as anguishing for Weir as seeing Sterling pale and helpless against the doorframe, gripping his arm, trying to keep the blood and pain inside his body.

It took everything Weir had to get through the next few minutes. His leg and arm ached to a distracting degree. The emotional overload of Raven and Sybil breaking down, Sterling being carted away in an ambulance, and the arrival of a very grim Adam had him tied up in knots, made his stomach ache.

Really, if he was honest, the only problem was the ambulance bumping away from him, carrying Sterling and Raven to St. Joe's. Adam could yell all he wanted. Weir's heart was being painfully yanked out of his chest.

TWENTY-FIVE

When he found out Bailey had been arrested, Darren Potts couldn't get his story out fast enough.

Virtually the first words spilling out of his mouth were, "Stephen Bailey made me do it." Who actually says something like that? Weir wondered if they'd let him take a shower or if he'd sat in the interrogation room covered with rotting-trash smell and a potential rat bite. Least of the fool's worries at this point.

A transcript of the interrogation landed in Weir's in-box a few hours after they returned to the house. Sammy had removed himself to his hotel room, leaving Weir at loose ends, giving him more time to think. Micah was upstairs "helping" Adam shower. Which Weir was thankful for, since it meant there was a remote possibility Adam was done yelling. Very remote.

Sterling had needed several stitches and a mild pain medication. They were so fucking lucky the shot hadn't hit anything vital. The thought of Sterling getting hurt made Weir's insides freeze and twist uncomfortably. It would have been his fault. It *was* his fault. He felt close to vomiting. The bullet had grazed Sterling's upper arm. The handsome ER doc had cleaned it up and closed the wound while Weir hovered unhelpfully in the little exam room. Sterling hadn't needed to stay overnight at the hospital as long as he promised to rest at home. Which was what he was doing right now.

Weir was studying the tragicomic downfall of Darren Potts and, soon enough, Stephen Bailey. Contemplating how truly unoriginal people were, and questioning why Potts hadn't been drowned at birth. While a constant buzz of worry about Sterling hovered in the background. And Raven, too.

Potts had been contracted by Bailey to perform the kidnapping. Weir wondered if it was coincidence that Bailey had hired the very same person who had outed his son years earlier. After leaving Patty's, he'd driven directly to the plantation, where he'd deposited the teens. Raven and Pony were blindfolded, their wrists and ankles duct-taped so they couldn't escape from the carriage house. Which was why the Tesla and Lexus had been parked outside when he and Sterling paid their visit, exactly as Weir had thought. Wouldn't want kidnapping to get on your cars.

Bailey had given Potts instructions on how to demand the ransom and told him to lie low for the next few days. He'd lured the teens by telling them there had been an accident, although apparently Raven had argued with him about details, which led to the scene in Patty's. Potts had been camping at the old ranger station before the kidnapping—Sterling hadn't been wrong about that—but the weather had turned colder, and he was bored, so he'd decided to spend the day inside. At the casino. It had not occurred to Potts that being at the casino was *not* lying low. Bailey had promised him a cut of the ransom, just enough to pay off Potts's debt to Charlie Herb, and they would go their separate ways. No one would know any better.

Weir snorted.

Right.

No way would Bailey have given him that money. Not with the amount of debt he was in and his current lack of capital. Weir didn't know exactly how desperate Bailey was, how much of a hardened criminal he'd evolved into, but he thought it was a lot more likely that Potts would have disappeared, along with a pair of specially fitted cement boots. Or whatever creeps used in the Pacific Northwest.

Stephen Bailey had been arrested, Sybil taken in for questioning. Pony's mother and father were questioned, too, but their worst offense appeared to be neglect. They did not seem to care that their child had been abducted. Adam had pulled strings, so, tonight at least, both teens were coming to Micah's. Once the team sifted through the physical and digital evidence, statements, and paperwork, the various federal and state entities involved would have a better idea of where Pony, especially, would land.

How Sterling had emerged whole from the fiery ashes of his childhood, Weir didn't know. He brought to mind of a piece of kintsugi pottery, purposely broken, then repaired with gold and lacquer, resulting in a piece stronger and more beautiful than the original.

* * *

HE HEARD the commotion before either Raven or Pony reached the porch. Poor Micah, he was always going on about his nosy neighbors, and now they had given the little old ladies another gossip item: two teenagers escorted to his house by the SkPD.

The front door crashed open. At this rate Micah was going to have to have it replaced, or at least replaster the wall behind it. Raven burst in first, Pony more tentatively on her heels. Sterling must have heard them, too, and he appeared from the bedroom to engulf Raven in a fierce one-armed hug. Weir watched the two siblings. The envy he felt surprised him.

In the kitchen, before powering down his laptop, he made sure the tiny code he had inserted was live. Shutting the lid, he tucked the laptop under his arm and made his way back to the bedroom. Sterling and Raven were sitting together on the couch, Sterling cupping her face, running a hand along her bare arms, checking that she was really in front of him. Raven was demanding details about his visit to the ER. Pony sat off to the side, in one of the smaller chairs, Micah and Adam trying to make them comfortable.

Micah was succeeding.

The bedroom was a sorry mess. Even though he was exhausted, his leg and arm aching, Weir began packing up his belongings. He had allowed himself to become far too comfortable here at Micah's, in Skagit, and he had no place in a family reunion.

Soon enough his meager belongings were stuffed back into his suitcase. The few extra things he'd picked up during his stay he shoved into a plastic bag the hospital had provided. It was too late tonight; tomorrow he would make plans to head home.

Much later, he heard a soft knock on his door before it quietly opened. He felt, more than saw, because he was a coward feigning sleep, Sterling checking on him. The door shut again, and he released a sigh and tried to sleep for real.

As soon as the sky began to lighten, he called a cab. A blanketed form was snuggled on the couch; from the size, Weir thought it was Pony.

Unlike Sterling, he was able to sneak out of the house without anyone chasing after him.

Once he was in the back of the cab, his bags tucked into the trunk, Weir asked the driver to drop him at the airport. He couldn't face another anonymous hotel room right now, not while his nerves and emotions were raw.

Lucky him, all the nonstop flights that morning were full, but if he wanted he could go via Phoenix, for a travel time of just under seven hours to LAX. He put the flight on his personal credit card. Maybe he would get reimbursed for it later.

As the flight was getting ready to take off, he sent a text to

Mohammad letting him know he had decided to go back to LA. Mohammad would let Adam and the team know. After all, he *was* still on medical leave.

* * *

THERE WAS SURPRISINGLY little fallout from his decision to return to LA. He had expected a barrage of phone calls and text messages, but by the time he landed, tired and aching, he had just one voice mail from Mohammad.

Listening to his boss's sexy voice was always enjoyable, even when he was in a crappy mood. He had strict instructions to finish out his physical therapy, check in with HR, stay away from his laptop, and basically get back into fighting shape. Also, he needed to report to the staff psychologist for his quarterly evaluation by the end of April.

Okaaay.

Ironically, when he reached his tiny condo, a few blocks from Hermosa Beach, it held virtually the same appeal as the no-name hotel room he had fled Skagit to avoid.

TWENTY-SIX

Swept into the torrent of events surrounding Raven's return from the police station, the eventual arrest of both his parents, the impending doom hovering over the Loft, and the ache in his arm reminding him he had been shot, Sterling didn't register Weir's absence until late the next afternoon. In fact, it wasn't until Micah mentioned the downstairs bedroom being clean that he understood Weir had left. He'd assumed Weir was working on his laptop or resting. Even then, he supposed Weir had gone to a hotel, not vacated Skagit entirely.

It was a relief, really. It was.

Weir was a distraction Sterling couldn't handle. The man-child-genius-surfer-runner dude would only cause confusion while he pieced his life back together. While he fought the state over where Raven should live, figured out what had happened to his savings, and tried contacting Rick so he could hopefully renegotiate a purchase timeline for the Loft. At one point during the afternoon he was holding a phone conversation with a social worker, texting Rick, and receiving a voice mail notification from the local bank loan officer, all at the same time. Weir would have been one thing too many.

He'd gotten comfortable around Weir: his ridiculous sense of humor, clever brown eyes, and sharp intellect. Too comfortable. Being used to something didn't mean it was good for you. Familiarity bred contempt; he'd heard that growing up, although he was never certain exactly what it meant. Come to think of it, anything his parents quoted should probably be taken with a grain of salt. Sounded more like an excuse to avoid people, cheat, or treat others like crap. Regardless, it was for the good that Weir had left. Sterling didn't miss him.

Sybil was released from custody after being charged with collusion and obstructing an ongoing investigation. Adam didn't think there would be jail time if she could demonstrate remorse and establish she had been coerced. Over the past few days the most pressing issue had become housing, for both his sister and Sybil.

The money?

Where it had all gone was still partially a mystery. Stephen had invested a great deal in an IPO a buddy claimed was a "sure thing." It failed spectacularly. That had been four months ago; he had not been able to recoup his losses. He also would probably be investigated for tax evasion, as there were several shell companies money had been funneled to with remote or nonexistent addresses and fictitious owners. The house payments were behind and far out of Sterling's reach. Sybil would have to put the house on the market immediately; the Tesla and Lexus would have to go, too.

Shit. Car. He still had Buck's car. Fuck.

"Buck, I'm—shit, with all the stuff happening I forgot I still had your car." Sterling cringed; he hardly knew the guy and he'd accidentally *kept* his *car*?

"Hey, Sterling." Buck's lazy drawl was clear even on his cell phone. "It's no big deal. I meant it, I always help out a friend. If I needed it, I knew where to find it."

"I, uh, appreciate the generosity. I really do." He debated with himself for a few seconds before adding, "Sybil, my mother, she is going to have to sell their cars. Any chance you have something reliable she can drive?"

Not that she would be driving soon. His mother was wandering around in a persistent daze. Sterling almost felt sorry for her and found it darkly ironic that helping her find a place to live had fallen on his shoulders. He had a moment when he considered not lending a hand. But he wasn't able to do that. Seeing her attack Stephen had been epic, although not worth getting shot for. He still couldn't believe Stephen had threatened them all with a loaded gun. The scene had been so unreal. He rubbed the bandage covering his stitches. He also couldn't believe how much it had hurt.

"Yeah, man, I got a couple things. Come by tomorrow, bring Sheila, we'll figure it out." Sterling almost teared up at the unconditional offer.

Stephen had seen his last free sunlight for years, Sterling hoped it was for the rest of his life. Sterling didn't feel an ounce of pity for him. He could rot in fucking hell. Sterling would be in the front seat with popcorn and a giant box of Hot Tamales.

* * *

STERLING FINALLY ASKED Adam about Weir.

"Took you long enough."

Sterling rolled his eyes. He didn't have time for Adam's crap. He was back in his own apartment, which felt unusually lonely. Raven was staying with Sybil in a tiny house Sterling had been able to rent with the proceeds from the cars and the blood of a newborn. He was managing the bar, what was left of his family— or maybe what his family had grown into—and sorting out his finances. The finances were confusing, because he had seen with his own eyes that the money was gone, and yet... when he had checked just before payroll, there had been more money. Every day there was a little more. He couldn't figure out where it was coming from.

He had his suspicions, though.

"Just answer my fucking question."

Adam and Micah were sitting in their spot at the bar. With all the shit going on in his life, Sterling was still only working Mondays and Tuesdays.

"I thought bartenders were supposed to be chatty and under-standing. Worldly."

"You thought wrong."

"Adam," Micah warned with a smile. Because, yeah, fucking foam heart on his latte.

"Weir is complicated," Adam began, paused, tapped the bar top, then continued. "He's one of the smartest guys I've ever worked with. He makes lightning-fast connections, knows a lot, remembers more. Amazing with a computer. The guy has a PhD in statistical modeling. Which, while valuable, bores the shit out of me."

"But?" Sterling asked, filing the information away. Weir had never told him he had his PhD. Sterling only had an associate's degree.

"But. Yeah. But. I'm not sure he wants to be the federal wonder boy. I think he ended up a fed kind of on accident. And he's good at it, so it's hard for him to admit that maybe it's not what he wants. Plus..."

"Esther."

"He told you about Esther? I don't think he's told Micah about Esther." Adam looked at Micah for confirmation; he shook his head.

"I think it was the medication he was on, after the accident." Probably.

Adam appeared to have an internal debate before continuing for Micah's benefit. "Weir's older sister, Esther, disappeared when he was five or so. She never came home. His family fell apart. I know a lot of why he decided to become an agent was informed by that experience. I'm just not sure that, for Weir, it's the right reason."

"So?" Sterling prodded.

"He went back to LA. It was hard for him, I think, seeing you get Raven back." He held up a hand. "Don't misinterpret—he's happy for you. But it may have been harder than he expected, seeing you get what he didn't."

Huh. Sterling was an idiot.

"He's still on medical leave for a little longer. He'll be cleared for light duty soon."

"And then?"

"And then we find out."

Huh.

He thought he'd been relieved that Weir was gone, that they had drifted a little too close to relationship territory for Sterling's comfort. He'd even admitted to liking the guy, but neither of them was looking for a relationship, right? Fuck, he wasn't relationship material, not for someone as smart and focused as Weir.

Days stretched into a week, then nearly two, and Sterling found himself angry. Angry with Weir for abandoning him, that he would leave with no word, no goodbye. Stubbornly, he refused to call or text him.

Recently he had been remembering silly things: TV they'd watched, weird conversations about the relevancy of the Dewey system, the history of the American highway, why Weir thought honeybees were disappearing and what could be done about it. Actually cooking. Sterling missed Weir, missed even his ridiculous jokes, just didn't know what to do about it.

Then Raven ambushed him.

Needing to get away from the Loft and his tiny apartment, he had gone to the Booking Room. It was relatively quiet, and he was able to snag a table near the back. Foolishly, he chose to sit with his back to the door, or he would have had more warning than her plopping down in the chair on the other side of the table.

She had been a rock star through the kidnapping and the events that followed. She claimed she'd known they were being held in the carriage house from the smells and sounds. That knowledge had kept her from panicking, but not from plotting her fantasy revenge against Stephen and Sybil when she and Pony were finally released.

Sybil's involvement seemed to be peripheral, and the law didn't like putting two parents in jail when there was a minor child. Well, they did, but Sybil had a good lawyer and evidence that she was, at worst, an enabler.

"Why haven't you called Weir?"

"How do you know I haven't?"

"He told me."

What the fuck? "He told you?"

"Yeah, we were texting and I asked him."

"He hasn't texted me."

Immediately, Sterling knew that was the wrong thing to say. Raven's black eyebrows, identical to his own, quirked up in disbelief. Her mouth gaped open before she clamped it shut, instead taking a lungful of air in through her nose. Sterling recognized one of his own coping mechanisms and chuckled. Internally, because she was about to rip into him.

"I thought *I* was the younger kid. Are you kidding me now?"

"Can you keep your voice down?" Oh, yeah, his brain was not functioning properly at all.

Raven's voice dropped to a hiss that without a doubt could be heard across the café. Ira was wiping down tables and pretending not to listen, but Sterling could see his shoulders shaking with laughter. Asshole.

"You are acting like you're twelve. Did it ever occur to you that maybe you need to be the one to reach out? He told me about his sister." Sterling's eyes widened. "Gah, men, you're all useless and deserve to be miserable. You, specifically, quit taking it out on everyone around you. Poor Cameron."

Cameron had confessed that he had taken the liquor. But not to drink it. He had been trying to teach himself how to toss bottles and pour drinks. From what Sterling understood, he was very lucky the entire back bar hadn't gone down. "How do you know about Cameron?"

"Alex from GSA is his younger sister. He's why she's in the club."

"Were they right? About Pony's parents wanting to send them away and you were going to help them escape?"

Ha, finally he had the upper hand. He saw the guilty flinch.

"Yeah," she replied glumly. "We were at Patty's, planning. I was going to take money from my savings." They fell silent, thinking how much had changed in the past month.

They would be fine. Raven had a roof over her head.

"What's happening with Pony?"

"They're finishing the school year, then moving to Seattle to live with an aunt. I guess she left town a long time ago, but when she found out what was happening to Pony she drove up here and confronted Pony's dad. There was some kind of 'reckoning,' and suddenly Pony is being treated better and excited about moving to Seattle."

"You're gonna miss her—them—sorry." He cringed, hating it when he messed up the pronouns.

Raven smiled a little. "Yeah, we aren't like best friends or anything, but they will do way better down there." She shook a finger at him. "You are still on my shit list. Do something about Weir, and quit being a complete asshole to your employees."

She gave him a big hug before she left, leaving him to brood about Weir and contemplate how his view on life had changed since Weir had come into it. His eyes widened at his internal, unintended pun, and he snickered inadvertently. Quickly gathering his things before he could change his mind, he headed back to the bar to clear the air and see about the future.

TWENTY-SEVEN

The computer screen taunted Weir.

Strict instructions to stay away, let Sammy take over his open cases, notwithstanding, he knew he'd seen something: a tiny factoid that was important and could lead them closer to Peter Krystad's killer. He was still not convinced the murder had anything to do with those fucking geoducks. It was something he'd seen relatively recently. Maybe when Sammy had been at Micah's?

He was *not* thinking about Sterling Fucking Bailey.

Not.

Mohammad had asked him to think long and hard about his commitment to the team.

"It is your choice, of course." His deep voice rumbled across their connection. "You are an incredibly competent investigator and an asset to my team. Yet I am not convinced your heart is in it. Did you know I initially joined the military?"

No, Weir had not known that. There was a lot he didn't know about Mohammad.

"I wanted to prove, among other things, that regardless of my name and my religion, I was just as loyal an American as Joe Blow from Tulsa."

"Tulsa?"

"An example. I grew up in Dallas. Don't distract me. I did it, I qualified. Served for six years. But I wasn't happy. Many reasons. The overarching one was, being in the military made no difference to how anyone else saw me. I was still that Muslim with the funny name. And yet I was still from Dallas. Still a loyal American."

Weir was unsure why Mohammad was sharing this with him.

"Okaaay?"

He heard Mohammad's sigh. Could picture him rolling his eyes upward, trying to think of a way to get his point across. Weir waited. One did not rush their team leader.

"I often forget how young you are. When I was twenty-six, I had only just gotten out of the army. Ida and I hadn't met. I went back to school, where I eventually got a degree in criminal justice. You have done all of that and more, but you are still young."

Weir paced while he listened, looking out the sliding door. The beach was beckoning, a siren of sorts. He only had a peek-aboo view; the condo he'd bought with the money Ben left to him was tiny, with only a hint of balcony, but he knew the glittering sand and endless expanse of ocean lay just a few blocks away, waiting for him. At the same time, as much as he had bitched about the weather while he was in Skagit, he missed the craggy mountains and evergreens that dominated the landscape there.

What was Mohammad trying to tell him without actually saying the words out loud?

"I would like you to spend some time, over the next few weeks, considering whether being a federal agent is really what you want to do with your life. Have you ever asked that question of yourself, Carroll?"

Oh, man. Dude. He needed open space. Being cooped up in the condo wasn't doing him any good.

"Are you saying I'm not good enough?"

"No, Carroll." Fuck, he hated when Mohammad used that tone. "I supported your joining the team in the first place; do you think that is something I would do lightly? For someone I need to trust to have my other agents' backs? You are an excellent agent. What I am asking is for you to take some time to make sure that this life is what you want."

The conversation rocketed around in his head. He'd *always* wanted to be a cop, an agent, right? Ben was his hero. Weir *needed* to do something with his own life to honor the man who'd saved him.

Ben had been silenced too soon. Weir badly wanted to be able to ask his advice now. He felt rudderless. Since Ben died, he had swept from single point to single point, keeping his head down, managing through sheer force of will to put one foot in front of the other. *Was* he doing the right thing? Who was he living his life for, himself or the ghosts that haunted him?

* * *

BEFORE WEIR KNEW IT, April bled into May. He'd been back in LA for weeks with nothing to show for it except for a tan and a few missed calls he didn't care about. Fleeing Skagit had not brought him clarity. Well, it had: it had become abundantly clear he had no life here, either. He loved the surf and needed the open space, but there were no people here for him. He'd left them in Skagit. Now he couldn't figure out how to get himself back up there.

Raven had continued to text him. At first he had been confused as to why she would reach out. Once he had gotten over the weirdness, he accepted her overture for what it was: friendship.

They ended up having a lot in common. Not once did she mention her brother, except in passing. Raven was fun to talk to

—different from Sterling, but turning out to be a good friend; she was not your average sixteen-year-old girl. She quizzed him about living in California, coding, working for the feds, surfing. Every once in a while she had a question about the legal situation with her parents. Those he had a harder time answering.

He'd heard from Sammy that Mrs. Bailey had not been a part of the kidnapping. She hadn't known the teens were on the property. What that said about her powers of observation and her ability to keep her head buried so deep in the sand he worried about lack of oxygen to her brain, Weir wasn't sure. At any rate, she had been questioned and released. Raven had mixed feelings about living with her. She worried that by living with her mom she was hurting Sterling's feelings. And, man, Weir was not equipped to help her with that. His mother issues were deep and unresolved.

The beach, even late on a Tuesday, was far too fucking crowded. Weir recognized some familiar faces. Nobody he wanted to talk to, no one who made him laugh. A couple guys he'd fucked once and couldn't care less about. It was a good thing he had his sunglasses on while he detoured through the sunbathers and kids with buckets and shovels, so they couldn't tell how disgusted he was with their mere presence.

Eventually, he reached the ever-changing boundary line where the last vestige of each wave urged itself relentlessly and futilely toward dry land before sliding back to start again. Kicking off his flip-flops, Weir stood still, allowing the ocean to gently purge him. A sort of sacrament. Wave after wave rushed toward him, slowing as they approached where he stood, sweeping across the top of his feet before taking much of his bad mood and frustration with life in general back with them into the depths.

Weir sat in the sand as the tide went out, his arms across his knees as he stared out across the horizon. These past weeks had been the first in his adult life when he had time to think. He wasn't officially on a case; he wasn't in school, training, testing, planning a funeral. He was being.

The last rays of the setting sun stretched across the Pacific, tinting distant clouds a lusty pink, before he stood back up. The beach had emptied somewhat; only the diehards were left. Still a significant crowd, but at least the shrieking kids had been bundled up and taken home. He gathered his thoughts from where they had been spread along with the wisps of cloud and streams of rosy light. Brushing off his butt, he jammed his feet back into his flip-flops, not certain what he had resolved, if anything.

Before Sterling, before landing in Skagit, he had ignored his lack of friends, but with nothing to do except twiddle his thumbs it was hard not to notice how empty his life was. Even if he'd been close with people from high school—which he wasn't—they wouldn't be local now. In college he had been the young freak. People thought it was so funny to call him "Doogie Howser." Ha fucking ha. And original, too. So, yeah, note to self, no friends in LA.

Mohammad's directive rang in his head: "Ask yourself, is this what you really want to do?"

He had no fucking idea.

Although the more he let Mohammad's words rattle around in his brain, the more he considered that maybe, possibly even likely, the answer was not in LA and not with the feds. It was nice texting with Raven, but would her brother be as welcoming after he had fled like a coward?

Screw it. He was going back to the condo and brooding over his laptop until he figured out what it was he'd seen in Sammy's notes.

TWENTY-EIGHT

How hard could it be to find one guy on the beach?

Really fucking hard. The beach ran for miles and was packed with humanity.

He'd stopped by the address Adam gave him. After he'd spent five minutes buzzing the intercom to no avail, some guy leaving the building told him Weir could often be found on the beach this time of day. Surfing, probably. In a black wet suit, like fifty other guys along a mile stretch of beach.

With nothing better to do, he waited in a kind of numb haze, sitting on a bench where the sand gave way to a strip of grass before the pavement began, watching the runners, skaters, skateboarders, even old-lady speed walkers, zip by. These people were religious about exercise. He stood out like a sore thumb in all black with no tan whatsoever. He'd smeared sunscreen on his exposed skin, but he was pretty sure he could feel himself starting to turn pink.

Watching the surfers was mesmerizing. Once, when he had been very young, his parents had taken a family trip to Hawaii. They had spent one day on the North Shore watching a surfing competition. These waves didn't seem as big, but he had been much smaller then. And, if he remembered correctly, he'd sported a horrible sunburn by the time the day was over.

The sun was edging toward the horizon. Checking his phone, he saw it was after seven. If he didn't find Weir before dark, he would just have to go back and lurk around the entrance to the condo.

One of the surfers made his way out of the water. Sterling squinted into the settling dusk trying to make out features, something that would tell him it was Weir this time. All he could see was a very sexy body wrapped up in a wet suit, and a huge surfboard in his hands.

"Did you come all this way to ogle sexy men in wet suits?" A mocking voice asked from behind him.

Sterling almost fell off the fucking bench. He had been so intent on the guy coming out of the water, he hadn't been paying attention to his surroundings.

"What the fuck, Weir? You scared the shit out of me! How did you know I was here?"

"Old loose-lips Riley on the second floor told me he'd sent a 'hot guy wearing all black' down to the beach looking for me." He stared out at the surf, a look of intense longing on his face. "I'm not cleared for surfing yet," he said with a pathetic pout.

"Oh. Uh, I'm sorry?"

Weir kept looking out at the waves, his hair, white-blond from the SoCal sun, blowing around his face. "Nah, s'okay, I'll get back soon enough." He turned to look at Sterling, "So, why're you here, in LA, at my fucking beach?"

Right. This was the part Sterling had been practicing, repeating to himself during the flight to LA and the cab ride to the address Adam had given him. With a helping of snark.

Adam and Raven, after a long night of no sleep and a whole lot of soul-searching, convinced him the only way Weir would truly believe Sterling was serious would be if he heard it from him in person. He'd booked the flight before he could change his mind.

Over the phone, email, any number of other (less terrifying) methods Weir could blow off as not serious. Sterling had thought a lot about why he was the one who had to travel down to the hellhole of SoCal—he was going to bake to death—when it had been Weir who left without saying goodbye.

The conclusion he arrived at was stark: no one, not one single person in Weir's life had ever come for him. Esther had disappeared, leaving him behind. As young as he had been, Weir must have felt abandoned and guilty, because he was safe at home. Then his mother. Sterling wondered again if Weir had ever looked for her; if he wanted to see her again. Followed by his father and even Ben Tompkins—the man had been killed in the line of duty, but still, it was a long list of people who had left and never returned.

So, if Weir was going to believe that Sterling really wanted to build something with him, Sterling had to be the one to go and get him.

Leaving Skagit, Sterling hoped, had been a self-protective measure. If Weir didn't allow himself to get attached, then he wouldn't get hurt. And, yeah, Sterling knew that because it was one of his own classic moves. But they had gotten beyond that, he hoped, even if neither of them realized it until they were stupidly, accidentally, in a relationship only Micah had identified.

Sometimes he wanted to punch himself. In the face.

Weir looked good. The bruises, scratches, and general pallor had been replaced with a nice tan. He was wearing board shorts and a tank top, which did absolutely nothing for Sterling's concentration. Weir was still lean, but he didn't lack muscle.

"Look, uh." Come on, *man up*, he reproached himself. "Can we go back to your place?" On second thought, maybe he should do this out in the open. "No, wait." He grabbed Weir's arm as he started to turn. "Here is fine."

Weir looked at him like he had grown a second head, which Sterling would, too, if he was Weir.

"Sit with me?"

Weir sat, his thigh brushing Sterling's, sending a little shiver through him.

"You okay? You're acting a little weird. Even for you," Weir said.

"Shut up, fuckhead." It was go big or go home (did he just *think* that?). He had to just start talking and not stop until he said it all. "That night, when you handcuffed me—"

Weir snorted.

"Fuckhead," Sterling repeated, with no heat behind it. "That night, I told you something I've never said to anyone before. I meant what I said, even if it may have seemed to be in the heat of the moment. I like you, Carroll Weir. I'm not smart like you, or athletic, or much of anything, but I think we have a connection, a real one. Not just incredible sex—which, by the way, I am not discounting. So, I was wondering…" He stuttered to a stop, not sure if he could get the corny words out of his mouth.

"Are you," the fucker was actually snickering, "are you asking me to go steady? Because I think we live in the twenty-first century, not the 1950s." He doubled over, breathless. "I'm sorry for laughing."

"Asshole. You are not. How about, Carroll Weir, will you be my permanent fuckbuddy?" Sterling may, or may not, have accidentally raised his voice just as two extremely elderly ladies in hot-pink athletic gear creaked by with their little rat dogs. They glanced over at them but kept walking, seemingly unsurprised by his outburst. Dusk was falling, the neon of the neighborhood businesses gleaming brightly, outshining any stars that could have been out.

Weir didn't reply, although he had stopped laughing. Sterling started to get nervous. Had he made the trip in vain? Misread everything? Weir shifted next to him, Sterling started to look at him instead of focusing on the neon, and suddenly he had a whole lot of man all over him. Weir grabbed his face with both hands and started kissing him hard. His lips were hot; his tongue demanded entrance into Sterling's mouth. Sterling opened gladly; when he got over his surprise, he wrapped his arms tightly around Weir. He moaned, it felt so good and so right.

"Get a room!" a gruff male voice shouted, although Sterling could hear laughter, too.

"Yeah," Weir said. He stood, pulling Sterling up with him. Weir didn't let go of his hand the whole three-block walk back to the condo, Sterling's backpack stuffed with a change of clothing dangling from his other hand. They didn't talk, either; they needed to get somewhere private before they embarrassed themselves and the entire neighborhood. What needed to be said could be said later, after.

Weir's condo was on the third floor. Instead of waiting for the elevator, they jogged up the stairs, giggling like idiots. Luckily, they didn't see anyone in the lobby or in the hallway outside the condo while Weir tried to unlock the door with Sterling pressed up behind him, pressing his erection into Weir's ass. Arms around Weir's waist, he fumbled with the snap on his shorts. They needed to come off immediately.

Weir groaned, leaning his head against the door. "Dude, I can't, I can't open the door with you doing that."

Sterling dropped his backpack and pressed harder into Weir's back. He grabbed the set of keys with one hand and stuck his other hand down Weir's shorts, stroking his erection, luxuriating in the soft steel under his fingers. Weir braced them against the door while Sterling jammed the key into the lock and turned it.

"We have, we have to stand back or we're going to end up on the floor..." Weir ground out.

"We're gonna end up on the floor." Sterling needed to touch Weir, to breathe him in. He wanted to be naked *now*.

"As much as I—fuck, need to feel you—I don't want to break anything. Again."

Fine. Sterling leaned away about an inch. Weir flicked the door handle and they were inside. Good thing, too; Sterling saw the elevator door open and "loose lips" Riley was getting off. Didn't he live on the second floor? It didn't matter; the door slammed behind them, and it was Sterling's turn to be manhandled up against the wall.

"In case you were wondering—" Weir pressed their foreheads together, "I'm in. We'll talk, but I gotta—feel you…"

Yeah, whatever the boy genius wanted. Sterling was putty in his hands. Also, *not* a boy.

Sterling had no idea what the inside of Weir's condo looked like. He could have been a serial killer displaying creepy maps with red pins marking very specific places and human skin taped to the walls for all he knew. Didn't care. He pressed himself back against Weir; they needed to have less clothing on. Grabbing Weir's shorts again, he pushed them down as far as he could. Sterling whimpered when Weir stepped back, but then Weir kicked his shorts off all the way, tossing them aside. His tank top followed.

Naked.

The small entryway echoed with their pants and whimpers. Weir struggled with Sterling's jeans.

"Jesus Christ, dude, these things are too fucking tight. Off now," he demanded.

Crap, his boots were still on. This was a clusterfuck. As quickly as possible, Sterling divested himself of his Doc Martens, jeans, boxers, and T-shirt. Weir was impatiently running his hands across Sterling's head, ruffling his hair, stroking the sensitive skin of his neck.

Finally, his clothes were off and he was able to press his naked self against Weir. Time slowed. Sterling shut his eyes so he could just feel. Feel the pulse of Weir's heartbeat, the silk of his skin, the scent of him. This he had missed. Missed so much.

"We could do this here, against the wall, but I have a really big bed," Weir whispered into his neck, before gently biting his earlobe. Sterling's cock throbbed.

"Bed."

They fell into bed with reckless abandon, touching hands, kissing, rubbing, both needing to feel the other. To remember. Weir rolled Sterling onto his back, straddling his hips, before leaning down to attack his mouth while rubbing their erections together. The heat was building so quickly. Sterling didn't want this to be a fast fuck, not anymore. He wanted to take his time, to feel everything.

"Stop, stop a sec," he managed to gasp. "I'm going to come already, it's been too long."

Weir whimpered again, pressing their groins together, before he shoved a hand between them, searching for Sterling's sensitive nipples. "You leaving soon?"

"Nahg, no."

"Then give it up for me, please."

Fine, fuck.

Grabbing Weir's slender hips, he used gravity and the upward motion of his body to create the friction he needed. It wasn't much. Weir slipped down so he was between Sterling's legs, sucking one nipple while playing with the other. Giving up, Sterling threw his arms over his head and wrapped his legs around Weir's, allowing their sensuous motion to take over. It was all friction, sucking, and the scent of the man he had let into his heart.

Leaving his nipple, Weir slipped a hand between them, around their dripping cocks. A little pressure was all it took, a few tugs, though Sterling's orgasm still almost took him by surprise. He arched into Weir, letting himself go, feeling come pulsing from his balls.

Weir came a moment after him, his body seizing while he kept grinding against Sterling until there was nothing left but the sound of their breathing, heavy and sated.

"Fuck."

"Yeah. Dude."

Weir was still lying on top of Sterling, his head tucked against his chest. Sterling didn't know if he had ever felt this content.

"I should probably tell you that I love you," he said. "I hope that doesn't scare you. When I said 'like' before, I meant love."

TWENTY-NINE

Those words.

Weir couldn't remember when he had heard them last. From anyone. Probably before Esther disappeared. Ben loved him, he'd understood that, but those words had never been uttered between them. Ben had been a police officer and his foster dad, not his real parent, and certainly not a poster child for how to communicate. He had shown Weir in other ways, like supporting his crazy athletic dreams, getting him into college, and making sure he wasn't put in juvie by the feds.

He assumed his parents had loved him at some point. The loss of Esther had overshadowed their own abilities to function as parents or normal humans. Who knew, maybe they had been having troubles before Esther disappeared. Weir would never know. His father had died in prison.

Sterling said he loved him.

Weir continued to half lie on his lover, the shadows in the bedroom blanketing them. He didn't want to move from the safe space they had created. He didn't want to speak and ruin the moment. Sterling's breathing evened out, indicating he had drifted off.

"I think I love you, too," he whispered.

"I know," Sterling murmured back. Weir smiled into his chest, and Sterling tightened his grip around him.

Eventually, Weir rolled off, going in search of a warm washcloth and supplies for later. When he returned, Sterling had pulled the covers aside and nestled into the sheets. After wiping him off and tossing the cloth aside, Weir crawled in next to him, pulling the covers over them both.

Later came a few hours after midnight. Weir awoke to a hot mouth on his cock. He let himself lie there and revel in the feeling of Sterling giving him everything, until he was too close. He tugged at Sterling's hair, demanding his attention.

"Hey, uh, I, can I—" Sterling chose that moment to stick his tongue into the slit of Weir's steel-hard cock before sucking only the head, making Weir lose his train of thought and moan loudly. Sterling chuckled before popping his mouth off with a lewd smacking sound.

"You want something?"

"I really want to be inside you. If that's okay?"

Sterling sat up, straddling Weir's hips, his own erection dripping only inches from Weir's face.

"You'd be the first in a very long time. But yeah, let's do that."

A minor comedy of errors ensued as they changed positions. Weir's foot got caught in the sheets, but soon enough Sterling was on his back underneath him. Weir lay on top of him for a moment before slipping to the side, lost again in a passionate kiss Sterling initiated. Fuck, Sterling could kiss. It turned Weir on even more, having his tongue in his mouth, caressing him from inside. He bolted up.

"Jesus, you are distracting. Your mouth..." He trailed off, leaning to grab a condom and lube from the nightstand.

Sterling laughed, his eyes dark, full of passion.

Weir tossed the condom onto Sterling's chest. "Put it on me."

"You think you can handle that?"

"Fuck, shit, no." He snatched it back, fumbling with the slick packaging before finally getting it open. Sterling tried reaching for it, but Weir backed away, grabbing his own cock and rolling the condom on carefully.

Scooting up between Sterling's legs, he pulled Sterling's hips over his thighs so he could stretch him. He traced Sterling's hole with his thumb, teasing, suggesting, massaging the lube into him, promising. Sterling clenched around his thumb and Weir muttered whatever carnal words came into his mind, telling Sterling how fucking beautiful he was, how his ass made Weir want to come, how he wanted to fuck him.

He wasn't normally one for a lot of dirty talk, but something about Sterling, how vulnerable and trusting he was in the moment, how he responded, kept Weir's mouth moving. He poured more lube into his hand—they would be lucky if they didn't slide off the bed—before slowly pushing one finger inside.

Sterling kept his eyes locked onto Weir's. Weir pushed slowly past the initial ring of muscle... ah, he was hot inside. Felt amazing. He almost couldn't wait to get his cock in there.

"Hurry up, you're killing me," Sterling panted, reading his mind.

"In a sec." He wanted to find the G-spot first. He inserted a second finger.

"Relax," he crooned. Sterling flipped him the bird. "Oh, don't you worry." Finally he found the little bundle of nerves, sliding his fingertips across it, pushing delicately, circling.

Sterling shouted something unintelligible, which Weir was going take as "Don't fucking stop." Sterling's erection, which had flagged when Weir started to open him up, returned in full force. Leaning over, Weir licked the tip of his shaft, savoring the taste of Sterling's precome.

"Weir, *please*."

Begging was good.

Giving Sterling one last lick and the gentlest suck, he pulled his fingers out. One hand on Sterling and the other on his own wrapped cock, he slowly began pushing inside. Like a champ, Sterling bore down, opening up for Weir's needy cock.

"Oh, fuck." Weir was panting, too, because he really wanted to push all the way inside. All the way. It felt like hours, his forehead beaded with sweat, before he was fully seated. Waiting another moment for Sterling to get used to him took the absolute last of his self-control.

When his lover nodded, Weir pulled out a little before pushing back in. Setting a rhythm met by Sterling. The hot, gratifying pleasure of Sterling's hole clenching around his cock was intense and heady. Made him lose focus, his sac tapping against Sterling's ass, sensation everywhere. On his tongue, against his skin, the scent of them together, sweat, come, whatever it was that made Sterling smell so good. It was too much—Weir was going to come—everything was exponential, and he had wanted to be inside Sterling for months.

He grimaced, trying to hold back, but Sterling grabbed his dick and began jerking himself. The sight of him together with the press of Sterling's hips against him sent Weir over the edge, tumbling fast and hard, filling the condom. Sterling shook beneath him, and the warmth of Sterling's come spread across their bellies.

They lay together, breathing hard. This time Sterling got up for a towel. Weir was going to need to do serious laundry. Soon.

Sated, they fell asleep again, wrapped around each other, waking hours later without having moved.

WEIR'S STOMACH GROWLED, giving him away. He'd been watching Sterling sleep, something he had never witnessed before. At the faint noise, Sterling's eyes fluttered partially open. At first glance they seemed cold, but Weir knew this particular shade was the hot blue at the base of an acetylene torch, so scorching your body confused it with ice. Never again would Weir make that mistake.

"Mmmm. Somebody needs to eat."

"All that sex and no dinner." Weir pouted.

"Growing boy." Sterling palmed Weir's morning erection, making him shiver.

"Dude," he rasped out, "I need fluids. Food."

Apparently he also needed one more blow job.

The morning light sneaking past his curtains caressed Sterling as they lay in his bed savoring what they had just done. Weir could see the fresh, pink scar on Sterling's bicep. He stroked his index finger across it. What if the bullet had been farther to the right or higher up? He had done that—he had almost gotten Sterling killed. Weir shivered, feeling like he had been doused in ice water.

"Hey." Sterling's bright, laser-sharp eyes were intent on his face. "You didn't do that. Stephen did that. First, what kind of bottom-feeder releases the safety while he's running—that's what happened, right? Second, he pointed that gun at you. At you, Weir. I saw the look in his eyes; he didn't care that you were a federal agent. He was—is—so caught up in his own fear that he was instinctively lashing out, like an animal. I hope he rots in hell."

"I shouldn't have gone there without backup," Weir whispered. "I wanted to be a hero; I wanted to be the one... the one who brought your sister back to you. I was being selfish. Instead I got you hurt."

"I would have gone by myself, you know—if I'd found out you were calling Adam or whoever, I wouldn't have waited—and then what would have happened?"

They were both quiet for a few moments. Weir turned on his side, burying his face in the curve of Sterling's neck. "I'm always scared. I'm scared this isn't real, we aren't real, or that I'm going to mess it up, because it's something I've always wanted and couldn't have. I hate being scared all the time. Running, surfing, being so focused on something that I can shut the world out... those are the only times I'm not afraid." Since he was mumbling this into Sterling's skin, Weir didn't know how much he had understood.

"What's your middle name?"

"What?" He sat up a little bit to look Sterling in the eye.

"What's your middle name? You don't want me to call you Carroll; I can't keep calling you Weir, so what's your middle name?"

"Uh, Evan?"

"Evan. Mmm, I like the sound of that. Plus, I'm the *only* one saying it. No one else gets to call you that. When you hear 'Evan,' you need to remind yourself who is saying it: me, Sterling Thaddeus Bailey. That I have your back. You don't need to be scared anymore, because I love you. Evan, Evan, Evan... Should I keep saying it? You've been scared because you didn't have anyone. Now you have me."

Weir had to clench his eyes shut to keep the tears from squeezing out. Sterling seemed to understand; he murmured nonsense and ran a soothing hand across his back until he got himself under control.

"*Thaddeus?*" Weir finally asked.

"Shut it. Sybil must have been reading a bodice-ripper when she named me."

Weir loaned Sterling an extra pair of ratty cotton sleep pants and a T-shirt. Walking around naked was too distracting. If they were going to eat breakfast, they both needed to be dressed. As it was, dressing took far too long; both their stomachs were rumbling before they made it out of the bedroom.

Unfortunately, the contents of his fridge were meager at best. Living on takeout and fruit smoothies, easy when he was alone, meant he had next to nothing to eat in the condo. Somehow he didn't think Sterling would appreciate a kale omelet.

"Not much in there," Sterling said over his shoulder.

Weir turned, kissing him quickly but soundly on the lips. "Mmmm."

"If I'd known you were coming, I would have bought groceries."

"You do know that whether I was here or not, you still need groceries? Scrambled eggs. Then we can go to lunch."

They ate at the tiny kitchen table, knees bumping underneath it. Yeah, they, he, was going to have to go to the store. Weir was bemused that Sterling had come all the way from Skagit to find him. It felt weird, and right, to have him in his condo.

The weird part made him want to keep touching Sterling to make sure he was really there. It made him nervous, the *wanting* to touch, but he couldn't help himself. Or maybe that was just the part where he knew more words needed to be said. The *right* part... that scared him, too, but it *did* feel right and Weir wasn't going to discount that.

Sterling must have sensed his rising anxiety, because he snaked his hand across the table to twine their fingers together. "We don't have to figure everything out today, Evan. Or even while I'm here, okay?" It was kind of pathetic how much he loved hearing the name Evan fall from Sterling's lips. *Evan* was someone with more possibility and future than Weir had ever envisioned for himself.

"Yeah," he answered, nodding around the lump in his throat. He was afraid he was going to mess this up. He wasn't sure how he would mess up something he'd never had before, but he could find a way to do it.

"Hey." A gentle finger lifted his chin. Caught in the calm promise of Sterling's eyes, he found courage.

"I do, too, you know. I mean, I'm pretty sure I'm in love with you." His world fell away with those words, out in the open for anyone to hear.

Sterling smiled at him and tugged his chin. "Aren't we a

messed-up pair? We'll be good, okay? Coming here and finding you has already gone beyond what I imagined could happen."

"Yeah, okay."

The words were sealed with a kiss. It should have gone on longer. Weir welcomed that kiss forever, a promise.

They were interrupted by the harsh ring of Weir's cell phone, blaring from the entryway where their clothes were still strewn in chaos. He picked up his board shorts and shook them, and the phone fell out of a back pocket. He recognized the number as the same one he'd been getting a lot of calls from over the past few weeks. Whoever it was never left a message, Weir debated not answering again, but it seemed like they were going to keep calling until he told whoever it was to fuck off.

"Weir here."

There was silence on the other end. He checked the screen; maybe the call had dropped.

"Um, am I speaking to Carroll Weir?" a hesitant female voice asked.

A frisson that could have been dread, or maybe anticipation, ran down then back up his spine. Goosebumps popped up on his arms, making him shiver, despite the warmth of the spring day. "Yes."

The line went quiet again, but he could hear faint breathing, so she was still there. When she began to speak, Weir only heard the first few words before her voice turned to a white-hot slurry of noise. He had no idea what else she said.

Sterling came up behind him, his hand to Weir's lower back, a question in his eyes. Weir didn't know how to answer it, Sterling or the voice on the other end of the line. Mutely, he handed the phone over.

THIRTY

"Hello?" A woman's voice crackled across the connection.

"Hello? This is Weir's boyfriend, Sterling."

He watched Weir—*Evan*—walk slowly to the couch and slump onto it. He kind of crumpled, his elbows resting on his knees, head in his hands. He was trembling. Sterling followed closely behind, the phone to his ear.

He stopped in front of the sliding glass door and stared out at the sliver of sand and ocean while the woman on the other end of the line explained she was Amanda Smith, formerly Amanda Weir, Carroll Weir's mother. She had been looking for him for several years. Was hoping they could meet so she could explain. Get to know each other.

The words were hurried and breathy. It was obvious she had been practicing them.

He turned to see Evan still shaking, the magic of their morning dissipated by the call. "No; I don't think he is ready."

"Oh." A pause. "All right. Would it be okay if I left a number? Or an email? I could try calling again?"

Grabbing a pen from the tiny counter that divided the living room from the kitchen, Sterling scribbled down a phone number and an email before clicking off the call. He carefully tucked the slip of paper into his wallet before sitting next to Evan on the couch.

"Sorry to make you deal with that," Evan muttered in the direction of his bare feet.

"I'm glad I was here." He really was. "Let's go for a walk. Get out of this place a for a little while."

"All right. Beach?" When Evan looked at Sterling like that, hope in his eyes, he had no chance.

"Yeah, beach." After he put on a gallon of sunscreen.

* * *

THE BEACH HAD way more people on it now than it had the evening before. Evan tugged on Sterling's shirt, indicating the direction he wanted to go. Silently but companionably, they walked down to the tide line. Sterling had borrowed a spare pair of flip-flops but resisted shorts or a short-sleeved shirt. Not only would he burn, he would blind anyone not wearing sunglasses.

Evan sat down on the sand. Sterling stared.

"What? You're not made of glass, we can shower later."

Against his better judgment, he sat next to Evan. They watched the waves come and go and listened to the crashing surf. A few seagulls overhead flew closer, hoping for a snack.

"What did she want? My mother?"

"She wants to meet you, explain, get to know you again."

"Yeah, very much not ready for that." He ran his fingers through his tangled hair. "Maybe a few years ago, or when my dad went to jail, I would have been more forgiving, but not now. Not anymore. Where was she when I needed her?"

"You don't have to forgive her," said the man who had a very complicated relationship with his own mother.

"I know. But I bet she wants it." He chuckled darkly and looked over at Sterling. "Until she called, and I heard her voice for the first time since—" he rolled his eyes up, calculating, "—in seventeen years, I had no idea how angry I was. Still am. Very fucking angry."

Sterling nodded like he had an inkling of how Evan felt.

"Thanks for bringing me out here."

"Hey, it's what boyfriends do. I read up on it, since I don't have any actual experience."

"Yeah? Boyfriend, huh? Me either—no experience, I mean." Evan bit his lower lip, looking more vulnerable than he had… maybe ever. His world had changed a lot in the past twenty-four hours. Sterling couldn't help but lean in and kiss him soundly, sucking in that abused lower lip and stroking it with his tongue.

"I'm sorry," Evan said when they broke apart.

"For what?" They were still close enough for Sterling to feel the thrum of Evan's skin, the beat of his heart.

"For leaving when I did, leaving Skagit without saying good-bye. Or anything. I was scared."

Sterling cupped Evan's cheeks, the rough stubble chafing his palms. "Apology accepted. It gave me time to think, to realize I missed you and want you in my life. Anyway, I'm pretty sure I'll mess up sometime soon with the whole relationship thing." Fuck, just saying the word out loud was enough to give him dry heaves.

"Aww." Evan bumped him with his elbow.

"Asshole. I'm pouring my guts out right now."

Evan shifted closer, leaning his head on Sterling's shoulder. Sterling put an arm around him, pondering the magnificent perfection of the moment.

"We should go," Evan said. "You're going to get sunburned. Besides, I'm still hungry and, regardless of the neighborhood being awesome, some asshole from the Inland Empire—which is a fancy name for *way* too far from the beach—here with his impressionable kids will get his boxers in a wad if we start macking again. Which I want to."

"Yeah, all right." Sterling still held Evan's hand all the way back to the street.

* * *

THEY STOPPED to eat at a little place just off the beach Evan said had a pretty good menu. There was a patio not too packed with late brunchers and, thankfully, an umbrella-covered table so Sterling could stay out of the sun.

Putting off difficult conversation for a while, they sat and enjoyed their food, which for a touristy neighborhood was surprisingly delicious. Sterling took note of the chicken sandwich. Maybe Mac could put something like that together for the bar.

"So, the money?"

Evan immediately looked guilty. Swallowing his bite of salad, he replied, "Yeah, complicated. But, fuck, I wasn't going to let that asshole steal everything from you. I followed where some of it went, found a loophole. That's what I was doing before Adam got back that day. My worm followed your money and wherever it is now, when that balance goes above a certain threshold, the worm kicks the slush back to you. Through a very circuitous route. It should have stopped, though?"

"Yeah, it stopped, right at the balance I had before shit happened."

"Good." Evan beamed, pleased with himself.

"So I guess I was right not to mention it to Adam? Probably not within your scope of work?"

"Yeah, no." Evan put his fork down. How that meager salad satisfied him, Sterling had no idea. "If Adam finds out I could get in big trouble. Who am I kidding? He probably already knows, or suspects." he said glumly. "Mohammad asked me to think about whether I want to keep doing this job or not, if this is really what I want to do with my life."

"Is it?"

"Maybe?" Evan winced. "How long can you stay?"

"Probably not long enough for you to decide what you want to do. I've got a flight out tomorrow afternoon. Can't leave the bar for too long, no matter how responsible Kent and Kevin are."

"Are you still going to buy it?"

"Yeah, thanks to a certain federal agent. Rick and I pushed it back a bit, though. It probably won't happen until summer."

"Will you wait for me?"

Sterling frowned. "What do you mean?"

"While I figure stuff out?"

"You know where I live."

"Actually, I don't," Evan pointed out with a smile.

"Ha. I have an apartment above the bar. It's about as big as your condo."

"Will you?"

Sterling wished they weren't having this conversation in public so he could pull Evan close, reassure him the way he deserved. Because yes, Sterling would wait. He had waited this long for someone without realizing it; he could wait a little longer. Besides, he figured it was close to a sure thing.

THIRTY-ONE

Sterling left too soon; the condo was barren without him. Emptier than it had been before. They *had* managed to have sex on almost every horizontal surface before he left for the airport. Now all Weir had to do was look around his home to be reminded that Sterling was in Skagit and Weir was alone with decisions he needed to make. Because Mohammad was right. Weir didn't know what he wanted to do.

Weir hadn't wanted him to go, but he did have some thinking to do.

Sterling had left the scrap of paper with Amanda Smith's phone and email address tucked under a magnet on his refrigerator.

Weir had not been tempted to call or email.

All these years and now she shows back up? He had zero interest in hearing her "side" of the story. What kind of person, grief-stricken or not, abandons their family? As far as he was concerned, she had left them and never looked back. Still, he didn't toss it away. He let it sit there. Instead he went and visited his father's grave.

He'd laid his father to rest at the Rose Hill Memorial Park in

Whittier. Located on a nice hill, the site looked westward, with a view of LA. Weir thought his father would have liked the aloe and yucca that dotted the landscape, as well as the open sky.

Forgiving, or at least coming to terms, with his father hadn't been easy, but Weir had eventually come to understand that the sheer weight of it all had been too much for him, that he had broken. When his mother walked out on them to make her own new life—and, for all Weir knew, an entirely new family—his dad had died. Even before he'd been sentenced, he had withered inside.

"Hey, Dad, I think I'm going to move to Skagit," he said. "I thought you might want to know. I met a guy, Sterling, who gets me. It's a little weird, actually. I never expected to meet anyone like that. I think you would be happy for me." The wind was blowing, as usual, making his jacket flap and chinos press against the back of his legs. "If it works out, I won't be able to visit you as often, maybe only in the winter." A particularly strong gust of wind pushed against him; he chose to take it as a sign his dad was okay with the arrangement. "Amanda called a few days ago." He refused to call her Mother, or Mom. "She wants to see me and explain. I think you'd understand why I can't do that. You and me, we don't owe her anything. Maybe someday I'll change my mind, but I don't think so. And, hey, I'm going to see about doing something with my degree." A second gust pushed even harder against his back. Weir couldn't help smiling a little as he turned to make the walk back to his car.

* * *

IT TOOK him a month to tie up all his loose ends in LA. Thirty days longer than he wanted. He decided against selling his condo yet; he could drag his boyfriend down in the dead of winter for some sunshine and beach time. In the meantime, he would rent it short-term.

Boyfriend.

They talked or texted almost every day. Which was surreal. Weir wasn't used to being a part of someone's orbit. He'd never been amused by something random and thought, "So-and-so would like that." He'd never had someone to talk about his day with or have phone sex with. Because they did that, too.

Late spring in Skagit was… well, it was better than December *and* it had Sterling. He'd driven up, which Adam had warned against, but Weir didn't see a way around it. Not if he was going to bring most of his stuff. Most.

He wasn't hedging his bets, but bringing his surfboard seemed a little too hopeful. Weir was hoping to rent an apartment close to Sterling. Or something. They'd talked about it. They had talked quite a bit over the past four weeks. Weir was the one nervous about moving in. They'd lived in the same house for a few weeks, sure, but Weir didn't want to curse anything. Sterling Bailey, confirmed bachelor of Skagit, had chuckled.

"I flew all the way down there, that didn't convince you?"

Sterling found a place for him within walking distance of the Loft (and by default his own apartment). The place wasn't available for a couple more weeks, but Weir hadn't wanted to be in LA any longer. He maybe had a surprise for Sterling, but didn't want to tell him until he was sure.

Sterling's apartment was tiny and perfect in that it had a bed in it. A nice large bed that the two of them made use of immediately and vigorously. After years of anonymous sex, Weir couldn't imagine falling into bed with anyone else. No one else smelled like Sterling.

The bed was separated from the main room by a rice-paper screen. The wall next to the bed had several bookshelves. Unlike the staged bookshelves at the former Bailey mansion, these were lined two deep with well-read paperbacks and a few hardbacks. Sterling's taste was eclectic, ranging from mass-market thrillers and horror to memoir and a variety of local history tomes. For a guy who claimed to be "not so smart," he sure had a lot of books proving otherwise.

"That was incredible," Sterling said, his chest rumbling under Weir's cheek.

"Yeah, wow."

Weir was tired from the drive. Without traffic it was twenty hours. Key words: *without* and *traffic*. As far as he could tell, every county, city, and town between Hermosa and Skagit had begun their construction season. Weir had spent as much time waiting for the guy (or gal) in the bright orange vest to turn their stop sign around as he had on the open road. The stretch between Portland and Skagit had been especially brutal. Instead of arriving at a reasonable hour, he rolled in after midnight on a Friday.

Seeing Sterling's familiar form behind the bar was exquisitely painful. His heart had actually clenched at the sight. All Weir had wanted was to jump his frame and get naked. Instead he'd calmly sat at the bar and planned how he and Sterling were going to spend their first available hours in bed. Naked.

"What's going on inside that complicated head of yours?" Sterling asked, nudging him.

"Sex, lots of sex. If I hadn't already come like a fire hose I would want to again. Sadly, I think I'm done for the night."

Sterling chuckled, a sound Weir had grown fond of.

* * *

THE NEXT MORNING, or early afternoon, both of them having slept far past the break of day, Sterling took Weir on a walking tour of his neighborhood. Aside from the Loft, there was a coin-op laundry that hailed from the early '70s—maybe the machines did, too—a couple insurance offices, the Beaver (which Weir had not yet been to), and a Goodwill-type used-clothing place.

Most businesses on the back side of the block were more industrial, a bearing manufacturer (the imagination runs wild), two collision repairs (which explained the insurance on the other side), and a cabinetmaker, all interspersed with empty storefronts and anonymous offices. Farther along there were two (!) actual vinyl record stores, a fish market (claiming the freshest fish in Skagit)... and, be still his heart, something called the "Health Hut."

Weir stopped in his tracks. "Dude, you did not tell me this was here."

"I forgot because I don't generally eat seaweed and whale cock," Sterling muttered, but he was smiling.

"Check it out, they have smoothies!"

Inside smelled like every health-food store Weir had ever been in. It was impossible to tease apart the various scents, a mix of vitamins, health "tonics," and every possible variety of bulk yeast. "A-fucking-mazing. Let's get a smoothie."

"You get a smoothie, I'll stick to coffee," Sterling grumbled.

Back outside, Weir clutching his green apple–spinach–wheat grass smoothie like someone was going to try and steal it from him, they sat in a couple of chairs set out for customers to enjoy the spring sunshine. A sunny Saturday afternoon gave them a lot of people to watch while they drank their beverages. A few of them knew Sterling from the bar and waved at him, looking long and hard at Weir.

"Am I going to be an object of curiosity?"

"Probably. Do you care?"

"Nope." He grinned before taking a healthy suck on his straw, making his cheeks cave and Sterling laugh.

THIRTY-TWO

Evan was up to something. Big surprise, the guy was a natural-born practical joker. He'd departed that morning, Monday, saying he would be back in a few hours. He'd been wearing one of his federal-agent suits that made him look hot and in charge. Sterling was left to wonder how much trouble Evan could manage to get himself in, and could he bail him out?

His phone pinged.

- When are you inviting me over?
- Never, Raven.
- Fine come for dinner 2nite
- Weir's cooking?
- …………
- lol

Evan returned from his secret errand a few hours later. Sterling was dying to ask what he'd been up to, but Evan avoided his questions with skill. Mostly the skill involved his mouth and Sterling's cock.

He'd never been a napper, but he had a sudden appreciation

for "afternoon delight." A drowsy, content Evan was tucked up under his arm. If he weren't painfully aware that Raven would be there in less than two hours, he would have suggested they stay in bed and order dinner in. But he did not need his sister catching the two of them like that. He wasn't a prude, and he knew Evan wasn't against a little PDA, but no, Raven did not need to find them in bed.

Evan murmured something nonsensical as Sterling ran his fingers up and down his back. Lying in bed with another man, a man he loved, was something Sterling never expected in this life. A wave of emotion threatened. He rolled over, taking Evan along with him. Sterling pressed him into the mattress for a few long seconds, his nose pushed into the sensitive crook of Evan's neck. Sterling was pretty sure he was the only one who knew this particular spot. It was his alone.

"Something you wanna tell me?" Evan chuckled.

"We gotta get up. Raven's coming for dinner," Sterling whined.

They made a quick stop at the Health Hut for fresh vegetables, and salad ingredients for fuck's sake, then went to the Fish Market for something he could cook in the oven—his lover had better appreciate the smell of fish lingering in a five-hundred-square-foot apartment.

The Fish Market—which literally was its name—was one of those old-school places not seen much anymore. Cold cases lined two walls and were stocked with a variety of colorful fish and shellfish. There were large buckets, almost like fifty-gallon drums, full of ice with several kinds of oysters, clams, and mussels crammed in the top. They also sold fresh poultry. The wall across from the frozen counter was full of jars of sauce, so many sauces. Hot, BBQ, local and international. The display was colorful and awe-inspiring.

Sterling picked out a salmon fillet and an older guy wearing a plastic apron and a bad attitude wrapped it carefully in paper and answered his pathetic questions about how best to cook it. Evan was no help, as he was held in thrall by the jars of hot sauce. There was a tense moment when Sterling thought the guy might refuse to sell him the salmon, like only experienced chefs were allowed to touch such precious fish. Luckily he left the shop with his head held high, the fish safe in a plastic carry bag along with a lemon, fresh dill, a head of garlic, and a pound of butter.

DINNER WAS FUN, except for the part where Raven and Evan reenacted their *not-so-funny* April Fool's joke. Sterling would have been mad at being the butt of their joke, except he loved having them laughing in his apartment. It was its own kind of sunshine.

Of course he didn't tell them that; he called them fuckers and stomped over to the kitchenette to sulk and clean up. Who knew broiling some fish in the oven would make this much of a mess? He'd been trying to chop the dill, but the feathery bits of the herb had kind of exploded everywhere, and the butter accidentally left on the top of the stove melted, leaving a greasy pool to mop up.

He felt more than heard Evan come up behind him. Strong arms wrapped around his waist, and soft lips kissed the back of his neck.

"We're sorry." But he could feel the lie in the smile pressed against him.

Sterling smiled, too. "You aren't. But I forgive you anyway."

Suddenly Evan pulled away. He grabbed the fish wrapper, with its "TFM" imprint all over it, from the back of the sink where Sterling had tossed it in his cooking frenzy. "Where'd you get this?" he demanded, his voice serious.

Raven came over to see what he was asking about. Three people in this tiny corner of his apartment was two too many.

"Uh, the Fish Market? That's from the salmon. You were there when I bought it?"

Evan's expression was pure amazement.

"Why? What's wrong?"

"Nothing is wrong! This is amazing." He pulled out his phone, took a picture of the paper, then stuffed the paper into the plastic bag Sterling had brought the fish home in and took off. The front door slammed, and he was pounding down the stairs before Sterling or Raven could react.

"What just happened?" Raven asked.

"I have no idea."

They came to their senses at the same time. Quickly ensuring everything was turned off, Sterling grabbed his coat, and Evan's, because the idiot had run off in a T-shirt and nylon track pants.

The Fish Market was their destination, of that Sterling had no doubt.

The older guy wasn't behind the counter any longer. In his place was a much younger male, similar enough that Sterling figured he was either a son or a grandson of the man who had sold him their dinner and given out a recipe. He was shaking his head, looking confused at whatever questions Evan was peppering him with. Also trying to close up for the night, if the half-empty cases of seafood were any kind of clue.

Sterling interrupted. "Hey, here's your coat." He handed it to Evan, who took it automatically, putting it on. It was early June, but that meant afternoon and evening temperatures in the '50s. Sterling didn't think Evan had acclimated quite yet.

"You'll have to ask my dad, but he's busy right now. I only work here after school and on weekends." The teen had wide blue eyes, messy brown hair, and that bone-deep *hungry* look that only a teenage boy going through a growth spurt has. Too skinny, too tall, this boy's body was still catching up with itself.

Evan looked frustrated, but nodded. "Okay, thanks."

"Come on, let's walk Raven to her car." The girl in question started to object. "It's a school night, and you promised."

"Fine."

Sterling wanted to roll his eyes but instead, like the mature person he tried to be, he ushered both Evan and Raven out of the shop and toward her car. They watched her drive off, taillights disappearing in the distance.

"What was that all about?" Sterling asked, once she was safely out of sight.

"I gotta call Sammy."

Sammy Ferreira was not in Skagit anymore, but Sterling knew from eavesdropping that he was the last agent assigned to the murder of a local Fish and Wildlife detective.

Together they rushed back to Sterling's apartment, where Evan changed from running gear to his other outfit of cargo pants, a T-shirt, and Vans. Sterling wasn't sure what the rush was about. The detective had been dead since February. Evan was trying to talk on the phone while he changed clothes. Sterling wasn't helping by actively ogling, but hey, a guy had to take what he could get.

"Yeah, I need to look at those notebooks again… I know, but I'm telling you I saw something and I think it matches… Yeah… Let me do this one thing… It's not official, come on!" He ran an impatient hand through his hair. "Fine… Okay, I'll grab the key from Poole. Sammy? Thanks." He clicked off the call. "Okay. I gotta go check on something over at the Fish and Wildlife office. Shit, where are my keys?" He patted himself down before shaking his head. "I'll just walk."

"I'm coming with you."

THIRTY-THREE

The evening was cool, but pleasant enough. It wasn't raining. Not that Weir paid any attention to it while he power-walked from Sterling's apartment to the Fish and Wildlife office on the other side of downtown. Sterling didn't try to ask questions or make small talk, which was a blessing. He matched Weir's pace as they made their way through the semi-industrial neighborhood. Weir had too many thoughts swirling around in his head to answer someone else's questions.

The office was located on one of Skagit's impossibly wide streets. City developers must have hoped the city would grow as large as Seattle. As a result, the street could accommodate four lanes of traffic and still have diagonal parking on each side. Tom Poole was meeting him at the office to let him in. But Weir already knew he was right. He might not have an eidetic memory, like Raven, but he had stared long enough at those doodles to know he was on to something.

Something that might just crack this stubborn case wide open.

"Let's cross here. The office is on the other side," Weir said. He was growing to love the late sunsets in this part of the world. It was still light out, and the sun wouldn't truly set until after

8:30. Skagit itself was starting to grow on him, not only the sexy bartender who'd become his boyfriend.

A big SUV rolled slowly past them heading the other direction, turn indicator flashing. Weir recognized Tom Poole's bald head. Focused on Tom and reaching the office as soon as possible, he didn't register the squeal of tires coming from his left. Weir stepped out into the street, intent only on his destination.

Time slowed down in a way he supposed only happened to people who were about to die. The car was a mere silhouette, its daytime running lights creating a halo he couldn't see past in the quickly falling dusk. He had the impression of two bright lights speeding toward him while he stood there frozen, literally like a deer in the headlights. Funny how he had never really understood that phrase before.

Someone—Sterling, of course—grabbed the back of his jacket and yanked him backward far enough that, instead of being flattened by several thousand pounds of car, he only felt the intense heat of the engine, tasting hot motor oil as the air around the moving vehicle caressed the front of his legs and torso before continuing its forward motion.

"Jesus fucking Christ, what the fucking fuck was that?"

With a screech of tires, Poole reversed his own vehicle and raced off in the same direction as whoever wanted Weir dead.

"Jesus fucking Christ," Sterling repeated, quieter this time. Weir was still stuck in his head, seeing the car coming toward him. He had almost died, again.

Snapping himself out of his daze, after looking both ways he ran across the wide street. Sterling followed, sputtering curses. Some of them quite creative; Weir was impressed with his breadth of knowledge when it came to swearing.

While they stood in front of the Fish and Wildlife office, Weir put a couple of calls through, first to Adam and then to Sammy. Sterling leaned back against the plate-glass window, his chest heaving as he tried to collect himself. His face was pale, even for him, and he was shaking. The wailing sounds of sirens approached; hopefully that was Poole's backup.

Weir pulled Sterling into the small entryway. "Hey, it's okay. *I'm* okay." He cupped Sterling's cheeks with his cold hands. "I'm right here." Because he needed it as much as Sterling, Weir leaned in and kissed him. It was meant to be a gentle reminder that they were both alive and on this earth together, breathing the same air. Sterling grabbed him, fingers digging into his hips, returning the kiss fiercely. He wanted to respond, to lose himself in this moment of victory where he was alive and uninjured, but he had an asshole to catch.

Even so, he might have been distracted from the chase, except the sound of screeching tires followed by the unmistakable grind and squeal of metal on metal brought him to his senses.

Weir snapped to attention, training making him automatically alert. "What the hell? Stay here, I'm going to see if that's our guy."

"Hell fucking no, someone has got to watch your back." Sterling was in no mood for an argument and, frankly, Weir didn't want to leave him there. Together, they jogged toward the flashing lights and sirens.

The scene was chaotic. Poole's enormous Land Rover was smashed into a line of angle-parked cars two streets over, a second, smaller car trapped in between. The two cars' driver's-side doors hung open. Weir winced at the property damage, recalling an incident from his very first case, Adam's reaction, and the lecture the entire team had heard from Mohammad. Jason Bourne-style car chases were very much frowned upon. Weir recalled the phrase "budget nightmare" being thrown around. Luckily it hadn't been him behind the wheel.

A small group of people huddled at the far end of the block were being held back by a uniformed officer, proving that even in a city as small as Skagit, people would always come out for police activity. Two SkPD squad cars squealed into position, blocking off each end of the street as Weir and Sterling arrived. Weir flashed his badge and kept moving.

There was no sign of Poole or the unknown driver. Weir had some ideas about the identity of the driver, but only time would tell. He was uneasy. Sterling had stopped swearing and was walking quietly next to him. Weir glanced over at him, his expression grim.

One of the onlookers shouted, "They ran inside that building," pointing to a nondescript two-story brick building that looked to have been built in the 1970s. It was ugly; not even gentrification was going to save it. Regardless of the FOR LEASE/SALE/WILL BUILD TO SUIT signs plastered all over it, the building remained stubbornly empty.

"I need you to stay here."

"I'm not staying here if you go in there. You need to wait for backup."

"Sterling," he began, frustrated that Sterling wasn't listening. Instead, he was looking over Weir's shoulder.

Sterling smiled, and it wasn't at him. Weir looked. Adam and an agent Weir hadn't met were standing directly behind him.

"Oh, hi."

"Yeah, 'Oh, hi,'" Adam growled. "No, you're not going anywhere. If I let you even close to whatever is going on in there, Mohammad will string me up by my balls. I happen to like my balls."

The agent standing slightly behind Adam swallowed nervously. He was tall and slender, with a shock of red hair kept under control by a buzz cut. His handsome face was covered in freckles that looked like a splash of stars across his nose and cheeks. It was hard not to stare. Which was when Weir realized he was staring. Luckily, Sterling was staring, too. The man was striking.

Adam smirked. "Weir, Sterling, this is Agent Nate Richardson. He's joining us from some hellhole back east. Welcome him to the team, Weir. Nate, this is Weir's boyfriend Sterling Bailey. Not really sure what he sees in Weir, but I'm glad somebody is taking him in hand."

"Adam," Weir growled back.

"Right. You two, stay right fucking here. Richardson and I will find out what's going on." As Adam and Richardson moved closer to the uniformed officers and where Weir suspected Poole and the perp were, a thunderous cracking sound came from above. The window didn't shatter—presumably it was safety glass—but everyone below had a clear view of a man's back and shoulders where his body was smashed against the window. The abused glass bulged outward, and there was a tinkle of shards hitting the sidewalk as the window creaked under the strain of Tom Poole's massive frame.

"Fuck, that's Poole," Weir exclaimed.

Richardson did what Weir wanted to, bolting through the building's open door, pounding up the stairs before Adam could stop him.

"Jesus fucking Christ." Adam pointed a finger at them, "You two. Do. Not. Move." He ran after Richardson. His speed and athleticism always shocked Weir until the next time he witnessed them and was reminded the guy made up for his stature with rampant competitiveness.

A few minutes later Adam called down, "Weir, get an ambulance, then get up here. Bailey, you're going to have to stay where you are."

Weir patted his boyfriend on the shoulder before moving to do Adam's bidding.

THIRTY-FOUR

"The perp thought Krystad was on to him. Well, Krystad *was* on to him but hadn't put the whole thing together. So Marcus Franks, owner-operator of the Fish Market, took things into his own hands. We found the rifle in his trunk." Adam paused for a second. "Why are criminals so stupid? Why on earth would you keep that kind of evidence in your car?"

Weir didn't have an answer to that. The guy claimed he didn't want his son getting a hold of it. Like, it was okay that *he* had killed someone with it, but he was all about gun safety otherwise? He'd only been in questioning for a few hours.

Franks had concocted a get-rich-quick scheme harvesting geoducks and selling them to foreign buyers. Not really a one-man operation, which was why he had brought his son in to man the shop when he was doing business.

"Poole will be all right. What the fuck was he thinking, going into that building with no backup?"

"I'm pretty sure he was thinking the guy had tried to run me over in the middle of the town in front of where his former partner had been killed. He made some assumptions about who the guy was, and he was right. Poole's not used to perps who don't just fall in a quivering heap when he chases them—you've seen him, he's huge," Weir replied.

"Yeah, well, Franks clocked him with a two-by-four and nearly shoved him out a window. Maybe he'll be a bit more careful from now on," Adam groused. He really did not like it when people got hurt on his watch. As much as he tried to be Mr. Tough Guy all the time, Weir knew he cared deeply for his team and, by proxy, Tom Poole, who had nearly gotten himself killed.

Richardson had gotten up the stairs just in time to stop Franks from pushing a concussed Poole all the way out the window. The two-story fall might not have killed him, but it would have hurt. As it stood, Poole was in St. Joe's overnight for observation.

Meanwhile, Franks was in custody for the murder of Peter Krystad and the attempted murder of a federal agent, namely him, Carroll Evan Weir. Franks tried to deny he'd hit him with his car back in March, but aside from Poole and Sterling witnessing a second attempt just a few hours ago, his son had admitted under questioning that in March, his dad's car had mysteriously been out of commission for a few days, and when it returned it had a new right side panel.

Franks wasn't going anywhere.

"I still don't get why he ran me over, or how he even knew who I was," Weir groused. Especially since he had only figured out the connection between the Fish Market and Peter Krystad in the last twenty-four hours. The entire case circled back to those doodles in Krystad's notebooks, one of which was a circle of fish with the letters "TFM" smack in the middle. "He must have thought I was closer than I really was."

It was late. Weir was ready to get home. Wherever Sterling was, Weir wanted to be there. Adam noticed his shift in concentration and chuckled. "Go home. There will be plenty left to talk about tomorrow. Be back here by ten. Bring coffees."

Here was a little office in a nondescript business park off of I-5.

Mohammad had authorized the expense after listening to Adam bitch for months about secure space.

Sterling was waiting for him at home. Fuck, he had ridden with Adam and Richardson, his own car safely parked behind Sterling's apartment and the Loft.

"I'll give you a ride." Adam said with another irritating smirk.

* * *

THANKFULLY, Adam didn't make any snarky comments on the drive to Sterling's apartment. Weir wasn't sure he could handle anything right now. Moving his stuff up to Skagit had been a very analytical decision. He thought. It was logical, right? His boyfriend lived here and soon would own a business here. Sterling would hate to live in LA. Weir could call Skagit home but still travel with the team, right? If he decided to stay with the team.

Except.

Except Sterling made him want more than that. Sterling, who had opened himself to Weir. Who had made the trip to LA for him. Weir knew Sterling's past now. The month he was in LA after Sterling's visit, just hearing Sterling's voice on the phone gave him shivers. He'd never known what people were talking about when they claimed their "entire body lit up," until the first time he saw Sterling's number flash across his cell-phone screen.

Not only did his body light up, he found himself smiling at odd times. Smiling at all was a new thing, really. Weir knew how to fake it, he had for years, but truly smiling? That shit felt different.

Sterling had saved his life today. If he hadn't been there, there was no doubt in Weir's mind he would be a smear on the pavement. Sterling, permanent bachelor of Skagit city and county, had asked Weir to move in instead of renting a separate apartment. He didn't know why he was dragging his feet. What was the difference between moving to a city—fuck, moving to another state—to be with someone, and sharing a home?

"You're pretty quiet over there."

"Yeah."

"So, you and Sterling?"

"Don't."

Adam pulled into the parking lot of an am/pm. Fluorescent light fell from the front windows; neon pulsed, advertising cheap beer and a special on nacho cheese. Weir shuddered.

Adam twisted to look at him. "I'm not. I think it's a good thing. Sterling's not my type of guy, but then, neither are you. I think you two fit well together. Does he make you happy?"

"Yeah," he muttered, not believing he was getting the dad/big-brother convo from Adam Klay.

"I like what I see since you've been back. Yeah, I know it's only been a couple of days, but he's good for you. I can tell he really cares."

Weir sighed. "It kind of doesn't feel real."

"You wouldn't know real if it hit you in the head. Fuck, Weir, you've been out at sea for so long struggling to stay afloat, you wouldn't recognize a life preserver if it landed right in front of you."

"Okaaay, what do you mean? I don't speak weird Adam Klay references."

"I mean since you were a kid you've been on your own. You're very smart and a little lucky, so you've managed. Shit, if I'd been through what you have I'd be curled up in a fetal position. Don't know how he did it, but Sterling managed to get past the shit you've piled up to keep anyone else from hurting you."

"Pretty sure it was the meds," Weir grumbled. He was not comfortable having his personal stuff aired out all over the place.

"Nah, nice try though. Quit trying to second-guess yourself. Take your own advice—what was it, 'Did you just figure out you love him? Tell him when you see him,' or some shit like that? Hah, anyway, it's okay to be happy."

"How's that working for you?"

"Fuck off, it's working fine. I just don't want you shutting Sterling out because you're scared."

"I'm not scared," he muttered. No, he was fucking terrified.

Adam raised his eyebrows in disbelief but didn't say anything further, instead restarting the car and heading back out onto the street.

WEIR EYED the steps leading up to Sterling's apartment. The light was on upstairs; Sterling was a night owl by nature. Walking up the stairs was somehow a momentous decision. Weir took them two at a time, not wanting to second-guess himself any further. He just needed to get in the door.

Sterling was curled on his tiny couch, reading. How had Weir never seen the reading glasses before? Weir moved closer and tugged the book out of his hand.

"True crime? Really?" He tossed the book onto the closest flat surface. It hit the floor with a smack.

"The hell, you better not have lost my place." But Weir could tell Sterling wasn't really angry.

He crawled onto Sterling's lap, pinning him with his weight, removing the sexy glasses and setting them aside. God, he smelled good. He wasn't in the mood for gentle. He wanted to possess Sterling. If he was doing this, he wanted it all; everything. Smashing his lips against Sterling's, he opened his mouth, licking until Sterling opened for him. Weir pushed his tongue inside, mapping Sterling's mouth—the sensitive roof, along his teeth and across his gums, tasting him.

Sterling allowed him to plunder for a few moments, most likely out of pure surprise, before his arms came around Weir, holding him painfully tight. They dueled for dominance, neither wanting to give in. Finally acceding to the need for oxygen, Weir broke the kiss.

"Clothes off. Now." Thank fuck, Sterling was wearing his not-going-out sleep pants instead of his far-too-tight "How many tips can I get?" black jeans. Weir had seen Sterling's closet; there were at least ten pairs of the fucking things.

The thirty seconds it took the two of them to get completely naked was a hundred years too long. Weir needed to feel Sterling's strong body against his own. He needed the reassurance of sex, of meaningless sounds.

"Lie down. On your back."

Sterling did as commanded, his pale skin and beautiful body glowing against the black sheets and comforter. He stroked his hard length, eyes locked on Weir's face. "You want to tell me something?"

"Yeah, I think I do." Weir dropped onto the bed and crawled over to Sterling, laying his body over his lover's. Sterling's arms came around him again, tethering him. Their hard cocks ground together, and for a few moments Weir reveled in just that, the two of them rutting against each other. Sterling moved his hands to Weir's face, lifting it so he could look into his eyes. Weir leaned on one elbow, slipping the other hand between them so they could fuck into his fist, keeping his eyes open so Sterling could see. He felt so vulnerable, exposed. There was no one else he could imagine allowing this for. Sterling had snuck inside him, stolen his heart when Weir wasn't paying attention.

"Don't stop," Sterling panted. Like Weir was ever letting go.

Weir grunted a response, letting the sensation building up in his groin expand. Sterling dropped his hands, instead grabbing Weir's ass, digging his fingers into it, forcing him harder against Sterling's hips and pulsing erection. He was coming in that instant, come flowing over his fingers. Sterling spread his legs apart even farther, rutting, grinding, coming arched into Weir. Weir held on to keep himself from floating away.

"Fuck," Sterling whispered some time later, still slightly out of breath.

"Dude." It was the best he could do.

Sitting up a little, Sterling grabbed tissues off his nightstand. Weir rolled so they could clean up.

"So, you going to tell me?" His eyes were half closed; he was still breathing a little heavily from their activity.

He tucked himself back against Sterling and pulled the covers up because, June or not, it was fucking cold. Weir knew he was stalling, but what he wanted to say felt like a boulder in his throat. Caving to his irrational need to hide his face, he pressed even closer to Sterling before speaking.

"I almost died today." The arms around him tightened, but Sterling didn't interrupt. "If you hadn't been there—" Weir shook his head at himself. "If you hadn't been there I would be paste."

He wasn't doing this right. Taking a deep breath, he tried again, except Sterling was stroking a hand across his ass and it was very distracting. Using the sensation to focus himself, he forged ahead. "I don't think I want to move up here." The hand stopped. Weir replayed what he'd said. "No, I mean, agghh, fuck, Sterling, I don't want my own apartment. If I'm moving all the way up here we should be together. In the same house."

After a pause, the stroking started up again. "You think?"

"Yeah, because... you keep me in one place. I left Skagit because I was being selfish and stupid, and then you came and found me when I thought I had fucked everything up. Seeing you on the beach that day, ridiculous in those black clothes, already sunburned... well, until that moment I didn't know I'd been walking around in the dark. Feeling my way through days and nights. So I wanna live in the same house and really be with you."

Sterling flipped them over so he was mashing Weir into the mattress. His hot mouth was on Weir's, a demanding, passionate kiss. Weir wrapped his legs around Sterling's hips, wanting Sterling's weight to keep holding him down. When he had run away to LA, he hadn't realized how his mind quieted around Sterling. Once he was alone in his apartment again, his mind had turned back on with its relentless cycle of activity. Sterling ground into him harder and smiled against his mouth before kissing him again.

"Quit being a smug bastard." But he wasn't really complaining.

EPILOGUE

It felt *weird*.

Sterling hadn't realized, when he convinced Evan to move to Skagit and get a place together, he would be inheriting a whole family. To be honest, he didn't think Evan had, either. Yet here they were in Ed Schultz's backyard at his annual summer barbeque. Sterling had heard stories about Ed; there was no doubt that this would be a serious party.

Being here with his boyfriend—who also happened to have landed an adjunct professor position in the Statistics Department at the local university—at a semi-family event, Sterling was left wondering what the hell had happened to his bachelor life, but not missing it.

Carroll Evan Weir had happened. How crazy was that? And now Sterling had a bigger family than he could have ever imagined. Raven was even invited, along with her posse of GSA friends. Hopefully the one kid wouldn't do a repeat performance and break an ankle. Also, oddly enough, there was a guy Sterling thought he recognized as Roberts, one of the EMTs who'd responded when Raven and Pony had found Evan after the hit-and-run.

He shivered, thinking for a moment what they both would have missed if Raven hadn't stopped that day. They'd found out Marcus Franks had been somewhat of a regular at the Booking Room. He must have heard some discussion of the case there, or just made the connection between Krystad and Evan, and decided to get rid of Evan as well.

Evan squeezed his hand. Neither of them was usually expressive in public, but they both needed reassurance today. Everyone and their dog was there, the dog in question being Joey James's mutt, Xena. The Russian foster kid was there, too. Konstantin, Sterling reminded himself. Xena was obviously the kid's tool, as they went from adult to adult procuring snacks for both dog and child. Joey's mother had dropped Kon off but claimed she had her own neighborhood event to go to.

Standing outside in the backyard were Buck and his friend Miguel. Sterling tugged on Evan's hand and pulled him outside, through the throng crowded onto the deck and down the steps to where all four of them could hide from the rest of the guests. Thank fuck there was a bucket full of ice and beers at the bottom of the steps.

"Hey, guys."

"Hey," Miguel replied. Buck looked nervous and a little flushed. Sterling wondered if he was sick or something. And how had he gotten away from his boyfriend, who seemed to have him on radar?

"There's a lot of people here," Sterling said uselessly.

"Yeah," Miguel said. "I think Ed went a little overboard on this beginning-of-summer shindig."

"Where's Sara?" Evan asked. And true, where was she? Sara and her dad were very close. Besides, he thought Miguel and Sara had been seeing each other.

Miguel looked uncomfortable. "Uh, we're kind of taking a break. She's in Seattle visiting friends for the weekend. Ed still wanted me to come, wouldn't take no for an answer. Irritating old man."

A throat cleared; the "irritating old man" had managed to sneak up behind the four of them. "I've been called worse, and not by any of you, so being rude isn't going to get you out of my party."

Miguel rolled his eyes, looking up to the heavens, Sterling supposed, for patience and support.

"It'll be fine, boy, you're both adults. I like the both of ya. Well, I like Sara better, but that can't be helped." He turned to Buck. "Everything ready?" Buck nodded. "All right then." Ed wandered away in the direction of the deck, muttering about "getting the meat on," which made all four of them bust out laughing like hyenas.

Sterling thought there was something a little *off* about Buck's laughter. Miguel must have thought so, too. He grabbed Buck and pulled him in close, tugging his head down and whispering in his ear. Buck seemed to need the contact, because he allowed Miguel to plaster himself all over him, nodding in response to what Miguel whispered. If Sterling hadn't known that Buck belonged to Joey body and soul, he would have been confused. More confused. Apparently Miguel had no boundaries and zero issues with how (or who) he touched. It was astounding how quickly Buck settled.

"Where is Joey?" Sterling asked.

"At the hospital, he'll be here as soon as his shift is over," Buck answered, a little out of breath.

Buck managed to pull himself together, shaking off whatever it was that had put him near hysterics. They shot the breeze for a little while. Buck and Miguel were deep in negotiations for a larger shop space. Buck and Sterling bonded about the world's most boring meetings, the dreaded Chamber of Commerce. Sterling had only been to one so far; luckily Buck had warned him to bring coffee. Sterling hadn't regretted the choice of a quad Americano.

By this time many of the guests had migrated down to the yard, and Kon and Xena were playing fetch. Sterling thought he saw Mrs. James again, but he had watched her drive away, so that couldn't be right. Most likely it was Ed's current girlfriend. For an old guy, he sure got around.

Evan and Adam were talking about something Sterling wasn't paying attention to; he was wrapped up in his own conversation with Buck and Miguel about the city plan to "revitalize" NOT. Neither of their businesses was affected, but the plan was half-baked at best.

Ed appeared from around the corner of the garage, Joey trailing behind him with Kon and the dog in tow. Sterling looked around, needing another beer, and his incredible boyfriend reappeared with a beer and a plate of chips. Sterling leaned in and kissed him on the lips. He couldn't help himself, he immediately wanted more.

Somebody grabbed his ass. It wasn't Evan, because his hands were full. Sterling glared at Miguel in astonishment. "What the fuck?"

"Pay attention." Miguel nodded toward Buck, who once again had that sick look on his face. Sterling *finally* got a clue, but Miguel squeezed his ass again for good measure. Now Evan glared at him, too. Heh. Sterling snaked an arm around Evan's waist, tugging him closer before snagging some chips.

"Joey?" Buck rasped out.

"Yeah? Buck, what's wrong? Are you sick, do we need to go home?" Kon was pulling Joey's hand in one direction and Xena was pulling the other.

Miguel ran a comforting hand down Buck's back before stepping away. Buck took a deep breath before dropping to one knee.

Joey froze. He resembled a man being crucified, but Sterling thought guests would overlook that. And it *had* been Mrs. James he'd seen lurking by the garage.

"Joey James?"

"Uh, yeah?" Joey whispered.

Buck dug around in his jeans pocket and finally pulled out a small box. He flipped it open before continuing. The dog came rushing over to slobber all over him; Miguel grabbed her, but he wasn't able to grab Kon, who vaulted into Buck. If the guy weren't built like a Mack truck, he would have fallen over.

"Joey—" One hand held the box out, the other held onto Kon. "Will you marry me?"

Sterling had never thought he would see Joey at a loss for words. There was a palpable heartbeat of anxiety amongst the partygoers before Joey recovered himself.

"Oh my god, yes!"

Joey threw himself at Buck, who only just managed to push Kon to the side before his boyfriend/fiancé landed on his lap, passionately kissing him and crying at the same time.

"Yes, yes, yes!"

Sterling had to turn away from the sweetness. It really was too much. *His* boyfriend was right there next to him. He certainly wasn't wiping his eyes.

Evan grinned. "You ever ask me in public like that, and I will snuff you."

Huh, somehow that sounded like a challenge he could overcome. Grinning, he kissed the living daylights out of Evan until they both had to come up for air.

* * *

Keep reading, Shielded Hearts continues on in, As Sure as the Sun with US Marshal Sacha Bolic and free spirited Seth Culver. An older/younger romance about finding a physical home as well as a home in your heart.

* * *

IF YOU'VE ENJOYED the Shielded Hearts series be sure to check out Conspiracy Theory, the first in the Veiled Intentions series which follows Sheriff Mat Dempsey and ex-detective Niall Hamarsson as they solve crime and fumble their way toward their happily ever after.

A THANK YOU FROM ELLE

If you enjoyed Convergence Zone, I would greatly appreciate if you would let your friends know so they can experience Weir, Sterling and the rest of the gang as well. As with all of my books, I have enabled lending on all platforms in which it is allowed to make it easy to share with a friend. If you leave a review for Convergence Zone, or any of my books. on the site from which you purchased the book, Goodreads or your own blog, I would love to read it! Email me the link at elle@ellekeaton.com

Keep up-to-date with new releases and sales, *The Highway to Elle* hits your in-box approximately every two weeks, sometimes more sometimes less. I include deals, freebies and new releases as well as a sort of rambling running commentary on what *this* author's life is like. I'd love to have you aboard! I also have a reader group called the Highway to Elle, come say hi!

ABOUT ELLE

Elle hails from the northwest corner of the US known for, rain, rain, and more rain. She pens the Accidental Roots series, the Hamarsson and Dempsey series, and Home in Hollyridge all set in the Pacific Northwest. Elle is chief cook and bottle washer, the one always asking 'where are my keys and/or wallet' and 'why are there cats?' (This question not yet answered).

Elle *loves* both cats and dogs, Star Wars and Star Trek, pineapple on pizza, and is known to start crossword puzzles with ballpoint pen.

Thank you for supporting this Indie Author,

Elle

ABOUT CONVERGENCE ZONE

*Previously published as Spring Break, only the title and cover have changed!

Sometimes a guy needs a break. Carroll Weir got one--but it wasn't what he expected.

A weary FBI investigator, a permanently single bartender; the men have nothing in common except for their sexuality. They meet by chance; converging weather patterns creating a private storm of their own.

Agent Carroll Weir wants to escape the dreary damp town of Skagit for a warmer climate, instead, he's assigned to a cross-agency case involving smuggling and a murdered Fish and Wildlife Detective. Could things get any worse?

The spark between Weir and Sterling is electric and unless they're careful somebody's going to get burned.

"Elle Keaton brings the characters of Skagit to life, and shows the support, love and humor that this small town shares. The plot itself has danger, action, mystery, money laundering, kidnapping and makes for a page-turner. With each installment, this series has gotten better and better. There are some new investigators who have come on the scene, and a few interesting surprises in the Epilogue-ish final bit of the book. The author has left me curious, as well—I don't have any idea who will be featured in the next installment." 5 star Amazon review

*Convergence Zone was previously published as Spring Break – the content has not changed in any way.

  *HEA No cliffhanger

  *Intended for a mature audience, 18+

.

Copyright © 2021, 2022, 2023 by Elle Keaton

All rights reserved.

No part of this book may be reproduced in any form or by any electronic or mechanical means, including information storage and retrieval systems, without written permission from the author, except for the use of brief quotations in a book review.

Edited by Alicia Z. Ramos

Cover by Cate Ashwood

❀ Created with Vellum

Printed in Great Britain
by Amazon

35846020R00137